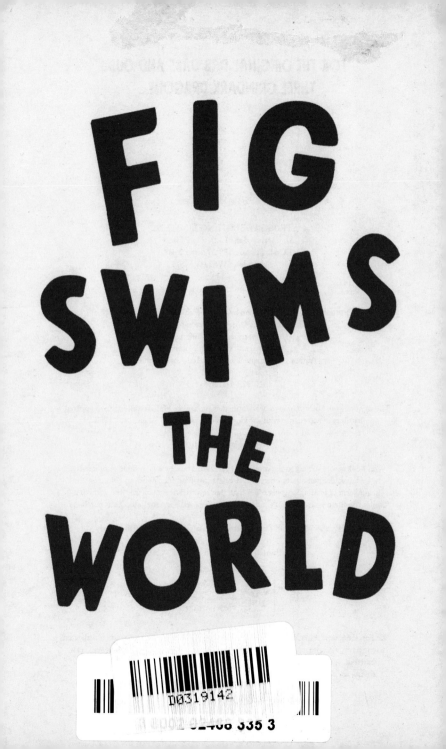

FIG SWIMS THE WORLD

FOR THE ORIGINAL DAB DABS AND OUR THREE GRIMDARK DRAGONS...

STRIPES PUBLISHING LIMITED
An imprint of the Little Tiger Group
1 Coda Studios, 189 Munster Road,
London SW6 6AW

www.littletiger.co.uk

First published in Great Britain by Stripes Publishing Limited in 2020
Text copyright © Lou Abercrombie, 2020
Cover copyright © Stripes Publishing Limited, 2020
Girl image © shutterstock.com
Author photograph © Lou and Ted Abercrombie

ISBN: 978-1-78895-153-1

MIX
Paper from
responsible sources
FSC® C020471

The Forest Stewardship Council® (FSC®) is a global, not-for-profit organization dedicated
to the promotion of responsible forest management worldwide. FSC® defines standards
based on agreed principles for responsible forest stewardship that are supported by
environmental, social, and economic stakeholders. To learn more, visit www.fsc.org

2 4 6 8 10 9 7 5 3 1

Lou Abercrombie

FIG SWIMS THE WORLD

Stripes

PART 1
SINK OR SWIM

"Twenty years from now, you will be more disappointed
by the things you didn't do than the ones you did do."
Mark Twain

RESOLUTIONS

At just under five foot, and with pretty much everything right about her, my best friend Stella is about as different from me as you can get. Even in school uniform, she looks chic and elegant, while I'm like an awkward giant.

"Fig!" she giggles, extracting herself from my enormous hug. But I'm just so thrilled to see my one and only friend after ten days of being stuck at home. "Gutted you couldn't come to the party," she says. "What happened?"

"Mubla happened," I mutter. "Her usual *You don't need to see the date change to know a new year has begun.* She doesn't trust me, Stella. I'm fifteen and she still thinks I need supervising!"

I'm sick of my mother controlling me. She's hacked into my life for too long, insisting on her 'It's my way or the highway' rules; on me having to follow *her* timetable; dressing the way *she* suggests; achieving the New Year's resolutions *she* makes for me.

"She hacked into my phone," I tell Stella, who gasps. "It was supposed to be the one private area of my life. Dab Dabs promised he'd get her to leave my phone alone."

"What was she looking for?"

I smile grimly. "She wanted to check whether I had a boyfriend. Now that *would* have been a hideous betrayal, but – shock, horror! – the truth was far worse. That I *don't* have one. And that I'm the biggest nerd in school."

"You're not," murmurs Stella but I know she's only being kind.

"D'you know what she said?" I continue. "'You're a loser, Lemony. And I was always so popular at school. I expected more from a Fitzsherbert…' Honestly, I came *this* close to pointing out how ironic it is that my *bullying* mother was disappointed that I'm being *bullied* at school."

"What *did* you say then?"

I shrug. "Shouted at her for calling me Lemony."

"Why won't she call you Fig?" asks Stella, frowning. "Your family's all about the nicknames."

"Dunno," I sigh. "I should start calling her Mother. See how she likes it…"

Of course I probably won't. Jago, my little brother, gave her the name Mubla because he felt sorry for her after I'd given Dab Dabs his nickname.

Stella grins sympathetically and changes the subject. "Good Crimbo?"

"Effervescent," I say. "You?"

"Meritorious," she replies.

Every day we try to out-word each other. It's a game we've been playing ever since Year Five, when Mubla put me into the World Championship Spelling Bee competition. I had to read every page of the *Oxford Dictionary* for eight months but faltered at the World Quarter Finals, on the rather easy word 'neurotic'. For the record, I got stage fright, and put the 'e' and the 'u' the wrong way round. Hilarious really, since Mubla uses the word to describe me all the time.

"I've made the mother of all resolutions," I say. "It's going to blow your mind!"

Stella frowns. "You can't mean you actually *like* the resolution Mubla's given you?" She cringes. "It's not another maths challenge, is it?"

She's referring to last year when Mubla wanted me to be the youngest person to get an A* in maths A level. I got an A. I do love maths, though. Give me an algebra problem and I will happily sit there for hours.

"God, no," I laugh. "She's signed me up for acting classes. Wants me to get over my 'silly stage fright'."

"You? Acting! Is she insane?" Then the bell sounds for registration and Stella turns to me. "So what *is* your resolution?"

"I'm going to swim the world," I reply.

"Flip, Fig!" she shrieks. "Where'd that come from?"

"It was that *Inspiring Women* seminar we had before Christmas," I say. "The fourteen-year-old girl who became

5

the youngest person to sail round the world single-handedly. Got me thinking."

"That's a flipping awesome resolution," says Stella. "My one sounds lame by comparison."

"Why, what's yours?"

"Drink more water, eat less sugar," she replies.

We end up doubled over with laughter, until Stella stops suddenly. "Hang on. Isn't there one tiny problem here?"

I grin. "Yeah. I can't swim…"

NICKNAMES

Stella walks away, laughing her head off. I knew she'd understand. She's the only one who's ever got me. Unlike most of the people who go to this school. A few years ago, I overheard a conversation between a couple of clones in my class, Maisy and Daisy. They were having a good old giggle about how much of a *loser* I am. They started talking about Dab Dabs and how he freaked them out, and I finally realized why no one, except Stella, had ever come to my birthday parties. They were scared. Of the dead bodies in the basement. Seriously! I mean, they're *dead*.

Dab Dabs, you see, is an embalming artist (self-proclaimed) and a funeral director, which makes our house the *Fitzsherbert Family Funeral Home: Putting Your Mind and Body to Rest*. The basement is where the dead bodies go for him to work his magic on them. It's quite a fascinating place and I'm more than happy spending time down there. It's a bit like a theatre dressing room, with bright lights, make-up and prosthetics everywhere. Dab Dabs has covered the walls with pictures of his creations. There are some really rather stunning portraits. You just have to see past the fact that all of his subjects are *dead…*

"Well, if it isn't Grim!"

I turn towards the voice, my shoulders automatically sagging. It's Cassandra, the so-called school beauty and one of the many girls who like to mock me. Grim is her nickname for me. Something to do with the Grim Reaper on account of Dab Dabs. By her side, acting like two simpering bodyguards, are Maisy and Daisy.

"Your dad work on any *dead* people recently?" Cassandra asks with wide eyes.

"What?"

"*Dead* people. Many of them for Christmas?" She takes a sidelong glance at her giggling mates.

"He doesn't do funerals at Christmas," I say. I don't know why she's so obsessed with death and me, so I add, "You're welcome to come and have a look in the basement any time, though. I'm sure he'd give you a guided tour."

Cassandra flushes red and mutters something about never being seen dead in my house. I'm desperate to say, "Your funeral *is* the most likely way you're ever coming to my house." But they've already stalked off.

Now I'm late for registration and I hate being late. My form tutor, Mr Harding, glares at me as I try to slope in unnoticed. Not easy when you're me.

"Fitzsherbert!" He practically hisses my name through gritted teeth. "Perhaps you might try 'being on time' as your New Year's resolution?"

"Sorry, Mr Harding," I murmur. "Yes, Mr Harding."

There's only about two minutes left before the bell goes when Mr Harding hands me a yellow card and goes into protracted detail about how my skirt length is not school regulation and something needs to be done about it. Quite what I don't know. I'm wearing the longest skirt they sell in the uniform shop.

As a result, I'm late for chemistry and have missed out on being put with a partner. Miss Denny looks desperately at the group, trying to resolve the issue. "Can't have someone working on their own, can we? Billy, can you share with Fig, please?"

"Ew!" he shouts. "I'm not sharing with Bug!"

Bug is another of my nicknames. Apparently it stands for Big Ugly Giant. Charming. Fug is another variant. Oh, and there's also Reaper, Boiled Sweet (on account of my name) and the usual obvious ones like Nerd, Jerk Face and Boff. Who knew one person could go by so many names?

"It's Fig," replies Miss Denny firmly. "And that's enough of your nastiness. Come and sit here, please."

Billy stomps across the room. "Fee-fi-fo-fum, Bug's gonna make me look very dumb!"

"That's enough!" shouts Miss Denny, glaring furiously round the room as everyone dissolves into laughter.

"It's all right, Miss Denny," I say. "Billy doesn't need *me* to make him look dumb – he does that all on his own." Well, that's what I say inside my head. What comes out of my mouth is, "It's all right, Miss Denny. I don't mind working on my own…"

PLANNING

Telling Stella my resolution has brought it home: this is an enormous challenge. If I'm going to succeed, I've got a lot of planning to do. So, after school, I pull out the list of swims I've begun compiling and plot them on a map of the world.

But it soon becomes obvious that I'm not really going to swim across all the oceans and seas in the world. That's a long way – just over 40,000 kilometres. Plus there's all sorts of things in the sea that would happily have me for breakfast.

Sea Creatures to Avoid

1. Sea snakes — if they bite you, you have to know exactly which type to get the right antidote. Don't get me started on water moccasins...

2. Vampire fish aka piranhas — apparently they'll only

11

attack you if you're bleeding or weeing, but I'm not taking any chances

3. Crocodiles — shudder
4. Portuguese man-of-war jellyfish — imagine being stung slowly to death
5. Sharks — I've already got one man-eating predator in my life (sorry Mubla). I don't need any more

There's also no way I'm swimming near the seventh and coldest continent, which doesn't even have any countries on it. No, I will just have to make do with choosing swims on the other six...

A quick internet search produces an astounding array of potential swims. Many of which I rule out immediately because I honestly can't imagine swimming more than ten kilometres in one go. Actually, I can't imagine swimming ten strokes, but I'll put that to one side for the moment. Clearly, I need some criteria for how to choose my swims.

Criteria

1. Interesting swimming names
2. Mixture of iconic swims and races
3. Interesting locations
4. At least one swim on every continent bar Antarctica
5. 10km maximum distance for any one swim

6. Twelve-month duration for entire adventure
7. Logical route round the world to minimize flying

With these in mind, I compile an enormous chart, laying out where and when each swimming event is in the world, along with the distance, event duration and entrance fee. And, by bedtime, I'm pretty certain I've got a list I can work with.

Fig's Swims Round the World

1. Dinosaur Island
2. The Jailhouse Rock
3. Mount Storm Rough Water
4. The Red Canyon swim series
5. La Isla Bonita
6. Turtle Bay
7. The Greatest Archipelago on Earth Clearwater swim series
8. Malokodaidai Island 10k
9. The Big Swim series in the Land of Koalas
10. The Lazy River
11. The Cold Drop
12. The Whale Isles
13. The Hot Fjords
14. The Ancients Trail swims
15. Island-hopping

16. The Sunriser
17. The Mermaid Canal
18. The Pilgrimage
19. The Squirly Whirly
20. The Cross-continental

I've decided to ease myself in gently with the first one. It's organized by a company called Voyage of the Water Treaders, who will provide full coaching and lifeguard support in the event that I might actually drown. It's a month before the rest, giving me plenty of time to assess whether I really can do this. And it's only a two-hour train ride from home, unlike some of the journeys it looks likely I'm going to have to endure. I'm a nervous flyer, so I'll be taking the land route as much as possible…

Just looking at the list sends excitement and nerves shimmying through me. I begin pacing round the room, feeling jittery. I can't wait to show Stella.

DOUCHEBAG

"Tell me what it's called again?" asks Stella the next day.

"Turtle Bay," I reply. "It's a six-kilometre swim alongside turtles. Sunshine, sand, blue sea and insane scenery. Your basic paradise."

"Except the swimming bit," laughs Stella.

Our mutual disinterest in swimming is just one of many things we agree on, and, considering we live in Old Mare, a small seaside town most notable for its large swathes of keen swimmers, we number among the few. Mubla included.

"Flip, Fig. That sounds, well ... *prodigious*!"

"I'm glad *you* like it," I sigh. "I'm a bit *vacillant*."

"Why?"

"Because I'm not prepared."

"You will be," says Stella. "You know you always are. You've just got to write some more of your lists."

"The lists I can do," I say. "It's the learning to swim part I'm dread—"

I'm interrupted by Billy, who catches us up and throws his arms round our shoulders. Well, *my* back, Stella's shoulders.

"Hello, ladies! You're looking particularly lovely today," he gushes, gaping longingly at Stella. "Is that a new haircut?"

"Just my usual trim," I laugh.

Billy snorts. "I wasn't talking to you, Fug."

"Don't call her that," says Stella, pulling away from him.

"Why not?" he counters. "It's true, isn't it?"

But Stella stands her ground. "Well, if we're telling the truth, Billy, maybe I should start calling you douchebag? You know, on account of how *pestiferous* you are."

Billy stares back. "I don't know what that means."

"It means annoying, you *douchebag*," I retort. OK, I don't actually call him that. Besides he looks a bit hurt. I think he's got a massive crush on Stella.

She laughs at him, which makes him blush even more. "See?" she says. "Not very nice, is it? Now bog off."

Billy slopes away, muttering under his breath, while Stella turns to me with a triumphant smile. "You were saying?"

I laugh. "That I've got cold feet."

"You will have if you swim in weather like this," agrees Stella. "Are you going today?"

I shake my head. "I told you. I'm not prepared. This is my biggest fear, Stella. It's going to take a gargantuan list before I'm ready to go near the water…"

To be fair, I have a few fears. They include, but are not limited to:

1. Swimming
2. Performing onstage
3. Being on my own
4. Being murdered
5. Jellyfish, crocodiles, water moccasins and pretty much any water creature
6. Spiders
7. Mubla
8. Life

Stella grins sympathetically. "Well, look, I'm not the best swimmer in the world but … if you ever want some support, let me know and I'll come with you. OK?"

LISTS

My family is all about the lists. Mubla is a very organized person. As a top-level criminal lawyer, she has to be. She also writes Dab Dabs's lists for him. Apparently he's incapable of writing his own. I don't know why. Jago is a mini-Mubla so he loves them too. He's a high achiever and the cleverest boy in his school. I'm pretty good at lists too, which is about the only thing I have in common with Mubla. That and being the same size as her. I could easily borrow her clothes if grey, boxy barrister suits were my thing.

I read somewhere that swimmers like making lists.It helps prepare them for the next challenge ahead. Personally I find they help control my anxieties. However, the list I wrote while staring at the New Year fireworks is rather pitiful in the cold light of day and I'm going to have to give this a whole lot more thought.

<u>To-do List</u>

1. Learn to swim
2. Learn how to swim further
3. Learn how to swim in open water

What is more convincing, however, is my list of reasons *why* I should do this swim.

<u>Reasons to Swim Round the World</u>

1. It's about time I learned to swim
2. I may as well put looking like a daddy-long-legs to good use
3. I need to do something that hasn't got Mubla's fingerprints all over it
4. To prove that I'm not defined by my fears
5. School is boring

Then, underneath yesterday's swim list, I begin a new to-do list.

<u>Fig's To-do List</u>

1. Write equipment list
2. Write main to-do list
3. Write contact list

So far so good. All I've done is write a list of lists and it seems rather straightforward. It's when I start researching what to add to the equipment list that I really begin to feel terrified.

Equipment List

1. Swimming costume x 2
2. Swimming hat
3. Swimming goggles x 2 (including different lenses depending on the weather)
4. Fins
5. Tempo beeper
6. Paddles
7. Bands
8. Pull buoy
9. Kickboard
10. Wetsuit

Who knew there was so much stuff needed to learn to swim? I naively thought I'd get away with a swimming costume, hat and goggles. I've no idea how half the things will help me, but I've just ordered them off the internet, thanks to a leftover birthday gift voucher, and they're arriving tomorrow, so we'll see…

I can't even begin to think how to write my Contact List, so I make do with the Main To-do List.

Main To-do List

1. Complete 'How to Learn to Swim To-do List'
2. Book place on the Swimmers Show motivational talk with the Boss
3. Details. Where will I live/sleep between swims? What will I eat?
4. Obtain fake passport
5. Write Contact List
6. Budget — how am I going to pay for all this?
7. Book round-the-world ticket
8. Plan escape
9. Swim the world

Items three and four give me the most cause for concern, alongside the obvious learning-to-swim bit. I've never been self-sufficient before and the idea of breaking the law to get a fake passport is frankly terrifying, but I can't exactly use my own. I'm pretty sure, with technology these days, I'd be picked up within hours.

Next up is working out the timetable and how long I've got to learn to swim proficiently. My first swim round Dinosaur Island is at the end of July. Apart from the name and amazing scenery, I chose it because it's fairly local and will give me a taster of what's to come. The second swim, the Jailhouse Rock, takes place on 25th August. That one is on the other side of the world and, since I have to get there, I base my calculations on the 24th:

$E^* = T + 232$
*Where E = Day of Escape/Exit/Exodus (delete as applicable) & T = today

With all my lists written and calculations made, I reluctantly turn to the actual task in hand. Learning to swim. There are countless step-by-step tutorials on how to do it and I spend the rest of my evening soaking up breathing rates, swimming postures and kicking techniques. I feel strangely exhilarated and can't wait to get in the water. I even go into a daydream about how well I'll be able to swim, now that I've researched it so thoroughly.

BEGINNINGS

I don't make it to the pool the next day. Or the following three. My argument being that any kind of new habit should really begin on a Monday. And my equipment doesn't arrive until the Saturday morning. I virtually hover by the door for the delivery, feeling so much excitement I can hardly contain it. But, when I open the giant box, there's no chorus of angels to serenade my new beginning. Just the rip of cardboard and a slightly terrified sigh from me.

Then my first swim, having spent so much time triple-checking plans and going over the theory, doesn't go well. Apparently, having all the equipment and know-how doesn't make you a swimmer. Instead, I sit on the side of the pool, literally quaking, and don't even make it into the water.

When I said I can't swim, I meant that I am completely terrified. You see, I had a bad introduction to it.

When I was a baby, Mubla thought it would be a great idea to get one of those underwater photoshoots done. You know, the kind where they stick the baby in a tutu and drop them in the water with a photographer waiting to capture the moment. There's a photo somewhere of me dressed in a pink net skirt, eyes wide open, bubbles streaming from my mouth as I tried to scream.

I didn't go in the water for eight years after that. When I was nine, we had compulsory swimming lessons at school. I turned up to the first lesson, knees knocking, blubbing away in my life vest and armbands. Obviously, I got laughed out of the changing room and didn't even get near the water. Then in Year Six, my teacher, Miss Sally, said I had to learn to swim. Something to do with the 'school inspectors'. It still didn't convince me to get in the water though and, since then, I've managed to avoid it.

Now on day five of my swimming plan – or, as I call it, barely getting my feet wet – a little old woman shuffles over and lowers herself down beside me. She's got an intense look about her and has different coloured eyes – one blue, one green – and she's wearing one of those weird swimming hats that has giant flowers attached to it.

"Are you getting in?" she asks.

I shrug.

"Swim here often?" she adds.

I shrug again.

We sit together for a moment in companionable silence, both considering the water. She no doubt thinking about the swim she's about to do. Me running through the reasons why I shouldn't get in.

"Bubble, bubble, breathe," says the old woman suddenly.

I frown. "Eh?"

She gestures at the water. "You're scared, aren't you, my love?"

I nod.

"Bubble, bubble, breathe," she repeats. "It's a mantra lots of swimmers use. Helps them get their breathing right."

Given I've got nothing else, I decide to give it a go and mumble, "Bubble, bubble, breathe," under my breath.

The old woman cackles. "That's the ticket! Bubble, bubble, breathe!"

We end up reciting it together, over and over, until we're both laughing and I don't feel quite so scared. Then the old woman grins and eases herself into the water, and, with a wave goodbye, swims off.

"Bubble, bubble, breathe," I murmur. The words feel quite nice. Maybe I should give it a try...

~~~

Later, in the swimming pool café, I sit, looking down at the water, watching the swimmers pound through their laps, and I can't help smiling. I need to tell Stella.

Me 17:35

I did it!

Stella 17:36

What? Told Billy he's a douchebag?

Me 17:36

LOL. Good one. No. I sat on the bottom of the pool and blew bubbles. With all that water above me! Didn't come up shrieking for air either

I grin at my phone, unable to contain my happiness.

Stella 17:38
OMG!

Stella 17:39
I am *exultant* for you

Me 17:40

Thanks. Positively *euphoric* here. Going to have a banana milkshake to celebrate

Stella 17:42
Enjoy. You've earned it. Come for dinner? Mum's cooking your favourite...

Me 17:43

Peanut satay?! 😋 Can't though. Mubla. Wish I lived with you…

Stella 17:43

 If only! I'll try to go on without you. Will maybe only eat half of them. As an act of solidarity you understand

Me 17:44

🖤

DEFLATION

Mubla is on the prowl when I get home from the pool and my feelings of elation soon turn to misery.

"Where've you been, Lemony?"

"It's Fig," I mutter. "I was with Stella, if you must know."

Mubla tuts. "Again? What about your homework?"

"It's Friday."

"You won't get anywhere with that attitude, you know." She gestures at the table where our nanny is casting an expert eye over the layout of plates, cutlery and water glasses. "Aurora needs your help, Lemony."

But Aurora growls, "Don't you dare touch it." She's got the ruler out tonight. Her exacting standards are one of the reasons Mubla continues to keep her on. And the fact that, when Jago came along six years ago, two children were more than she could handle *and* have a high-flying job.

"Evening, all," announces Dab Dabs loudly. "Dinner

smells delectable, darling."

Dressed in his camel lounge jacket and favourite T-shirt with the slogan 'I put the fun in funeral', he beams at Mubla, while she manages a tight smile as she scrutinizes him with a perfectly arched eyebrow. "Tom. I see you've made your *usual* effort. I thought the beard was coming off after Christmas?"

Dab Dabs grins back. "I could always go and shave now?" This earns him an eye roll.

"And let the food spoil?" mutters Mubla. "No, thank you."

Dinner is a stilted affair. Mubla's not a fan of conversation. We're not allowed to look at our phones at the table either and I think Aurora's dying inside with nothing to say. I know how she feels… Jago sits looking at his plate in miserable silence, a deep frown burrowing beneath his floppy blond fringe.

"Eat up, darling," says Mubla brightly. But Jago harrumphs, lifting his little shoulders up round his ears, then letting them fall with his arms stubbornly folded across his chest.

"No?" she asks, her smile temporarily falling. "No," she answers her own question and nods at Aurora to make him a sandwich. Then, with peanut butter smeared round his face, Jago starts nattering about a history book on the Second World War that he's been reading.

"My grandfather was a spy, you know," says Dab Dabs.

"Parachuted into enemy territory and ordered to obtain secret information."

"Epic," murmurs Jago, his face alight with curiosity. "Was he any good? What did he find out? Was he ever caught?"

Dab Dabs frowns. "Er ... no. But he wouldn't ever speak a word of what he found out afterwards. That's code of honour for you."

"I think I'd make a good spy," says Jago dreamily.

"I'm sure you would," I laugh. "Bet you could read my mind if I let you."

Jago grins and I cross my eyes, sticking out my tongue.

"Lemony, don't do that," says Mubla, fixing me with her disapproving glare. "I have news for you actually."

And then she drops her bombshell. I should have been prepared really. Because, as soon as I start to feel a bit more positive, something negative always comes along to redress the balance, and I'm back to teetering on the brink of anxiety.

"I've enrolled you in the Old Mare Am Dram Society," she tells me. "Starts the first Saturday in February."

I stare back, literally screaming inside my head. Why is she still trying to take over my life?

TORPEDOES

E = T + 213

It's been two long weeks of visiting the pool every day and my patience is finally wearing thin. I haven't made any progress beyond blowing bubbles at the bottom of the pool. What's wrong with me? I know all the theory and I know I've got the strength, but, when I try to lift my feet off the floor, it's like they're stuck in concrete.

The next step in the tutorial says to make like a torpedo and push off from the edge of the pool into the middle. But, since that requires me to lift my feet off the ground *and* not hold on to anything, I can't do it. My breath is stuck in my throat and I end up retching at the side of the pool.

It's at this precise moment Mubla decides to make her usual check on my whereabouts, and my phone, which I've left with my towel, rings loudly.

"What?" I snap, when I answer the call.

"Lemony. That's no way to answer the phone. Least of all to your mother."

31

"Sorry, Mubla," I say, gulping down my frustration. "Hello, Mubla. How are you?"

"That's better. And I'm fine, thank you for asking. Where are you?"

"At the pool," I answer, quickly adding, "Stella wanted to swim. I'm just watching."

Mubla snorts. "I was going to say. You can't swim! And are you doing your homework while she's in there?"

I frown. "Er … no?"

"Come off it, Lemony," says Mubla. "You're wasting your precious time in a swimming pool of all places? There'll be plenty of time for that sort of thing when you've left education."

She goes into her usual long lecture about how I've got to make myself stand out from the crowd, give myself the edge, or I'll never get a decent job. All the while, I'm standing there, shivering in my swimsuit, my goggles pressed firmly to my face. I'd be tempted to laugh at how ridiculous I must look if they didn't hurt so much.

"No phones in the pool," says the lifeguard approaching me.

"Sorry, Mubla," I say, interrupting her. "That's Stella. I've got to go. I'll see you at dinner time!" And I end the call before she can protest.

"How are you getting on with your swimming?"

I look down into the multicoloured eyes of that little old woman. She's smaller than I remember and I tower above her.

"Oh, hi," I say.

"Sage Olander," she answers, offering me her hand.

"Fig Fitzsherbert," I reply.

Sage beams. "Hello, Fig. So?"

It's at this point that I break down in tears and tell her how badly I'm doing and she ushers me into the changing rooms. Before I know it, I'm sitting in the café having a piece of cake thrust in front of me.

"What's wrong, my love?" asks Sage, resting her hand on mine.

"I can't do it," I sob, my bottom lip wobbling like mad. "It was a stupid resolution. I'm *never* going to be able to swim."

"Ah," she replies. "The age-old New Year's resolution quandary. You do realize most people give up on them."

I nod miserably. "Yes, but my mother never allows it."

"Is this her resolution?" asks Sage.

"No. It's mine." I begin to sob again, feeling hopeless. "But I can't do it."

"You can," says Sage. "And you will. But Rome wasn't built in a day. You're here, in the water. That's your biggest hurdle. It might only seem like a mini victory but you've got to take your triumphs where you can get them. Maybe stop trying so hard, Fig. It's supposed to be fun, isn't it? Give yourself the week off. Have a think about how much you really want this."

Deep down I know she's right but it takes me until Saturday to work it out. Cue Stella to the rescue.

~~~

"Are you coming in then?" she calls.

"Give me a minute," I say.

I stand there for at least ten. As usual, my breath is stuck. I try to yawn and end up gagging as my throat constricts with panic.

Bubble, bubble, breathe.

Slowly, the words begin to take effect and I manage to take a deep breath. Then a little girl suddenly jumps into the water beside me. She makes an almighty splash, which scares the life out of me. But, when she comes up for air, her eyes aren't frightened at all. They're filled with energy, like she's just had the biggest buzz of her life. Maybe I can do it…

With another deep breath and a call of, "Get a bloody move on," from Stella, I jump in. It isn't a pretty sight. I forget to hold my nose and a ton of water goes up it. I come up, gasping for air, with snot bursting out of me and a spout of water shooting out of my mouth, because I tried to breathe too soon and now have a lungful of chlorine-flavoured, and God-knows-what-else, water.

The fearless little girl swims over to me and asks in her cutesy baby way if I'm OK. I can't answer because I'm still gagging.

"Are you a mermaid?" she asks.

I shake my head.

"I think you are," she giggles. "You just have to think like one."

"How does a mermaid think?" I want to ask but she's already swum over to her mum. Without armbands!

"You're in!" shrieks Stella. "Now what?"

"Torpedo into the middle," I reply.

"OK. Let's bomb the crap out of this pool then!"

I giggle nervously. "Stella," I hiss. "You can't talk like that here."

"Oh, don't be such an old fogy!" laughs Stella. Then she dives under the water away from my swipe.

Before I know it, I've dived after her. She's swimming away from me, still managing a big grin under the water, and I kick my legs quickly to try and catch her. I don't manage it for long because I suddenly realize what I'm doing and swallow half the pool again.

"Flip! You did it," shrieks Stella. "Fig! You did it. You just swam."

"Did I?"

Stella nods rapidly. "Yeah. You really swam. Kicked your feet and everything."

"Flipping heck..." I gasp. "I swam!"

And that's it. It's like a switch has been flicked on and I'm no longer scared to lift my feet.

WISHFUL THINKING

Perhaps buoyed by my success in the pool, I decide to try convincing Mubla to cancel the looming drama class, deeming my best moment to be after Sunday lunch, when she's had a glass of red wine.

"Mubla," I say in my sweetest, most conciliatory voice. "Can I talk to you about something?"

"Your drama class starts next week," she replies, as if reading my mind.

"Yes," I say. "About that. I'm not sure…"

"Lemony," interrupts Mubla. "You know the rules on resolutions. No giving up. It's little wonder succeeding at them isn't your strong point."

"That's because they're yours not mine." Actually, I don't say that because that would start a row. Instead I remain silent. Like I always do. My resolve crushed, as usual, by Mubla.

"It's a three-hour class," she says. "I'll take you. I need

to make sure you go. Oh, actually…" She frowns. "Scratch that. I have a meeting at work. Tom. Can you do it, please?"

Dab Dabs looks up with that vacant expression he uses when he doesn't want to engage with the conversation. "Hmm?"

"Acting classes," snaps Mubla. "You'll take Fig next week, won't you?"

"Oh. Yes. Of course," he replies, sending me a sympathetic look, which I return with a miserable scowl.

"What's wrong with you?" asks Mubla, catching it.

"I don't want to go," I moan. "I'd rather see Stella. I'm tired."

"Perhaps, if you spent less time socializing and more time focusing on your studies, you might have more time to sleep. What's Stella doing texting you at ten o'clock at night? And in that weird coded language you insist on using. What does WTAF stand for anyway?"

"You're not allowed to look at my phone. You promised after last time. Dab Dabs," I say loudly, "you said you'd have a word with her. She's not allowed to look at my phone."

"And who's she?" snaps Mubla. "The cat's mother? Less of that rudeness, thank you."

"You're the one who's being rude," I argue. "Dab Dabs!" This time I prod him sharply in the arm. "Tell her."

Dab Dabs glances uncomfortably between us. "Now, Wendy," he says, clearing his throat, "we did promise…"

"I did no such thing," retorts Mubla, her face colouring slightly.

"Yes, you did!" I yell.

Dab Dabs rests his hand on mine. "Fig. There's no need to shout. That won't get us anywhere. Wendy. Darling. Fig's fifteen. Don't you think it's time we trusted her just a smidge more?" He says this with a wink and a smile, as if that's going to change her mind.

Mubla shakes her head unwaveringly.

I growl my frustration. Thank goodness I've deleted any messages where I might have mentioned my resolution. I need to remain vigilant.

"Fine, I won't use it then," I say. "I'll turn it off. Then you won't be able to ring me at all. Just think about that, Mubla. No more daily five p.m. phone calls…"

I can see her wrestling with this and, for a moment, I feel victory within my reach. That is until Mubla says, "Fine. Then I'll send Aurora to pick you up from school and see you home."

"Wendy," mutters Dab Dabs.

"And what about Jago's clubs?" I reply, thinking quickly. "You've got him doing something every day of the week. Are you going to take him to them while Aurora is being my prison guard?"

"You're not a prisoner, Lemony," snaps Mubla. "Aurora is your nanny. And besides you know I'm at work. I can't possibly be in two places at once. You're being ridiculous."

"You're the one who's being ridiculous!" I shout. "And she's not my nanny. I'm fifteen. I can leave school next year—"

38

"Over my dead body. You will be in school until you have all of your qualifications."

"Wendy," mutters Dab Dabs again.

She grimaces at him, then says, "Well, fine then. I won't look at your phone… Much. Take it or leave it."

"Only if you stop calling me every day," I counter. "Take it or leave it…"

I leave the table with a deal of sorts, having promised that I'll ring Mubla every day when I've finished my homework.

"Fig."

I look down to see Jago clambering up the stairs after me like an eager puppy.

"Why don't you change your passcode from a number to a mixture of characters?" he asks. "So that Mubla can't work it out. I'll show you how."

"Thanks, Jago," I say. "Brilliant idea."

Jago beams. "Happy to help. Will you do one thing for me in return?"

I nod.

"Play Lego with me?"

DRAMA DRAMA

I haven't had a single phone call from Mubla all week and, for the first time ever, I actually feel … independent. I mean, I'm not totally ready to be on my own yet, but it's a start.

The dreaded Saturday morning drama class comes round far faster than the weekend usually does. If I wasn't studying relativity at school, I would say that this week has gone by at precisely five times the normal speed. Clearly my nerves are getting to me.

Dab Dabs and Jago come with me to the theatre, where a man dressed in black, with a yellow silk scarf and a giant grey handlebar moustache, is already instructing everyone to do some kind of ridiculous warm-up, involving shaking their bodies about and making silly noises with their lips.

I don't want to do this. But Dab Dabs gently presses me between my shoulder blades, propelling me towards my worst nightmare.

"Hello," he says, pumping the man's arm up and down in

a firm handshake. "Sorry we're late. These are my kids, Fig and Jago."

The man beams at Jago, who has come specially dressed in his astronaut outfit, complete with helmet and jetpack. "Hello, young man. Ready for take-off? My name's Andy. And you," he says, turning to me with a smile, "must be Fig."

My face is frozen into a grimace and all I can do is quickly nod my head. I woke up this morning, anxiety descending over me like a fast-spreading fog. I haven't been able to speak a word all morning. Thank goodness Jago has been doing all the talking.

Andy chortles at me but, when I still don't smile, his expression changes to sympathy. "Ah. Your mother said you were a bit nervous."

A bit nervous? I'm petrified.

"Um," murmurs Dab Dabs. "She suffers from severe stage fright. I, er…" His voice trails away as Andy realizes what he's up against. There's a stifling silence between the four of us, drowned out by the ridiculous chirping noises coming from the other actors.

"Well," says Andy, laughing nervously, "we'll soon get you over that. Nothing to worry about in the slightest."

I respond by dashing to the nearest toilet cubicle. A bitter taste fills my mouth and I spit the resulting bright yellow liquid of 'nothing left in my stomach' into the toilet. My throat is so tight I can't swallow. I feel like my muscles have tensed up and I can only make very small movements. The effect is horrendous, rather like rigor mortis, I'd imagine. Then I have a miraculous idea as the words 'bubble, bubble, breathe' float into my brain. Slowly, I can feel my shoulders relax as the oxygen finally reaches my lungs.

Bubble, bubble, breathe.

Andy is waiting for me in the foyer, Dab Dabs and Jago nowhere in sight.

Bubble, bubble, breathe.

"All set?" he asks. "Let's get you onstage to meet the Old MAD crew."

"Mad?" I ask.

"Old Mare Amateur Dramatics."

"Oh," I reply unenthusiastically.

"Come on. We're about to pretend to be jellyfish. You know. Relax your body and let yourself go – that sort of thing. You're going to love it…"

Erm…

BUBBLE, BUBBLE, BREATHE!

I'm not sure screaming the mantra inside my head is helpful. As he leads me towards the stage, my stomach lurches and I clamp my eyes shut. I don't want to do this.

BUBBLE, BUBBLE, BREATHE!

"This is Fig, everyone," says Andy.

I open one tentative eye, then the other to see a group of kids my age staring at me like I'm an alien from another planet. I exhale a long wavering breath. Nope. I definitely don't want to be here…

Progress Report   Date: 25th February

Swimming Outcomes

Perform a torpedo glide on back for 5 metres ✓

Perform a horizontal stationary scull on back ✓

Tread water for 30 seconds ✓

Swim 100 metres front crawl, face in the water ✓

Swim 100 metres breaststroke ✓

Demonstrate an action for help ✓

Time spent swimming	36 hours
Swimming distance achieved (by front crawl)	1,000 metres
100-metre time trial	4 mins
200-metre time trial	8 mins, 20 secs
400-metre time trial	Incomplete

Fears Encountered

Swimming	✓
Performing onstage	Incomplete
Water creatures — if you count pretend ones!	✓
Mubla	0.6%*

*Nominal value awarded for getting her to stop checking my phone

MATHEMATICAL NIGHTMARE

I wake with a jolt in the middle of the night, my phone buzzing by my ear. Tonight is the moment Stella celebrates the fleeting passing of her birthday, the 29th of February, which doesn't exist this year.

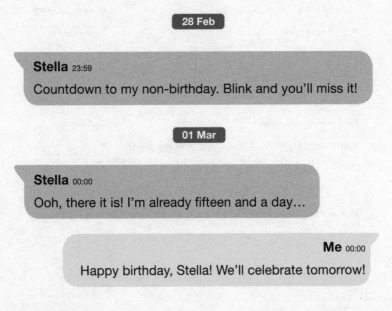

28 Feb

Stella 23:59
Countdown to my non-birthday. Blink and you'll miss it!

01 Mar

Stella 00:00
Ooh, there it is! I'm already fifteen and a day…

Me 00:00
Happy birthday, Stella! We'll celebrate tomorrow!

But trying to go back to sleep soon proves difficult with my stomach growling and every muscle in my body aching, no matter which position I lie in. Then my brain springs into action. Midnight, and the hours beyond, are exactly the time it's likely to do its most panicky thinking, and in this instance it's: *How am I going to afford this trip?*

I grab my budgeting notebook from its secret hiding place, the desk. You might think that's not secret, but it's a double bluff. Mubla won't look in it because it's *on display*. She's far more likely to go looking in drawers and cupboards. And besides it's in an old maths exercise book and I know she won't look there. Maths isn't her strong point...

Most of the money for this trip is coming from a savings account, which technically I'm not supposed to touch until I'm eighteen, but that's only a *few* years away. My parents have been paying into it since I was born. And my grandfather, Mubla's father, who has only met me once, pays rather handsomely on birthdays and at Christmas. I think that's out of guilt.

I log in now to check the current balance. I'm not

supposed to know the password or the login details but, as this used to be Dab Dabs's laptop, all the login details are saved. Computers really aren't *his* strong point.

I begin jotting down numbers in an attempt to estimate my budget.

<u>Known Quantities</u>

Savings: £10,000
Total price of admission for the twenty swims: £2,000

<u>Unknown Quantities</u>

Round-the-world ticket (guesstimate £5,000)
Cost of fake passport (guesstimate £250)
Cost of accommodation
Cost of food
Leftover money for sundries

I'm beginning to see why my brain is panicking...

$$£10,000 - £5,000 - £2,000 - £250 = £2,750$$

$$\therefore £2,750 \div 12 = £229.16/month \text{ or } £229.16 \div 30$$
$$= £7.64/day$$

Somehow I don't think that's possible, so I decide to work

out my travel ticket, hoping that will make me feel better.

<u>Travel Ticket Conditions</u>

1. Only fly where necessary (not my favourite mode of transport!)
2. Bus and train where possible
3. Cheapest option as long as time available and safe

Slowly, I piece together a possible route round the world, the cost of which is immense, even choosing the cheapest option. And the worry that has been slowly growing in me now screams inside my head like a siren. I've got to steal from Mubla. Use her credit card to buy the round-the-world ticket. It's the only way.

What will she say? What will she do? Press charges? I wouldn't put it past her. She's going to be so mad. I begin to pace the room, feeling wired. How am I ever going to get back to sleep?

I sit down again and work out the sums, this time taking out the travel ticket.

$$£10,000 - £2,000 - £250 = £7,750$$

In other words, £645/month or £21.50/day.
Well, it's a bit better.
I climb into bed, feeling weary. I have to get up in four

hours. But my tired brain won't stop whirring and the thought that I'll have to convert my money into all sorts of currencies suddenly floats into my head. Now, on the face of it, that should obviously send me into a tailspin because I have *no* idea how to do that. Then I think of all the possibilities of doing maths – I'll have to work out the conversions for every new country I go to! That's heaven for my brain! I feel myself finally begin to relax. It's going to be OK.

FAITH

E = T + 171

These last few months of learning to swim haven't been easy. Once my feet were off the ground, I found it hard to put my face in the water. Lying horizontally just felt weird and I couldn't control my breathing. And the arms! Trying to coordinate them and kicking my feet while turning my head to breathe? Impossible! That's three things at once. But I'm finally getting it. It doesn't look pretty and I'm very slow, but I can swim four lengths of the pool.

I'm treating myself to an extra large banana milkshake with whipped cream today, having completed three sets of four lengths, all using front crawl with the middle set using the pull buoy, a float in the shape of a figure of eight, which I have come to rely on heavily. (Mainly because it makes me feel like I'd at least have something to cling to if I started drowning.)

My phone grumbles with a quick succession of texts. Mubla. I knew it couldn't last. At least she's not *ringing* me.

Mubla 17:34
Where are you?

Mubla 17:35
Have you done your homework?

Mubla 17:45
Your English assignment is due tomorrow.

My shoulders sag. I don't understand why Mubla's on my case so much. I'm doing well in school. I've already got an A Level in maths and I'm taking English GCSE a year early. I'm just not competitive like she is...

It's her next text that causes my breath to catch in my throat and I have to force down the mouthful of milkshake, which is like pushing a bathtub of water through a pinprick-sized hole.

Mubla 18:10
I've read your essay. It's only worthy of a C. B if your teacher is feeling generous.

I sink my head into my hands. She doesn't even trust me to write my own essays...

Oh, what am I doing? Why did I think I could take on such a big challenge? Mubla clearly doesn't have any faith in me. I may be able to swim two hundred metres but the first swimming event, which is in less than five months, is ten times that!

An involuntary sob bursts out, as my feelings of hopelessness swallow me up.

"You all right there, Fig?"

I look up to see Sage hovering in front of me, her tray laden with a pot of tea and numerous slices of cake.

"May I?" she asks, and pulls out the chair opposite. "You're still coming swimming then? Most people would have given up by now."

"I'm not most people," I sigh.

"So I see," she chuckles. "You're doing brilliantly. The last time I saw you, you were stuck blowing bubbles at the bottom of the pool. Now look at you. Swimming laps. And front crawl at that. My goodness, you've come a long way."

"Doesn't feel like it," I mutter. And then, for some reason, I find myself telling this complete stranger everything about my crazy resolution and how I have only 144 days until my first event.

"But I can hardly swim," I finish. "Two hundred metres

at a snail's pace. How am I ever going to be able to swim two kilometres?"

Sage nibbles on her chocolate cake thoughtfully. "Well, you're not aiming to be the fastest person to swim the world, are you?"

"No, but…"

"So stop worrying about your speed. Just work on your endurance. The distance will soon come."

My phone, lying between us on the table, buzzes angrily and we both lean over to read the message.

Mubla 18:25

And I mean now, Lemony. Come on. We've got work to do.

Sage eyes me with sympathy. "Overzealous mother?"

I nod miserably.

"The reason why you're off to swim the world?"

"In part," I say with a shrug.

"Then I think it's time," she says, handing me a flyer for a swimming club. "Come and swim with the Mermaids, Fig. We'll help. Guaranteed…"

MERMAIDS

Old Mare is a place most notable for four things:

<u>Old Mare Facts</u>

1. It is the hilliest place in the country
2. It has a giant Victorian sea pool carved out of the rocks
3. It is home to the Professional Open-water Talent Scout Association
4. Perhaps because of point 3, a high number of coaches and elite swimmers have grown up here, the most famous being eighty-three-year-old Fred Willoughby who swam the Channel — there and back

The swimming club that Sage was talking about is the Old Mare Mermaids, who train three times a week at my pool until mid-April when their open-water season starts and they shift to the sea pool in the harbour.

By some stroke of luck, Mubla has landed a big case that's going to hold her attention for months, keeping her working late and (hopefully) unable to watch over me quite as closely. The sixty-minute sessions will be over by 6 p.m., which means I can get home, shower and do my homework in time to see her coming through the door at 8 p.m., none the wiser about where I've been.

I manage to talk Stella into coming with me for the first session because, even though I already know Sage, I'm feeling beyond terrified. My throat rapidly constricts with fear of the unknown and I'm afraid that I'm going to be sick. What if they laugh at me? What if I don't fit in?

"You all right?" Stella frowns when we meet outside the pool. I must look as green as I feel.

"Qualmish," I mutter with a grimace. "You?"

"Trepidatious," laughs Stella.

"What are you nervous about?"

"I'm not much of a swimmer, Fig," shrugs Stella. "Not like you. I don't mind coming to use the slides and splash about, but swimming? I hate it. I hate the way chlorine mucks up my hair colour. Soz…"

"Why didn't you say something?" I ask. "You don't have to get in the water. Just watch me from the café upstairs."

"Really? You don't mind? But I thought you said you were terrified of meeting these amazing swimmers? That you've only ever swum two hundred metres and they can probably swim ten times as much…"

And, with that reminder, I rush off to the loos to actually be sick, while Stella mutters sympathetic cooing noises from outside the cubicle.

~~~

There's a group of ladies doing a warm-up at the side of the pool when I arrive and they're not the young, lean athletes my panicky brain is expecting. The Old Mare Mermaids, I am relieved to see, are, in fact, all plump old ladies, with wobbly thighs and loose skin hanging from their arms.

I take a deep breath. "Hi," I say. "I'm Fig. I'm looking for Maud? Sage sent me."

The middle-aged woman leading the warm-up looks up at me from her toe-touching exercise. She's got a big round face framed by a short greying bob with a blunt fringe. Her cheeks are already bright red from exertion but she has really kind eyes and her face is immediately alight with a welcoming smile.

"Hello, Fig," she exclaims. "I'm Maud. Welcome to the Mermaids."

She goes on to introduce me to each of the women. There are about twenty of them, all with similar old-fashioned names along the lines of Sylvia, Mildred and Susan. I spot Sage and give her a big wave but she looks at me blankly as if she doesn't know me.

"Pop your stuff down there," Maud tells me. "We'll just

finish this warm-up and then we'll get going in the water."

Honestly, I feel completely ridiculous doing the exercises alongside these women. I must be at least sixty years younger than some of them and a good fifteen centimetres taller than most. I really am beginning to wonder whether Sage has played a very good joke on me. Or maybe it's worse. Maybe she's got dementia and doesn't even remember inviting me…

"OK," calls Maud. "We've got a tough session today. Sorry, ladies, but it's time we put a spring in our swim. It's time to kiss goodbye to our winter blues!"

She claps her hands together and, with a playful glint in her eye, bursts out laughing. The other ladies soon join in and the volume rises as they natter about how much they're looking forward to the summer.

"So, let's do one hundred easy, one hundred pull, one hundred kick, then one hundred easy and then we'll begin the main set. We're in lanes five and six, so let's get going." Maud smiles at me. "Did you get that, Fig? Sage told me you've just learned to swim, so do what you can, OK?"

I nod. Thank God I read up on swimming terminology. Surely it can't be that hard. If these women can do it…

EAT CAKE, SWIM

I'm wheezing like an old lady with a two-packet-a-day habit. I can't even hoist myself out of the pool and have to use the ladder. I can barely stand up I'm so exhausted. The other ladies, in contrast, look flushed and tired, but they're all beaming.

"How did you do, Fig?" asks Sage. "Did you enjoy it?"

I'm still panting too hard to really answer and can only grin at her, feeling thankful that she's finally remembered me.

"You've got tons of potential, you know," she continues. "Big tall girl like you. Get your speed up and you could be an Olympic swimmer."

I frown. What's she on about? Sage is the one who told me *not* to worry about things like that.

"You coming, Myrtle?"

And suddenly I see where my confusion has arisen. There's another Sage getting out of the pool. She looks identical, right down to the swimming hat.

"Hello, my love," says the actual Sage, pulling me into a hug. "I'm so glad you could make it. I see you've met my sister."

"Come on, you two gasbags," calls Maud. "We don't want to miss the best part…"

The best part turns out to be cake. We pile into the café, where we commandeer four tables and I'm told to have a seat while Maud takes everyone's orders. I order my usual banana milkshake and wave at Stella, who is patiently reading, to join us.

"How'd it go?" she asks.

"Knackering," I laugh. "These ladies can swim!"

I introduce Stella to everyone, as giant slices of coffee cake are pushed in front of us.

"I-I didn't order this," I stammer.

"That's why we swim," says Maud. "So we can eat cake. Burn the calories then fill up again. It's genius if you think about it."

"Why can't you just eat cake?" I ask, frowning.

This makes the ladies laugh even harder. I'm not sure why.

"How often do you swim then?" asks Stella, tucking into her own slice.

"Three times a week," says Sage. "Every day in the summer when we're in the sea pool. Then we usually head on down to the Summer's Point Café. I think we keep them in business with the number of cream teas that we consume."

"Which one's she again?" whispers Stella.

"Go on, eat up." Myrtle pushes the plate towards me. "You've earned it. That was a tough session today."

I take a bite of the brown sponge and buttercream and soon find myself wolfing it down. Cake has never tasted this good.

Sage and Myrtle grin at me and I notice for the first time that their different-coloured eyes are the opposite way round. If only I could remember which way Sage's were!

"See," laughs Sage. "Always tastes better after a swim like that. Have some more."

"Do you really swim three times a week?" I ask.

"Sometimes more," says Myrtle. "Depends on how achy I'm feeling and how mean Maud is being." She leans in to me secretively. "Maud's the one who writes the training plans. They vary according to how much cake she's eaten."

"What's that?" asks Sage, leaning in.

"I was telling them about Maud," laughs Myrtle.

"Sorry," interrupts Stella, asking the one question I'm dying to know the answer to. "Which one of you is Sage and which is Myrtle?"

"I'm Sage," says Sage, leaning forward with her eyes wide. "That's Myrtle, the one with the right green eye."

She goes on to tell us that she and Myrtle are mirror twins, which basically means they've got the same characteristics but reversed. Sage has the left green eye. She's also left-handed and has the same teeth as Myrtle but on the opposite side. She even says that her body's organs are opposite too and that she has what is called situs inversus.

"D'you think that's a real thing?" Stella asks me on the way home.

I shrug. "I'll ask Dab Dabs. He'll know."

"Is situs inversus a thing?" I ask Dab Dabs at dinner.

"What's that?" he shouts back. I think he might be going deaf. The other day I asked him to pass me the potatoes and he started talking about an old man he'd been working on, something about needing to reconstruct his nose.

"Is situs inversus a real thing?" I reply loudly.

"Lemony, please don't shout at my dinner table," says Mubla quietly.

I stare at her. "But..."

Mubla sighs heavily. "Are you going to argue with me too? Because I've had a day and a half of it."

"But Dab Dabs..." I say, trying to get my point across.

"Lemony," says Mubla with a warning tone. "What did I just say?"

I bite my lip.

"Yes, it is a real thing, Fig," says Dab Dabs, breaking the tense silence. "It means the heart and other organs are on the opposite side of the body."

"Awesome," squeals Jago. "Is that really possible? Does the body work in the same way, just in reverse? Have you ever worked on one, Dab Dabs?"

"No, but I'd love to," says Dab Dabs, his eyes alight. "I have seen one, though…"

This leads to a bizarre conversation about a dead body exhibition that he went to years ago. Jago goes wild for the idea. Me, not so much. Not sure I would really want to walk round a room full of dead bodies on display. Especially after Dab Dabs describes one of them being cut completely in half. I'm used to the funeral parlour, but that's taking it a step too far.

"Can we please end this conversation about bodies?" says Mubla with a yawn. "It's bad enough having dead ones in the basement but we don't have to talk about them incessantly as well, do we? Is this something you studied at school, Lemony? I'm not sure I saw it in the biology syllabus…"

"No, I met someone at the poo—" I stop short, making Mubla narrow her eyes at me. "I mean the pool table. Stella and I were playing pool."

"Where?" demands Mubla.

"Oh, just the youth club," I reply, trying to sound casual.

Mubla frowns. "On a school night, Lemony? How many times do I have to remind you?" She nods at the house rules displayed on the fridge.

<u>House Rules</u>

1. Complete all homework on the day it is given
2. Practise the piano
3. Exercise
4. Then, and only if there's time, engage in activities for pleasure

"But I got most of my homework done," I protest.

Mubla raises an eyebrow. "Like that English essay you got a B plus for?"

"It's maths," I reply. "You're welcome to check it. How are you on relativity?"

Mubla hardly bats an eyelid. "And what about your piano practice?"

"I'm just going," I answer, putting down my cutlery in defeat.

Practising the piano is a habit left over from the time when Mubla wanted me to be a concert pianist. She had me practising for three hours a day, every day for a year, double at the weekends. I didn't make it because of the aforesaid stage fright. But Mubla still insists I practise, though these days she insists on my using the soft pedal. I think it's because I'm learning Dab Dabs's favourite song.

'Scenes from an Italian Restaurant' sits untouched on the piano's music rest. It's an epic thirteen-page opera of a pop song, with numerous different styles, getting faster and louder throughout. Mubla loathes it.

I begin with relish but, by halfway, my forearms are throbbing with the unfamiliar fast-paced action and it's beginning to sound a bit, well, dodgy.

"What the hell is that racket?" asks Mubla, her scrunched-up face peering round the door.

"Billy Joel."

"Well, stop it," she growls. "How am I supposed to get any work done with that blasting out? You need to practise more. It sounds horrendous."

The irony of that statement is completely lost on her.

PACT TO ACT

"That sounded fantastic, Fig," says Dab Dabs enthusiastically when I emerge from the front room. "Triumph of a piece that is. Have you got a minute?" He motions to the basement. "I want to hear more about this person you met..."

As soon as we get down the stairs, he asks, "How old were they?"

"Early seventies," I say. "Why?"

"Oh, just trying to assess the likelihood of whether I might get to do any reconstruction work on them. Do you think you can put in a good word for me?"

"Dab Dabs," I scold. "That's dark. I can't exactly tell someone that they should use you when they die!"

Dab Dabs looks rather meekly at me. "Nothing wrong with a recommendation, Fig. Word of mouth isn't exactly the way to grow my business, is it? Not many seances these days."

I frown.

"Seances," he repeats. "It would be the only way the dead people I've worked on could review my work, wouldn't it? Word of mouth?"

I stare in disbelief. Quite how he manages to run a whole funeral director's business I do not know. "The word of mouth would come from the grieving family, Dab Dabs. Not the dead people themselves."

Dab Dabs stares at me for a long while. "Oh," he says quietly. "Yes. Quite right."

I pace slowly round the room, looking at the portraits on the wall, expertly lit by angled spotlights. They're in thin black frames with large white mounts. If you could ignore the strong smell of disinfectant, you'd almost think you were in an art gallery.

"You should put an exhibition together, Dab Dabs," I say. "You could call it *Death Becomes Them*."

"Fig," snorts Dab Dabs, wrinkling his nose. "Now *that's* in poor taste."

So photographs of dead people is a no go, but an exhibition of preserved dead bodies is fine?

I run my fingers along the vials of liquids on the workbench. "Your latest victim?" I ask, pointing at the body on the table.

Dab Dabs nods.

"What did he die of?" I ask.

He shakes his head. "Shouting at his mother at the

dinner table I shouldn't wonder."

We both dissolve into giggles.

"So," says Dab Dabs, looking up at me over his special magnified glasses, "how's the resolution going?"

"Terrible," I sigh. "I've tried, Dab Dabs. Honest. But it's been five weeks and I haven't been able to utter a word, much less do any acting. It's Mubla's worst resolution ever."

Dab Dabs grins. "Agreed. I've been pretending to keep up with mine too."

I have no recollection of what his is.

"Doughnuts," he says sheepishly. "Mubla wants me to cut down."

"Oh, you should try exercise then," I say, thinking of the Mermaids. "Burn the calories, then eat the cake."

Dab Dabs frowns at me, nodding slowly. "Mmm. That's not a bad idea actually. Yeah. I could probably fit in a run between surface embalming and moisturizing."

"What do I do about the acting, Dab Dabs? I hate it. I'm never going to be an actress."

"Well…" he replies slowly. "Why don't we just 'act' as if you're going?"

"Really?"

He nods and, before he can change his mind, I gasp, "Deal!"

TWO SUNDAY LUNCHES

E = T + 151

"I thought you two were going out for lunch," says Stella's mum, Nhu. She's frying up another batch of spring rolls for us because she knows I like them. I have to wait to finish my mouthful.

"Well, according to Myrtle," I say, "Sage is the worst cook on earth…"

Stella leans over to grab my phone. "Show me what Myrtle's text said again."

`26 Mar`

Myrtle 08:34
Eat before you get here.

Sage and Myrtle have become our new best friends. I suppose if you eat cake with someone three times a week, you really get to know them well. I have the kind of conversations with them that I imagine other people have with their grandparents. Dab Dabs's parents died when I was a toddler and my other grandfather lives miles away, so I've had little to no contact with older people.

Sage and Myrtle are full of hilarious stories about being twins, like the time they got arrested wearing only their bras when they were at a peaceful protest that turned nasty and the policeman thought he was seeing double. Or the time they ended up in a fist fight in the back of a van and Sage had to go to hospital to have stitches.

Anyway, we're going to Sage's house for Sunday lunch today and, thanks to Myrtle's warning, I've eaten a whole plate of spring rolls, much to Nhu's amusement.

Stella's so lucky. Her family life couldn't be more different to mine. Take mealtimes – where conversation is actively encouraged. I think Mubla would have us eat in silence if it wasn't for Jago's endless questions.

"Who is this Sage woman again?" asks Nhu, laughing as I help myself to a large chunk of pineapple upside-down cake.

That's another thing. When Nhu asks me a question, it's not to interrogate me or catch me out. It's because she's interested.

"Just someone we met at the pool," I reply, my mouth bulging like a hamster.

Stella stares at me with wide eyes. "How do you fit all that in?"

"Swimming," I laugh. "I can't seem to get enough food."

"Help yourself to as much as you like, Fig," grins Nhu. "You're always welcome."

"Thanks," I giggle. "I'd eat more but we'd better get going. Don't want to be late..."

～～～

It turns out Myrtle was telling the truth. The roast chicken is as dry as a bone, the vegetables have been boiled to death and the roast potatoes are still frozen in the middle. It's like trying to force down rocks.

"I'm sorry, Sage," I say. "I haven't got much of an appetite today."

Sage shrugs. "Oh well. Save some room for my crumble, won't you?"

Myrtle shakes her head very subtly.

"D'you know what?" I say, trying to choke down a giggle. "I think I'm even too full for that."

"Stella's been telling me you're on some crazy mission this year," says Myrtle, settling herself into an armchair after lunch.

I glare in Stella's direction. She grins back. "She forced it out of me, Fig. What was I supposed to do?"

"Not tell her?" I growl.

I can't help feeling scared. Aren't I running the risk that the more people I tell, the more likely it is that Mubla's going to find out?

"Go on, tell her about it," whispers Sage. "It's killing me

not being able to say anything."

"You haven't told her then?" asks Stella. "I didn't think twins could keep secrets from each other."

Myrtle snorts. "What, because we can telepathically read each other's minds? Utter nonsense." She points at Sage. "Keeping secrets was her job once upon a time."

Sage grins. "She's right. I used to work for the Secret Service."

"Really?" I say. "What did you do there?"

Sage smirks. "Well, that would involve me telling you a secret and I can't do that."

I narrow my eyes at her, which she returns with an arch of her eyebrow, until I hold up my hands in defeat. "OK, I'll tell Myrtle. But you have to all promise not to breathe a word to another living soul..."

THE SWIMMERS SHOW

APRIL 23 – 24 | AQUA EXCEL

POWERED BY
VOYAGES OF THE WATER TREADERS
SWIM RIGHT

BE ONE OF THE 50,000+ ATTENDEES AT
THE LARGEST WATER CONVENTION CENTRE
IN THE COUNTRY!
300+ BRANDS | SPECIAL GUESTS & EXPERTS
DEMONSTRATION POOL

The Swimmers Show proudly presents the perfect place to prepare for the swimming season. Whatever your level, come and explore the latest kit, take advantage of expert training advice and be inspired by our pro athletes.

Guests include open–water swimming guru turned motivational speaker, the Boss in THEATRE B8 at 12 p.m.

BIOGRAPHY

Nobody knows the Boss's actual name,
or if they do they're keeping it very quiet.
This woman is one of the most formidable
swimmers of her generation. Known for being the
only person to complete the Six Seas swimming
challenge within a year, she has gone on to swim
some of the most difficult open-water courses
available. With such incredible accomplishments
under her belt, and all before she turned thirty,
she has successfully reinvented herself as
the Queen of Motivational Speaking.

Come and be wowed by her stories
and be inspired to dream...

Swimwear can be purchased on the day.

Follow her on social media: @TheBoss

SPIES

E = T + 144

Annoyingly, my to-do list has hardly anything crossed off it so I'm focusing on a task I can do, which is to book a place at the Swimmers Show. It's where I can register for over half the swims on my list and where I plan to go to a motivational talk given by the Boss, a long-distance swimmer I read about. But I immediately hit a problem: I can't book a place on the talk because I'm fifteen and still a minor. Since I haven't yet figured out how to get a fake ID, I can't go down that route. There's only one person with the technical know-how that I can ask. Jago.

As I mentioned earlier, Jago is a child genius. When it comes to technology, you name it, he can do it. I blame Aurora for giving him her phone when he was eight months old.

He greets me with a huge grin, his blond hair standing on end like a troll and his eyes wide and glazed like he's been looking at a computer screen for too long, which he probably has. "Fig!"

"I need your help," I whisper.

"Oh sure, sure," he says, pulling me into his bedroom. "What can I do?"

"Well, firstly, you can't tell Mubla, Dab Dabs or Aurora."

"'Course," says Jago. "Are you playing a secret spy game?"

I nod quickly at him, grateful that he has provided the answer to my problem. "Yeah. Want to be in on it?"

He gasps. "Do I get to decide our spy names?"

"Absolutely," I say.

"Yay! What do you need then?"

"I need you to get me a place on this," I say, pushing the Swimmers Show leaflet under his nose.

"Sure. Two ticks." Jago taps away quickly at his keyboard, then looks up at me, the computer screen reflecting brightly in his glasses. "Done. Is that all?" He sounds disappointed – it was obviously very easy.

"Well, no," I say, thinking on my feet. "Obviously there's more to do. Can you find out how I can obtain a fake passport?"

Jago resumes tapping on the keyboard.

I stare at him, feeling flabbergasted. He hasn't asked me a single question! Does he really believe my spy story? And how does he even know where to look for such a thing as a fake ID?

"You need to talk to, um –" he peers closely at the computer screen – "someone called the Fixer. You'll need a photo and five hundred pounds."

"Five hundred pounds," I repeat. That's two hundred and fifty more than my estimate. My budget's dwindling and I haven't even got out of the country. "And, er, do you have a number for this Fixer?"

Jago shakes his head. "Nope. You'll have to ask around. Says here you'll find him at a bar called the Blue Lagoon."

"The Blue Lagoon," I repeat. "And how have you found this out?"

"You can find anything if you know where to look for it," replies Jago mysteriously. "Now about those spy names. I was thinking you could be Agent Rose Brown and I could be Agent Hugh Moonstone?"

"Excellent work, Agent Moonstone," I say, using my best posh accent. This appears to thrill Jago to bits. It seems that the easiest way to get a six-year-old genius to do anything is to just give them some attention. "Now, how about we work on finding some mysteries for us to solve?"

"Yes!" says Jago excitedly. "Let's write some lists. I'll do 'How to be a spy' and you can do 'Criminals we need to catch'."

We spend the rest of the afternoon playing spies, which mainly involves creating and colouring in ID cards, and running round the garden with Jago's walkie-talkies.

COUNTDOWN

E = T + 130

"How about an episode of *Countdown*?" asks Sage, holding up a videotape. "I've got an entire cassette's worth here."

Stella and I are spending the afternoon with her, as she's not feeling well and wants the company. I've brought Jago along too, since I thought he'd be over the moon to meet a real-life spy, though currently he's in shy mode and stuck to my side. He has, however, come dressed for the occasion in a flying hat, goggles and bomber jacket combo. He's literally flying with this Second World War spy idea.

"What's *Countdown*?" I ask.

"You've never heard of it?" asks Myrtle, plonking herself down next to me on the sofa.

"I have," whispers Jago in my ear.

"I would have thought you two would watch it every day," laughs Sage. "What with Miss Mathematical Brain over here and little Miss Word Bird over there."

"Fig's good with words too," says Jago proudly.

Sage snorts. "She's good at everything from what Stella's been telling me. Runner-up in an International Spelling Bee, top of her class in maths. Concert pianist aged ten. Where does it end?"

I glance at Stella. How much has she been telling them about me?

"What are your words for today then?" asks Myrtle eagerly.

"Perturbed," I mutter, worrying — if Stella crumbles so easily when questioned by a couple of little old ladies — what she's going to be like when she's interrogated by Mubla once I'm gone?

"Insouciant," counters Stella, unfazed by my glare.

Myrtle giggles. "Can I join in? Tickled pink…"

Countdown turns out to be a masterpiece of a game show, made up purely of finding words from letters and — the *pièce de résistance* — calculating a number from six random numbers, usually one large and five small.

"You could do that, Fig," says Stella.

"What's that?"

"Calculate sums while you're swimming long distances," she replies.

I glance nervously at Jago. I don't want him to know about this. Fortunately he's fast asleep. I glare at Stella. She's getting sloppy with this secret.

The question is still troubling me when I meet her at the school gate the next day. "Stella. You won't tell Mubla, will you?"

"Course not. Why would you think that?"

"It's just that you told Sage and Myrtle everything about me. And you mentioned the swimming in front of Jago."

"He was asleep," counters Stella.

"Yeah, but you haven't seen Mubla when she's really mad. She can squeeze blood out of a stone."

Stella laughs. "Sage and Myr are harmless, Fig. I think Sage really was a secret agent. She only asked a few questions and, before I knew it, I was telling her our life stories. Look, don't worry. Your secret's safe with me. And them."

I exhale slowly but I *am* worried. I've gone from telling no one about my secret to telling three people. Maybe I should start learning to trust my friends…

THE SWIMMING DEMONSTRATION

E = T + 123

The Swimmers Show is in a convention centre, about an hour out of town. It's gigantic, making me feel an equal measure of fear and excitement. Jam-packed full of stands selling every kind of swimming gadget you can think of. I'm glad I got Sage to drive me.

Safely settled in a coffee booth with two steaming mochas that cost a small fortune, we lay out the venue map on the table and inspect the schedule. We're both horrified to realize that there are two more halls like this and I can't help but wonder what on earth is in them.

Turns out they've got a giant, glass-sided, twenty-metre pool set up in the main exhibition hall, marked A on the map, and people are actually doing laps in it.

"Wow," I say, pressing my nose to the glass. "That's amazing. I wonder what it's like to swim in a glass pool?"

"Let's ask," replies Sage.

"What? I didn't mean now. I…"

But it's too late. Sage has marched up to the nearest official-looking person. The commentary stops as the bald-headed man covers his microphone to listen to her. Then he glances over at me and nods.

Sage returns, looking triumphant. "He says yes, you can. It's normally the Swim Right athletes in there, but he says, if you want to have a go, go right ahead."

"But, but… I haven't got any swimming gear," I say weakly.

"Hmmm," says Sage, looking around. "Now where would you find somewhere to buy a swimsuit? Hmmm. Where? You're right, Fig. You'll have to swim naked."

"Sage Olander!" I shriek. I stare at the pool. The water does look rather enticing and I can actually swim now. Why shouldn't I do it? "Fine," I say, sounding more decisive than I feel.

I find myself poised on the edge in a brand-new swimsuit and goggles, which Sage has negotiated a discount on. My dive is rather sloppy, a bit of a bellyflop actually, and it draws unwanted attention. I know this because I can see everyone peering in. It's a very strange experience, making eye contact with people on dry land, while I swim underwater, though Sage is there, giving me a big grin and a thumbs up.

As more people are drawn to the sides of the pool to watch, my stage fright kicks in and it starts to affect my breathing, so that I flail around in freestyle, my arms going all over the place, and water spurting out of my nose. I can't really make out what the commentator is saying because my ears are too full of water and all I can hear is my rasping breath. I can see people laughing, though.

~~~

Sage is waiting for me by the changing room when I've finished. She's bouncing edgily on her toes and won't look me in the eye.

"What?" I ask, a sense of dread spreading over me.

Her face goes all wonky while she considers what to say. It's making me feel nervous. "Did you, er, hear much of what was being said?"

"No, why?"

"Oh, that's good," she says, looking relieved.

"Why's that good?" I ask, my anxiety beginning to creep into my throat.

"Because they, er, used you as a, er, 'how not to swim' demonstration," replies Sage cautiously.

"What!" I shriek. "I wasn't that bad, was I?"

"*We-ell*," replies Sage slowly. "There wasn't anywhere to hide in that glass tank, was there? And you yourself said you get stage fright, so…"

"I'm not that bad a swimmer," I say, my confidence seeping into the floor.

"No, of course you're not," says Sage. But she pauses for just a little too long and I know she's just saying that to make me feel better. "What time did you say the Boss talk was?"

"Midday," I reply glumly. "Why, what time is it now?"

"Five to," says Sage. "Meet you back here in an hour."

THE BOSS

I arrive five minutes late for the talk, flustered and anxious from my swimming demo disaster. The auditorium is packed and I look around helplessly, trying to figure out where to sit. The woman onstage is playing a ukulele. Have I got the right room?

"Well, come in then," she says, making the audience turn and stare. "There's a seat here at the front. Chop-chop!"

My face burns as I make my way over. The thirty-something woman, who I assume is the Boss, takes me in in one glance and doesn't return my smile. "Now where was I?" She begins playing the ukulele again and launches into a funny song about swimming which has the whole audience laughing.

She's not at all what I was expecting. Shoulder-length brown hair and piercing blue eyes. I know this from the hard stare she keeps giving me. And she's small. Not built like an upside-down pyramid, just ... athletic-looking.

"Thanks, guys," says the Boss as the applause dies down. "So, why are we here?"

Silence.

"Well, let me start, then it's your turn." She giggles as if she's flirting. "*I'm* here to inspire *you* to fulfil your dreams."

It's like she's said some magic words because the room erupts into another round of applause.

"So what are my credentials then?" she says. "I'm the only person to have swum the Six Seas in less than twelve months. That's six swims of between twenty and thirty miles each, often crossing in some pretty awful conditions."

She goes on to talk about the amount of training she did, which I avidly note down word for word, then the floor is open for questions.

"What made you want to do this?" asks someone from the depths of the auditorium.

The Boss beams at the audience and, for the first time, says something that resonates with me. "Ever since I was a little girl, I wanted to do something different. Be different to the rest of the class clowns. But I didn't really start swimming seriously until I was in my twenties. I finished up at university, couldn't get the job I wanted and needed a focus in my life, so I joined a swimming club. I started doing the odd distance swim and found that I really liked the monotony of it. It was a time when I could meditate and sort my crap out."

She chuckles to herself. "And I, er, had a lot of that.

Anyways, I've come up with some of my best ideas while swimming. You see it's all about the head." She taps her temple with a well-manicured finger. "What's going on here will dictate how far you can swim, how you'll cope under pressure and who you can be. It's not about your body. Anyone can train to be an athlete. But it's who you are in here that counts."

"Can I just say," says a girl a few rows behind me, "that you're my hero. Your epic journeys have really inspired me."

"Thanks," replies the Boss happily, winking at her.

"Well, I er…" This girl is obviously completely in awe of the Boss. Funny, because I find her to be a bit smarmy. There's something about her that's annoying me and I can't quite put my finger on it. "Er, is there anything special about you that enabled you to achieve such an incredible goal?"

"Apart from my wingspan being longer than my height? No, nothing," replies the Boss, laughing, which everyone joins in with.

Fake. That's what it is! I instinctively don't trust her.

"What was the worst swim on the Six Seas?" calls out an excited voice.

"That would be the last one, crossing the Strait of Knar," replies the Boss, lowering her voice like she's telling a bedtime story. "The conditions were terrible. Everyone said we shouldn't do it, to leave it until the next day. But if I had done that I wouldn't be sitting here today as the only person to have completed the challenge within a year. So I insisted we continue. We weren't far in when I realized I was swimming towards a lightning storm. My coach wanted us to turn back but I couldn't do that. For two hours, I weathered that storm. The lightning flashed all around with waves three metres high. I had terrible seasickness, my head was throbbing and I was terrified I'd get struck by lightning. But I kept going. Stroke after stroke after stroke, I pounded my way across that sea. All twenty miles of it. I kept going because I had dared to dream. I had dared to dream that I could be the first woman, nay the first *person*, to complete this challenge. I wasn't going to let nature stop me."

Something about this story strikes me as untrue. You can't really swim in a lightning storm, can you? I mean, if the lightning hits the water, you're going to get fried. The water acts like a conductor. That's basic science. I put my hand up tentatively.

"Yes?" The Boss points at me.

"Isn't it dangerous to swim during a lightning storm?"

"Well, yes, it is," says the Boss. "That's the point of my story…"

"But," I say, interrupting her, "you were putting your coach at risk of electrocution by staying in the water."

"My coach," growls the Boss, her deadpan eyes fixed firmly on me, "would do anything for me." Then her voice lightens again as she looks about the room. "Anyway. Let's not get stuck on that one story. I'm here to help you.

I'm here to inspire you to dream…"

There are those magic words again and the rapt audience begin to whoop and clap.

I raise my hand again.

"Yes?" asks the Boss impatiently.

"What does the Boss stand for?"

The Boss bursts out laughing. "Ladies and gentlemen, this *ickle* mermaid doesn't know what the Boss stands for." I don't even flinch at the nickname or the condescending way she says it. I'm used to that. It's everyone laughing at me that I don't like. I sink lower in my seat, my stomach convulsing, feeling like I'm in my worst nightmare where I'm standing onstage naked while everyone points and jeers at me. "Let's tell her, shall we?"

Suddenly the whole room chants as one: "Big Ocean Sea Swimmer!"

"Right, does anyone *else* have a question for me?" says the Boss.

"What do you plan to do next?" says a man to my left.

"I'm going to be touring the world actually," says the Boss. "I'm an environmentalist. Swimming across the seas, I saw the litter that we've thrown away. We can't sustain that level of irresponsibility. The fact is, plastic's just not fantastic any more. My mission will be to raise awareness about that." Then she looks at her watch. "OK, now I want you to repeat after me: I can be extraordinary. I am extraordinary. I am inspired to dream…"

Progress Report   Date: 28th April

Swimming Outcomes

Successfully complete a tumble turn	✓
Successfully complete a standing start	✓
Swim 100 metres breathing (3/5/7/9)	✓
Swim 100 metres with bands	Incomplete

Time spent swimming	78 hours
Swimming distance achieved (by front crawl)	2,000 metres
100-metre time trial	2 mins
200-metre time trial	4mins 10 secs
400-metre time trial	8 mins, 35 secs

Fears Encountered

Swimming	✓
Performing onstage	Incomplete
Water creatures — if you count pretend ones!	✓
Mubla	3.2%*

*Based on the following calculation:

Number of phone calls from Mubla hassling me this month = 4

Compared with last month = 154

4 ÷ 154 = 2.597%

Add to that the random 0.6% from last Progress Report.

MURDERERS AND LOWLIFES

The big criminal case Mubla's been working on has been keeping her locked away in her study every night recently.

"Mubla?" I whisper at the door. "I've got your dinner."

The door flies open. Mubla is looking a little less tidy than I'm used to. Her red hair hanging down around her face in waves. Her shirt crumpled and make-up smeared. This is saying a lot. She always makes an effort with her appearance.

"Just put it there, would you, Lemony?" she says, pointing to a small space on her desk, which is almost entirely covered in paperwork.

"How's it going?" I ask.

Mubla growls her response. "Hmmm. Not well. I can't get my defendant to cooperate about someone who is the key to my whole defence. See this man?" She points to a photograph pinned to her vast office noticeboard, which has been taken hostage by reams of red string linking photos of different dodgy-looking criminals, and covered with

89

lists in Mubla's spidery handwriting.

I stare at the photo, beneath which is written:

<u>Defendant</u>
Name: Harry Milsom
Age: 26
Misdemeanours: 3 (2 shoplifting and 1 possession)
Felonies: 2 (aggravated and armed robbery)

"That's my client," says Mubla. "A dirty lowlife if there ever was one."

"Why are you representing him then?"

"Because that's what I do," she replies. "Anyway he won't give up the name of the Fixer. And the Fixer holds all the cards. Without him, I don't have much of a case."

"What does the Fixer do?"

"Everything." She stabs at the blank picture on the wall. Under it is a long list that makes my skin crawl:

<u>Alibi</u>
Name: the Fixer
Age: unknown
Convictions: 0
Known for (but found not guilty):
· Money-laundering
· Misappropriation of charity funds
· People-smuggling

- The Great Bank Job
- Fake ID including passports

"If I can just get him on the stand," says Mubla. "Get him to confirm that my client couldn't possibly have been in the building on the night in question and therefore couldn't have committed the murder..."

I frown at the pinboard. "Why couldn't he have been in the building?"

"Because he was busy committing another crime with the Fixer's help," replies Mubla bluntly. "But that's not what this trial is about."

"What was the other crime?"

"Bank robbery," says Mubla. "With aggravated assault."

I shiver. This guy really is a lowlife. "So the idea is to get him a not-guilty verdict for this case, then convict him for the crime he did commit?"

Mubla stares at me with disbelief, mid-mouthful. "The idea," she says after swallowing, "is to get him a not-guilty verdict full stop."

"Oh," I say.

"Well, thank you for my supper, Lemony. If you've nothing to add, I'll bid you goodnight." She kisses me on the forehead then gives me a firm shove out of the door.

It's only once I've walked past Jago's door that I allow myself to fall to bits. *I'm* supposed to find the Fixer for *my* fake passport...

THE FIXER

"Are we going in then?"

Sage and I have been sitting outside the Blue Lagoon for the last twenty-five minutes, neither of us showing much sign of being ready. As soon as I realized what I was up against, I texted her. It's a necessary evil that I need a fake passport and, of all the people I know, she's the only one I would trust to do this with me.

"Mmm-hmm," I manage, wanting desperately to scratch at my wig. Myrtle has worked wonders on my appearance. A full face of contouring make-up, so that I have actual cheekbones, proper shaped eyebrows and full lips. These, along with the dark brown bobbed wig, make me look like, well, an adult. Which I guess is the whole purpose of my getting a fake passport. But still I was unprepared for *this*. My breath immediately sticks in my throat. God, I hope Sage will do the talking for me.

"What can I get you, ladies?" asks the bartender.

"Whisky, straight up," replies Sage. "For both of us."

"Sage," I hiss under my breath. "I'm not allowed to drink alcohol. I'm fifteen."

"But you're pretending to be nineteen," replies Sage firmly. "You don't have to actually drink it..."

The familiar feelings of anxiety creep over me. What am I doing in a bar in the middle of nowhere? This is crazy. When the bartender puts the drink in front of me, I go into autopilot and take a sip. Oh my God. It *burns*! The back of my throat is on fire. That's disgusting!

"Bottoms up!" says Sage, raising her glass and downing it in one. "D'you like that?"

"No, it's vile," I say, resisting the urge to spit out the aftertaste lingering down my throat.

Sage rolls her eyes and motions to the bartender again, getting him to lean over so that she can whisper in his ear. "Same again for me, please. And I'm looking for the, er, the Fixer."

The blood drains from the bartender's face. Sage says something in a clipped accent and what sounds like gobbledygook. The bartender nods for us to sit in a booth located at the back. My nerves are better but I'm feeling a bit dizzy. Oh God. What if I'm drunk? Is this what it feels like?

"I think I'm drunk."

Sage snorts. "From one sip? I don't think so. Here, I'll drink yours – you take my glass."

"How can I help?"

We both snap back to attention. The most unassuming man has sat down next to me. Dressed in a dark grey suit with a black tie, he'd look more at home driving Dab Dabs's hearse.

"Well?"

"I, er…" I stammer.

"She needs some ID under the name Fay Olander," whispers Sage, glancing at me for confirmation. I nod. Fay is as close to Fig as I could get and Olander is Sage's surname. "The full works," she adds. "There." And she slides an envelope over the table. "The photos and five hundred quid."

The Fixer tilts his head at her with narrowed eyes. "Four months. I'll be in touch."

Sage mimics his stance and says something I don't catch, then adds, "Four weeks and *I* will be in touch."

The Fixer curls his lips in distaste but nods. Then, just like that, he disappears behind a red velvet curtain that I hadn't noticed before. My attention is suddenly drawn to the ring of a bell and I am frozen to the spot. Mubla is at the door.

I sit back, feeling terrified. "Sage," I mutter. "Mubla's here."

"What?" Sage cranes her neck round.

"Don't look!" I hiss.

"Oh," she says. "Wendy."

"You know her?"

"Doesn't everyone?" snorts Sage. "I definitely wouldn't want to get on the wrong side of her."

"Which is why we need to get out of here before she sees me."

"Oh, relax." Either it's the effect of drinking two straight whiskies – three if you count most of mine – in the middle of the day, or Sage doesn't realize what she's up against. "She won't recognize you in that get-up. Trust me."

"But it's Mubla," I hiss.

"Look," says Sage firmly, "she won't be expecting to see you here. Nor will she be expecting to see you in that disguise. It's called context. Now stand up and imagine you are nineteen-year-old Fay Olander, here for a drink. Then walk confidently out of the door and straight to the car. Got it?"

I nod slowly. I'm not sure I do visualize myself in the way Sage describes but I at least manage to place one foot in front of the other. It feels like I'm walking towards my execution. Closer and closer. Then Mubla looks directly at me and my throat constricts so that I can no longer breathe.

"Come on, you," says Sage, slurring her words, her arm slung round my waist. "You've had too much to drink."

Mubla looks away in disgust, muttering something about daytime drinkers. Then I'm back out in the car park, wincing at the bright daylight. I take a long, deep gulp of air, enjoying the fact that I have oxygen in my lungs again.

"I can't believe that worked. She didn't recognize me."

"I told you," says Sage. "Context. Now we need to ring Myrtle."

"Why?" Waiting for Sage to make a phone call is the last thing I want to do, knowing Mubla is sitting in a bar a few metres away, trying to catch herself a criminal.

"Because I'm as drunk as a skunk and I cannot drive in this condition…"

LAPS

E = T + 109

In preparation for my first-ever open-water swim next week, I'm swimming a 3,000-metre session in the outdoor pool. That's sixty laps in a thirteen-degree sea! I must be mad. And, as I wade in, the freezing cold water seeps its way into my wetsuit until all I can feel is sharp pricks of pain across my neck and down my spine. The doubts about why I'm doing this, and whether I even can, are flooding over me.

I begin slowly with breaststroke, the way Maud told me when I first swam here three weeks ago, trying to get used to the cold, but still too afraid to put my face in. After several minutes of acute discomfort in which I almost convince myself to get out, I finally relax into a stilted front crawl. By lap two, I'm feeling warmer and my face is comfortably numb, though my mind is still full of fear. I've never swum this far before. What if I sink through lack of energy? What if I freeze?

Bubble, bubble, breathe.

Lap three.

My mind's not on it today. I feel jittery and out of sorts. All I can think about is the deep open water of next week and how I won't get to touch the sides until the end...

Bubble, bubble, breathe.

It's like my brain is on high alert, alive to every single worry, and fear is rushing through me, making my fingertips fizz. Or is that adrenaline?

Lap four.

I've had a run of bad sessions. Maud had us doing this awful exercise the other day where I had to tie my legs together with a band. That was the worst. I thought I was going to drown for sure, but my 'bubble, bubble, breathe' mantra saw me through.

Lap five.

Sometimes I'm worried that I'll forget how to swim. That my arms and legs will stop working and I'll slowly sink to the bottom, unable to resurface.

Bubble, bubble, breathe.

My body is really changing, though, and I'm scared that Mubla's going to notice. Especially my arms and shoulders. They've become so muscly.

Lap six.

That's ten per cent done.

Mubla annoyed me this morning. "What are you doing, Lemony?" she said. "Stop lolling around on that sofa. Make yourself useful for once."

"I'm reading my set text for English," I replied. "For the exam next month?"

I think she hates the fact that I can use revision as an excuse not to do what she wants me to.

Lap nine.

I had the money nightmare again. Turns out calculating the same budget twice doesn't make the sums any different. I'm going to have to get hold of Mubla's credit card soon...

Lap twelve.

Twenty per cent complete.

I still don't know where I'm going to live throughout my swimming challenge. It's the one glaring problem that I haven't yet faced. Stella suggested camping. I think she's right but I don't like it. I mean, I could get murdered in a tent. And what will the loos be like?

Then there's the question of food. I'm waking up every night with hunger pangs. It's like I can't ever satisfy my stomach. How am I going to do so much swimming *and* eat on such a small budget?

Lap fifteen.

That's a quarter done.

I read that you're given food after these swimming events. Bananas, flapjacks, hot chocolate. I'll have to take more than my fair share, I suppose.

Lap twenty.

I've done a third already!

I wonder how fast I'm swimming. I've done those laps in what, just over twelve minutes? So, if twenty per cent is twelve minutes, if I can maintain the same pace, I should be able to do it in an hour. Wow. An hour?

Lap twenty-one.

Hang on, that means I'm swimming three kilometres per hour. That's slower than I walk. I can't decide if that's a depressing thought or not.

Lap thirty.

Halfway.

What was I worrying about again?

THE 'UN-FRIENDLY'

If Dinosaur Island is my taster swim, then my first actual open-water swim is a precautionary measure to double-check that I can do this at all. Laps in a pool is one thing; swimming in actual open water with miles of water surrounding me is another. And, because some of the swims I'll be doing are races, I need to get used to swimming in close proximity to others.

Freshwater Quarry is about forty-five minutes out of town, and would have been a nightmare to get to if Maud hadn't jumped in to help, citing it as an opportunity to visit a local friend. Mubla thinks I'm doing a science project at Stella's house. She even let me sleep over there last night. Her high-flying case comes to a head in the next few weeks and I think she wants all the space she can get.

I stand nervously alongside the group of triathletes doing their first 'friendly' of the season, though it feels more like a funeral, with everyone standing around in small groups, wearing black and murmuring quietly. I'm feeling incredibly conspicuous in my wetsuit on account of it being bright red. Something I thought might be advantageous when I saw it in the charity shop. It was insanely difficult to get on. I must have looked like a mad person trying to imitate a contortionist.

The quarry is a large lake surrounded by greenery with beautiful, crystal-clear water, which, with the sun shining through it, you can see goes down a *long* way. This place is a diving training centre and apparently there's an underwater sculpture garden at the bottom. Famous sculptors like Henri Matalan have contributed to it. The lady on the desk who gave me my safety bracelet said it's amazing and I should try it. I'm not that keen to be honest. I'll be focusing all my efforts on staying afloat.

I stare out at the shimmering, cool water. Under the heat of the mid-May sun, it looks so inviting that I decide to plunge in head first. Big mistake. I quickly realize that was the wrong thing to do because it's *absolutely freezing*. Even colder than the sea pool, and I was expecting *that* to be warmer by now. Suddenly I understand why everyone has been standing around by the water, gently splashing themselves. I scramble back to the jetty for my towel.

"I wouldn't do that again," says one lady wearing a bright pink swimming cap bearing the logo of a local triathlon club, the Old Mare Racers. "Cold-water shock can kill you. You need to ease your way in…"

I nod, feeling shy. I haven't yet plucked up the courage to talk to many other swimmers. At least nobody outside the Mermaids and none of them are here today. Sage laughed at me when I asked if she wanted to come along and Myrtle is nursing a hip injury.

"Nice wetsuit," continues the lady, with a smile. "I've never seen one like that before... I take it this is your first time here?"

I nod. Then I summon up the courage to ask her about her giant watch, which she keeps looking at and which everyone seems to have.

"Oh, it's a fitness tracker," she replies.

"What does *that* do?"

The lady smiles kindly at me. "Tells you how far you've swum, what course, what your heart rate is, that sort of thing."

I have to hold myself back from grabbing her arm and being overfamiliar. I love gadgets and this one sounds perfect. I could use it to map all of my swims.

As the whistle goes for everyone to approach the shore, the lady takes my hand. "Stay at the back of the group, sweetheart. Some of these triathletes are monsters at the start of a race and you'll get trampled if you're not careful."

I gulp and suddenly feel a thousand times more terrified. I thought this was supposed to be a 'friendly'.

The whistle goes and suddenly everyone is dashing into the water and I haven't even got my goggles on.

With shaking hands, I press them to my eyes and watch as the pack gets going. Then I'm off and swimming. The cold water rushes past my neckline and down my front, making me shiver and jolt. Why am I doing this again?

But I soon feel calmer because, having swum in the sea pool a fair few times now, I know what to expect. If I relax and move around, I won't feel it any more. Well, not much. It still amazes me how much a wetsuit helps, though, and I'm thankful for having borrowed Maud's swimming gloves. My fingers were like icicles after last week's swim. And, after a few attempts at plunging my face in, I settle into a comfortable pace, keeping an eye out to make sure I'm not left behind completely.

We're swimming three laps clockwise round the quarry. It should be quite straightforward swimming in a circle, but I find that I weave in and out of the course, sometimes veering too close to the shore, sometimes too close to the buoys in the centre. On the final strait of the first lap I even have to stop and take my goggles off so that I can see where I'm going. The sun shines directly in my eyes and I'm blinded. What am I doing wrong? How is everyone else managing it? I end up alternating between breaststroke and front crawl, which slows me down a lot, but does at least mean by the second lap I'm sticking to a straighter route.

When I come too close to a pack of swimmers, it suddenly gets a bit nasty. My hands keep tapping other people's feet and I get kicked in the face several times. Then out of the corner of my eye I see a couple of swimmers speeding round a buoy, gaining on me quickly. They must be swimming fast – they've completely lapped me. I don't think they've seen me and, before I know it, one of the swimmers virtually swims over the top of me and I find myself being shoved under the water. I snort in a ton of it and try not to think about how deep this quarry actually is. Too late. I start imagining myself sinking to the bottom, staring wild-eyed as I try to breathe, and coming face to face with beautiful art.

I snap out of it quickly and realize my arms and legs have lost the will to move. If I don't do something soon, I really will be seeing the *Mourning Mother* by Henri Matalan.

Bubble, bubble, breathe.

It doesn't work. It makes me splutter out even more water. Then I remember Maud's advice. "Lie on your back – your wetsuit will help you float – and stay there until you've calmed down," she said. "It's mind over matter."

So that's what I do. I stare up at the grey sky, allowing the tears to fill my goggles. After a few minutes, I'm calm again, although quite angry that that swimmer did that to me. I mean, hello! I'm wearing a *red* wetsuit.

When I eventually hit the finishing line, it feels like I've been swimming forever. I cringe when I realize I really am the last swimmer to come in – everyone else is standing around, chatting.

"Well done," says someone, who it slowly dawns on me

is the lady who was wearing the pink swim cap earlier. She hands me a steaming cup of soup. "Is this your first three k? How did you find it?"

"OK," I manage as I pull off my goggles, which feel like they've been surgically attached to my face. "I couldn't swim in a straight line, though."

"You need to learn to sight. Now, drink up – that'll get you warm."

In the changing rooms I get a first look at myself post three-k swim. I pause for a second to take that fact in. I've just swum three kilometres in open water for the first time ever. I feel triumphant, though my face says otherwise. My eyes are swollen into little slits and there are dark, bruise-like smudges around them. I grin at my reflection. I might look like I've been defeated in an exhausting ten-round boxing match, but I feel like the winner.

MAY HALF-TERM

$E = T + 87$

"Up, up, up!" shrieks Mubla at 6.30 a.m. on the first day of half-term.

Uh-oh. I know what that tone means…

Mubla proceeds to swoop through the house, with Jago and me in tow, while she declares what we can and can't keep. Decluttering. It's the first thing she does when she loses a big case.

"Lemony, you need to clear out some of your clothes. Anything that doesn't fit, get rid of it." She studies me more closely. "From the looks of things that's most of them. There are children starving in Africa, Lemony…"

I can't argue with that. After all this swimming, I'm getting bigger, with much broader shoulders. What worries me is that Mubla has *noticed*.

Oh my God. What if she starts asking me why?

By the end of the day, the house looks like it's been hit by a hurricane.

The following morning Mubla makes us get up early again, this time with the intention of giving us a full and educational week. Personally, I'd rather just read, eat, sleep and swim but this is the norm when Mubla's focus returns to her children and it's not good.

"We're going shopping," she tells me. "Then I thought we'd go to the local museum this afternoon. And there's a play I think you'd like. Oh and I'll need you to watch Jago on Thursday and..."

It doesn't exactly leave me much time for anything, is what flitters through my head. Instead, I say, "Sorry, Mubla. Stella and I have revision to do."

"Oh." Then, "And do you really think you should be doing that with Stella?" she asks. "Isn't that an activity best done alone? You'll just end up giggling over some nonsense."

Probably but I'm not going to tell Mubla that. Besides, I've done all the revision I need to do. It's only one English exam...

I had hoped that would put a stop to Mubla's unwanted attention, but she's still standing there, frowning.

"What is it, Mubla?" I ask, putting my book down flat so that I crease the spine.

"Use a bookmark," she hisses. "I, er, I wanted to say sorry."

Now she really does have my full attention. Mubla saying sorry is a rarity.

"Sorry for being ratty yesterday. That dreadful case really got to me. I was so close to winning but that dratted Fixer proved to be just a little too elusive."

I inwardly sigh with relief, knowing that, for a brief moment, the Fixer had had incriminating evidence against me that would have blown everything apart for both of us.

"I thought," says Mubla, "that we might go away in the summer."

"Really?" I say, beginning to feel excited. We never go away. "Where would we go?"

Mubla clears her throat. "Well, um, there's a Criminal Law Convention on corruption that I'd quite like to go to at the end of August. It's, er, it's quite a long way away actually. Not sure your father will make it, what with his aversion to flying."

"Where?" I ask.

"The Foggy City," replies Mubla.

I shrug. It means nothing to me. Then – hang on a minute! Isn't that the same time and location of the first leg of my planned escape? It's the one detail that has been preventing me from finishing my itinerary. Namely how to get to the Jailhouse Rock, my first swim on the other side of the world without being found out. It must be a sign!

"Isn't that where they have all the trams?" asks Jago excitedly.

"That's right, darling," says Mubla, squeezing herself between us on the sofa. "There's lots to do, Lemony.

I've already written you a list of what sights there are to see. You'll love it. And we'll take Aurora."

Something's going on. Why is Mubla being so pally all of a sudden?

"There's just one thing," she says.

Oh, here it comes!

"You need to tell Dab Dabs that we're going. Without him."

EXAM NERVES

E = T + 81

"Have you told him yet?" whispers Mubla under her breath.

"Told who what?" I ask, though I know exactly what she's talking about.

Mubla responds with a single menacing look.

I shake my head. Dab Dabs isn't going to like being in the house on his own. I'm not sure I want to be the one to tell him. "Why do *I* have to do it again?"

"Because," says Mubla with an exasperated sigh, "it'll be better coming from you. You've got a good understanding of each other. I asked you—"

"Actually," I interrupt, "technically you *told* me."

Mubla takes a nervous glance at Dab Dabs, who is deep in concentration, playing chess with Jago. "I'm asking you now, Lemony..."

"All right," I agree. "But only if you get off my back about the exam revision."

"I can't do that, Lemony," she says. "Qualifications are important. The exam's tomorrow."

"Yes. I know."

"Are you sure?"

"What, that the exam's tomorrow?"

"No," mutters Mubla through gritted teeth. "That you've done enough!"

"Yes, I have."

"How can *I* be sure?"

"You can't. You just have to trust me, Mubla." OK, so I don't say that last bit, but I think it.

"Tom," implores Mubla. "Tell your daughter to answer me. For heaven's sake! She's got an exam tomorrow. This is not a laughing matter…"

Dab Dabs looks up, his expression vacant as if he hasn't heard a word. "Sorry, what's that? Exam did you say? Yes, it's very exciting, Fig. We'll have a dinner to celebrate."

"But we won't know the result for months," complains Mubla.

"Quite right, darling. But still it's always nice to have a good excuse. We could open that bottle of bubbly you've been saving…"

"Yes, for a special occasion," scoffs Mubla. "All right. If you insist. Lemony, what time does your exam finish tomorrow?"

"Lunchtime," I reply. "I've got the afternoon off. I was going to go to the cinema with Stella. I told you that the other day."

"Yes, yes," mutters Mubla. "I don't need to know your every move…"

Really? I thought that's exactly what she wanted!

"Lemony. I need you to do the shopping for dinner tomorrow. I'll leave you my credit card and a list. Get everything on there and nothing else."

And it's as simple as that. The problem that's been waking me up, causing me to stress about what I'm putting myself through, and here it is being handed to me without a fight. I have Mubla's credit card! I can finally update my budget.

<u>Known Quantities</u>

Savings: £10,000
Price of admission for the twenty swims: £2,000
Fake passport: £500

<u>Unknown Quantities</u>

Round-the-world ticket (guestimate £5,000)
Cost of accommodation
Cost of food
Leftover money for sundries

£10,000 − £2,500 = £7,500
∴ £7,500 ÷ 12 = £625/month or £625 ÷ 30 =
£20.83/day

Beneath the budget, I meticulously note down the credit-card details. I then update my to-do list and feel exhilarated when I realize how many things I can cross off.

Main To-do List

1. ~~Complete 'How to Learn to Swim To-do List'~~
2. ~~Book place on the Swimmers Show motivational talk with the Boss~~
3. ~~Details. Where will I live/sleep between swims? What will I eat?~~
4. ~~Obtain fake passport~~
5. ~~Write Contact List~~
6. ~~Budget - how am I going to pay for all this?~~
7. ~~Book round-the-world ticket~~
8. ~~Plan escape~~
9. Swim the world

Now all I've got to do is tell Dab Dabs we're going away without him.

CODED MESSAGES

E = T + 74

"There," I say. "Looks all right, doesn't it?"

Stella shrugs. "If you like camping."

We're in her back garden, putting together a tent I bought in the Old Mare Bargain Basement. I've never camped in my life and Stella hates it, so we're novices together. It's taken us well over an hour to figure out that it's actually very simple.

I had hoped that, with my To-do List nearing completion, I'd feel a sense of satisfaction. I don't. Instead, the reality of saying goodbye to Stella in two and a half months fills me with dread. She's the one person who gets me through my anxiety – how am I going to cope without her?

"It'll be OK," I say. "Won't it?"

"Rather you than me," she replies gloomily, tears brimming in her big eyes.

"What's wrong?"

Stella shrugs, staring moodily at the tent.

"Stella?"

"Feeling gutted that you're leaving so soon," she eventually replies. "What am *I* supposed to do?"

I frown. "But you'll be fine. Everyone likes you."

"That's *not* the *point*," she snaps.

This is coming dangerously close to a row. We've never argued. Except for that one time when I got angry with her for not being able to come to my birthday party so I had to sit, looking at an empty table, eating birthday cake on my own.

"I'm sorry," I murmur. "I've got to prove to Mubla that I can achieve something on my own. You do understand?"

Stella puffs out her cheeks, deflating them slowly. "Yes… No… Oh, I don't know. It's a whole flipping year without you."

And it hits me – finally – how stupid I've been. What kind of a friend am I? I'm abandoning Stella and I haven't even realized it. She's always been there for me and I'm leaving her.

I feel awful. Why am I doing this again? Am I insane? I've learned to swim. Why isn't that enough?

"Maybe I shouldn't do it," I say.

"Of course you should!" shrieks Stella. "I didn't mean…"

"But I won't be there for you on your birthday or Christmas."

Stella waves her hand. "Oh, it's a non-birthday year anyway." She pauses, her eyes coming alive. "Why don't we talk every day instead?"

"How?" I ask miserably. "You can't contact me. They'll be watching you twenty-four seven, waiting to see if I get in touch, won't they? You know what Mubla's like. She's bound to question you."

"Instagram," Stella replies. "I'll set myself up with another account. They'll never think to look at that, will they? I'll send you coded messages about Mubla. We could chat every day."

"Brilliant," I laugh. "It'll be just like you're with me."

"Yeah, except I won't have to do the swimming or the camping…"

Stella agrees to come with me to the sea pool but only to watch me swim while she eats cake. The water is freezing – it's only June after all – and I'm not quite in the mood for it any more. What if I stopped doing all this now? No one would notice.

Myrtle is already warming up but there's no sign of Sage. She hasn't been swimming as much recently and I miss her.

"Come on, Fig," shouts Maud. "Get in the water already!"

I wade in and swim like mad until I can feel the heat pumping round me again. It's the only way when I'm feeling like this. Soon I'm much calmer and by the end of the session I have sorted my head out.

"Good swim?" asks Stella.

I nod. I'm tingling all over. It may have been cold and my

feet might be numb, but I'm buzzing with energy. And I've got my resolve back.

"We couldn't tempt you then, Stella?" says Myrtle.

"Flip, no," she laughs. "Too Siberian for me."

"Hyperborean," I agree.

Myrtle laughs and adds, "Gelid."

"I think Myrtle wins with that one," says Stella, looking impressed. "Ooh. And I've come up with my Instagram handle – @WordBird. What d'you think?"

"Your what now?" asks Myrtle.

I lean in to the table. "Stella was feeling bad about my, er, you know, my adventure? So we've agreed to stay in touch on Instagram. She's going to send me coded messages."

Myrtle still looks confused. "Oh."

"You will look after her, Myrtle?" I say.

"Of course," she replies, patting my hand. "So what's *your* handle going to be then?"

I pause for a minute, thinking about what the Boss called me and what Mubla would never guess. "@Ickle_Mermaid…"

THE ARGUMENT

E = T + 71

It is completely by accident that I tell Dab Dabs about the summer trip. It happens at the end of a particularly bad day at school, in which I endure no less than thirty different nicknames. I feel exhausted.

"Lemony! Your father asked you a question."

I've tuned out from the dinner-table conversation and missed the fact that Dab Dabs is talking to me. "I'm sorry. What did you say?"

"Oh, Lemony," mutters Mubla.

At that moment the mere fact that she refuses to call me by my preferred name is the final nail in the coffin and I end up yelling at her. "For the millionth time, it's Fig!"

"Don't be so melodramatic," retorts Mubla. "You can't possibly have told me that a million times. And I will call you by the name *I* gave you, and which is on your birth certificate."

"I hate Lemony and, and..." I push my chair away from

the table. "I hate you too. *Mother!*" Then I rush upstairs, tears streaming down my face, and throw myself on to my bed.

I don't know what's got into me. I'm not normally so disturbed by the name-callers at school and Mubla is, well, Mubla.

"Fig?" Dab Dabs leans over me with a loud rustling sound, placing one of his big hands on my back. He's taken to wearing a white shell suit and sweatband round his head these days and looks a bit like a tennis player from the seventies.

I frown up at him through my tears.

"What is it, my little Figaroo?" He hasn't called me that in a long time.

I grab a handful of tissues from my bedside table and blot my face. "Bad day," I say eventually.

"School?"

I nod. "I hate them."

"What – all of them?"

I consider this for a minute. Out of around two hundred people in my year, I'm friends with Stella, and I can have a normal conversation with maybe three others. "Ninety-eight per cent of them."

"That many? Wow," sighs Dab Dabs. "So why are you taking it out on your mother?"

"Because they call me names," I grumble. "And *she* does too. I hate the name Lemony. What on earth possessed you to call me that? And with a surname like Fitzsherbert."

Dab Dabs blushes. "Erm. Yes. Erm. Good point. I think it's something to do with the, er, lemon sherberts we ate on the night that you, er, were … conceived?"

"Oh," I manage to say. "*O–K…*"

Good grief. Well, I didn't need to know that!

"Mubla's always annoyed with me," I say. "I don't feel like I can do anything right."

Dab Dabs pushes the hair out of my eyes, brushing his fingers down my cheek, tracing the last of my tears, and gives me a sympathetic grin. "Maybe you're just a bit too much like me."

"But she married you," I argue. "Isn't that supposed to be a warts-and-all agreement?"

Dab Dabs grins. He's got that starry-eyed look he sometimes gets when he looks at Mubla. "You don't see her the way I do," he says dreamily. "She's the moon to my stars."

Suddenly I feel so irritated, I want to get back at Mubla. Make Dab Dabs see what I see. "Well, if she's so great, how comes she's organizing a family holiday to the Foggy City and she hasn't told you?"

Dab Dabs sits up abruptly, "What?"

"The Foggy City," I repeat. "Some criminal convention she wants to go to."

"But I never fly," says Dab Dabs, looking confused and rather ridiculous, his headband having shifted so that his hair has bunched up like a mushroom.

"You're not coming," I say, realizing instantly that I haven't handled this at all delicately, and the immense satisfaction I'd been hoping for, having successfully landed Mubla in it , doesn't materialize. Instead I feel awful for hurting Dab Dabs.

"Going away? Without me?" he sobs. "NO!"

OUT OF THE FRYING PAN...

Dearest Mother,

I'm sorry. I had no right to tell Dab Dabs about our Foggy City trip in such a negative way. I'm so glad that he's now realized you wanted him to go away with us and that I gave him the wrong impression purely out of spite.

You trusted me to handle it properly and I threw it in your face. Especially after everything you have ever done for me. I promise never to make such a stupid mistake again.

Your loving daughter,
Fig

The apology doesn't come easily and, when it's finished, I hurry down to the kitchen to check on the cake that I've been baking. It's Dab Dabs's favourite – a lemon drizzle. I'm making it as an apology. I feel the worst about hurting him.

I finish icing the cake, and sprinkle poppy seeds to make the word 'Sorry', then I put it on Mubla's special glass cake stand and take it down to him in the basement. He doesn't look up. I guess I'm still being given the silent treatment.

"I'll just leave this here," I say.

Dab Dabs doesn't reply, just carries on pumping. He's on the arterial embalming stage of his current client.

Upstairs, I clean the kitchen and begin to make dinner. I've been doing this all week, to demonstrate that I'm really ever-so-truly sorry. I don't know whether Mubla's ignoring my efforts or she just hasn't noticed. Hopefully, my apology letter will do the trick, where everything else has so far failed.

"Lemony, darling," says Mubla at dinner. "Did you make this?"

I nod, feeling hopeful.

"It could have done with a bit more seasoning…"

My hope drains away.

"Thank you for my letter," she continues. "Quite why you're calling me Mother, I don't know. However, it was very kind of you to admit to such wrongdoing. Can I be certain you won't do such a thing again?"

I nod my head.

"Then let's not speak of it any more. Pretend it never happened. Which reminds me, Lemony…" She pauses for a sip of wine. "How *are* your acting lessons going?"

My pulse rate shoots up, my breathing stops and all I can focus on is the blood rushing round my head.

"Lemony?" I look over at Mubla who is watching me closely. "Your acting lessons. Isn't there some sort of show coming up next month?"

I hold up a finger and point to my mouth to show that I'm chewing. But the piece of meat is stuck in my throat. It won't go down, no matter how hard I try to swallow. Mubla's face is slowly turning into a big frown as she waits for my response. I grab my glass of water and take a giant gulp but it's like trying to swallow an enormous pill and the meat remains firmly in my mouth. There's nothing for it: I have to spit it out into my napkin.

"Lemony!" cries Mubla. "Don't be so disgusting."

"I'm sorry, Mother," I murmur, making her wince. I may be sorry about everything else but I'm sticking to my resolution *not* to use her nickname while she won't use mine. "It must have been a tough bit of steak," I add. "You were saying?"

"Yes," she snaps. "About half an hour ago."

"Um, well, um," I stammer, looking over at Dab Dabs, hoping he'll back me up, but he refuses to return my gaze.

"Well?" asks Mubla. "Tom. Why's she looking at you?"

Mubla and I both stare at Dab Dabs. There's a long pause as he points to his mouth. It takes him just as long to finish his mouthful, although he at least doesn't spit the contents into his napkin.

"What's wrong with the two of you tonight?" asks Mubla. "My steak was all right. Except for the seasoning."

Dab Dabs clears his throat. "Erm, yes. I'm not sure about that show."

"No worries, darling," says Mubla, smiling sweetly at him. They've been acting like they're on their honeymoon since the row. "I'll see to it. You've got enough on your plate. Besides I want to see Lemony onstage."

It's now my turn to be furious with Dab Dabs. How could he? I haven't been to a single acting lesson in months! How the hell am I expected to slot myself into a play I know nothing about?

Oh my God, oh my God, oh my God.

Progress Report   Date: 25th June

Swimming Outcomes

Preparation for first event swim in 3 weeks	✓
Complete a 4k continuous training session	✓
Swim 100 metres with bands	✓

Time spent swimming	140 hours
Swimming distance achieved (by front crawl)	4,000 metres
100-metre time trial	1 min 50 secs
200-metre time trial	4 mins
400-metre time trial	8 mins 20 secs

Fears Encountered

Swimming	✓
Performing onstage	Incomplete
Water creatures — if you count pretend ones!	✓
Mubla	0%*

*Based on Mubla having decided to come and see me perform
in a play I have no knowledge of and in which I have no desire
to perform.

ACTING LESSONS
PART II

Oh my God, oh my God, oh my God. Oh my God, oh my God, oh my God.

Bubble, bubble, breathe.

Oh my God, oh my God, oh my God.

Bubble, bubble, breathe.

Oh my God, oh my God, oh my God.

It's not working. My swimming mantra is *not working*. Now that Mubla is involved in her resolution, there is NO WAY OUT. I am in the toilet at the theatre. Mubla is talking to Andy and there is NO WAY OUT. The only small mercy is that Dab Dabs managed to have a chat with Andy to make sure he would play along by giving me a short monologue to say at the start of the show. Dab Dabs might still be angry with me, but thankfully, he did at least realize that he'd be in trouble with Mubla too.

"All set there, Fig?" asks Andy when I eventually reappear.

I can only nod. I'm afraid if I actually open my mouth

I will vomit my insides on to the floor.

"Lemony," says Mubla, grabbing my arm. "I'm going to sit right at the back. Andy doesn't want me to distract you. Although I don't see why but there you have it. Can't have my little actress freezing up on that big stage, can we?"

Actress, freezing, big stage are the only words I hear and they send me straight back to the toilet, where I really do see my insides attempt to leave my body.

Bubble, bubble, breathe.

Still not working. My lungs are desperate for a decent amount of air, not the piddly amount I'm managing to gasp in. What did Maud say? Mind over matter. I should just visualize myself doing this.

I close my eyes and picture walking onstage. Then I'm saying the words. There are only fifty of them. If I say them at a word per second, it'll be over in under a minute. Just fifty seconds of speaking to a dark auditorium where I can't see Mubla watching me. It's just me, Andy and the giant stage.

∼∼∼

I really wish I could say that it went that way, but it didn't. Not with Mubla there, watching my every move. I chickened out. My feet wouldn't work. I couldn't breathe and my retching was getting out of hand. Andy just said that it was best if I didn't do it. That the show must go on.

Mubla is furious with me. I can always tell when she's

really mad because she holds her breath while she drives, like she's a volcano, storing up all her fury for one enormous eruption of anger. She doesn't say a word to me until we're in our driveway.

"I am incandescent!" she screams. "You've let me and your father down. You've let yourself down, Lemony Fitzsherbert. I have never been so embarrassed. NEVER! You know the rules. In my house, when you say you're going to do something, you damn well do it. Do you understand? I'm. Not. Letting. You. Off! Everything you do is a reflection on me and I will not have a failure of a daughter… How dare you lie to me like that? It's been months since you went to that acting class. That's what I got out of Andy. Months…"

~~~

"Figaroo?"

Dab Dabs appears at the door, holding out a plate of toast like a peace offering. The smell of it makes my stomach rumble as if it's never been fed.

I skipped dinner tonight and I'm hiding in my bedroom. I can't face any more of Mubla's tirade. I've had enough.

"Oh, Dab Dabs," I sob, flinging myself in his arms. "I'm so sorry."

"It's OK," he murmurs. "I understand." He wipes away my tears with his thumbs and peers at me. "Are you all right? What happened at the theatre, that's my fault.

We should never have made that deal."

"No, Dab Dabs," I say. "I'm glad we did."

And I really am. You see, I was beginning to wonder whether I should be doing this. Stealing money from Mubla and leaving my family. But today has just reminded me what I'm running away from and I'm more determined than ever. In just forty days I will make my escape. I'm ready for this.

PART 2
SWIMMING THE WORLD

"We may never meet again but for three hours
she was my closest friend…"
A swimmer

THE ISLAND GANG

SWIM 1 – DINOSAUR ISLAND
CONTINENTS VISITED: 1 | COUNTRIES VISITED: 1
$$E = T + 27$$

My first swim coincides with the first day of the summer holidays. I rise early and sneak out of the house, feeling a mixture of exhilaration and terror, with a healthy dose of nausea.

I've been up half the night, worrying and panicking. I even jotted down the times in a list because, as is usual for the middle of the night, only the reasons not to do this swim came to me.

<u>Times I wake up</u>

12.03 a.m.	Why am I doing this?
1.05 a.m.	I'm going to drown
2.34 a.m.	I can't swim that far
4.45 a.m.	I could give up
5.04 a.m.	If today doesn't go well, I will definitely call the whole thing off

I couldn't go back to sleep after that last one, so I thought I might as well get up and go through the stages in my head. I really didn't think I'd get this far and it's only because of the fact that I forgot my house keys and couldn't go home that I'm even on this train…

For some reason, I thought it would be easier if I wore my wetsuit and carried my clothes and towel in a bag. Turns out it's rather hot wearing a wetsuit out of the water and I soon begin to understand why people recommend the use of lubricant. I'm chafing everywhere! Plus, did I say I was hot? Maybe I shouldn't have put my swimming hat on yet. That may explain the odd looks.

I spot the Voyages of the Water Treaders swimming coach by the beach café – a chilled-out bald man with a big, red, shiny face and peeling skin on his shoulders. Barry, as he introduces himself, points out a group of men and women in varying states of contortion, i.e. pulling on their wetsuits. Then I see one lady – she's blond and petite – using a plastic bag over her foot to put hers on. It glides on in half the time.

"Just a little trick I learned," she says with a big friendly smile that puts me at my ease. A good thing, considering how jittery I'm feeling. "I like your wetsuit," she continues. "Never seen one like that before. I'm Zoe by the way."

"Fig," I reply. I like the way everyone talks to me as if I'm normal. I mean, obviously I'm normal, it's just that no one knows anything about me, and if they could hear my internal thoughts – a running commentary of *Abort! Abort! Get out of here now!* – I suspect their reactions would be rather different.

"Is this your first time?" asks Zoe.

Either she can mind-read, or my face is letting on how nervous I am.

I nod. "I only learned to swim in January. I've never actually swum in the open sea before."

"You what!" she exclaims. "Wow, did you hear that, Rach?" Zoe turns to another lady.

"You're kidding," exclaims Rach.

Then everyone else joins in and that's how I meet the self-named 'Island Gang'. We sit round, with Barry at the helm, telling everyone what our swimming experiences are. It feels a bit like a therapy session, and strangely I do feel better when I've told everyone mine.

"Right then," says Barry. "Welcome to the Dinosaur Island swim. We'll be swimming a course of three kilometres round the island in an anticlockwise direction, accompanied by two coastguards on paddleboards. I'll be in the motorboat. So, first up, let's run through some safety measures." He starts by making the letter 'o' with one arm and explains that this is the way swimmers communicate that they're OK. "If you're in distress," he continues, "wave one arm above your head."

The scenarios of why I might not be OK start to run riot in my head. Oh God, I feel sick. Maybe I'm not ready for this yet. What if the salt water goes up my nose? What if I get too tired and I need a break? What if…?

"There's always the option to take a rest in the boat," says Barry, looking directly at me. My face must have gone into panic mode. "There are some amazing landscapes to see on this swim, not to mention the art-deco hotel in the middle of the island, so take your time. The fossils on the beaches around here have been formed over the past one hundred and eighty-five million years, so giving yourself an extra ten minutes is nothing. Maybe take a moment to say hello to the seals."

The seals…?! Beyond the fish, which I think will be far too scared of me to come close, I hadn't expected any other creatures. Do seals like humans? I don't know. I haven't researched this possibility.

I feel wholly unprepared.

SWIMMING WITH DINOSAURS AND OTHER CREATURES

Bubble, bubble, breathe.

This is nothing like doing front crawl in the Old Mare sea pool. The giant swells are throwing me around and I'm terrified.

Bubble, bubble, breathe.

There's no going back: the tide is in and the current won't allow it.

Bubble, bubble, breathe.

I eventually settle into some sort of pace, and focus on keeping the island on my left and within a sensible distance. But the waves soon grow rougher and I'm thrown all over the place. I've swallowed so much seawater it's hurting my throat and I'm worried about how much my goggles are leaking. As my right eye begins to sting with the constant wash of salt water, I have to stop to deal with it. Treading water, being bobbed up and down with the tide, while trying to empty my goggles and put them back on securely, however, is like one of those impossible conundrums. Why hasn't anyone invented something better? It's no good. I'll just have to put up with both eyes being partially full of water.

I'm only just getting used to the number of fish darting around me when I suddenly spot a seal. It's sitting on a rock, looking directly at me! Before I know it, it's swum up to meet me and is looking me right in the eye. But rather than feeling fear, my go-to emotion, I feel exhilarated. It's the most amazing experience. The seal wants to play and keeps dashing round me, rubbing its body on me.

Crap! I'm not sure about this.

In my panic I swallow a huge gulp of seawater, which makes me splutter, and I start to flail around like I might sink. Funny, but it feels like the seal is pushing me towards the shore. Is it trying to help me?

I'm still snorting seawater out of my nose as I stumble over the pebbles on to the beach. High above me is a giant piece of rock that has been carved into an archway over a path leading to a small sandy beach. It appears that I have it to myself. It's a strange feeling. A bit like being on a deserted island I expect. Then I spot him. A little old man sitting in a wheelchair, legs tucked in with a red knitted blanket, white hair whipped up by the wind making him look like he's being electrocuted. He's saying something but his words are being stolen by the wind, so I walk over to him.

"Hello," I croak.

"Hello, young lady," says the old man in a very plummy voice. "I see you met Digbert."

I frown back. *Who's Digbert?*

"Digbert," repeats the old man. "The seal. He's lived on this island almost as long as I have. Here, would you like a jelly baby? It'll help your throat – something I learned years ago. I've been swimming these waters since the hotel was a new build."

"How old *are* you?" I exclaim before I can stop myself.

The old man chuckles. "Old enough to have been here when they dug up the dinosaur skeletons from this beach. They say there might be hundreds of them underneath the seabed, though I never found any evidence when I swam around here."

He stares wistfully out to sea. Must be awful not being able to do something any more. I can't imagine being that old. I silently vow to try to enjoy these swims more, and take a seat on the sand next to his wheelchair.

The old man glances down at me, his captive audience, and begins to tell me about his swimming adventures. Turns out he was the first man to ever attempt to swim the Six Seas and tried it three times before he eventually succeeded.

"The Strait of Knar was the worst bit," he says. "Riddled with thunderstorms that forced you on land for days." He hesitates, pointing a quivering finger at me.

"You're not used to the sea, are you?"

I shake my head.

"What are you scared of?" he asks.

I shrug. "Everything?"

"That's a lot to be scared of. Young girl like you should be carefree."

"I can't help it," I say. "I've always been like this."

"It's only your mind that's stopping you, you know. Fears are all up here," he says, tapping his head.

Funny how everyone keeps saying that to me. Like it really is mind over matter. It doesn't feel that simple when I'm in the middle of a panic attack, though.

"Hello! Is everything all right?" A voice suddenly echoes all around. It's Barry calling out to me through a loudspeaker from his motorboat.

I turn round and give him the 'OK' signal.

"It's been wonderful to meet you, sir," I say politely. "But I must dash. I've got a swim to finish. Thanks for the jelly babies."

"You're a good swimmer," I hear him call after me. "You just don't know it yet…"

Fig's Swims Round the World

1. ~~Dinosaur Island~~
2. The Jailhouse Rock
3. Mount Storm Rough Water
4. The Red Canyon swim series
5. La Isla Bonita
6. Turtle Bay
7. The Greatest Archipelago on Earth Clearwater swim series
8. Malokodaidai Island 10k
9. The Big Swim series in the Land of Koalas
10. The Lazy River
11. The Cold Drop
12. The Whale Isles
13. The Hot Fjords
14. The Ancients Trail swims
15. Island-hopping
16. The Sunriser
17. The Mermaid Canal
18. The Pilgrimage
19. The Squirly Whirly
20. The Cross-continental

THE ITINERARY

The time has come to buy the round-the-world ticket and I can't quite believe that I'm actually doing it. The ticket costs a small fortune, making me wince as I type in Mubla's credit-card details. She's going to be furious. But it's an anger I am willing to face because, with one swim already under my belt, I'm beginning to feel like I can do this. That feeling when I stumbled back on to shore! Oh my God, it was amazing. I felt like I was buzzing with energy. I could get addicted to that...

It's been a complicated process figuring out how to get to some of the more remote locations. It was impossible to completely avoid flying and, where I *have* been able to, I can look forward to some pretty gargantuan journeys ahead of me.

Swim	Date	Travel and accommodation	Duration (hrs)	Date of travel
DINOSAUR ISLAND	28th July	Train there	2	28th July
		Train back	2	28th July
THE JAILHOUSE ROCK	25th Aug	Taxi to airport	8	23rd Aug
		Flight to Foggy City	11	
		Taxi to hotel	1	
		Last hotel sleep for a year!	1 night	24th Aug
MOUNT STORM ROUGH WATER	2nd Sept	Train to airport	1	25th Aug
		Flight north to Rainy City	3	
		Bus to port	1	
		Boat to Mount Storm	3	
		Wild camping	10 nights	25th Aug–4th Sept
THE RED CANYON SWIM SERIES	6th–11th Sept	Boat to port	3	5th Sept
		Bus to Rainy City airport	1	
		Flight south to Monument	2.5	
		Sleep at airport	1 night	5th Sept
		Bus to Red Canyon	7	6th Sept
		Camping inc. in the trip	5 nights	6th–11th Sept
LA ISLA BONITA	17th Sept	Bus to Playa Abundancia	12	11th Sept
		Ferry to La Tranquila	6	
		Bus to La Isla Bonita	2.5	12th Sept
		Camping	6 nights	12th–18th Sept
TURTLE BAY	30th Sept	Bus to Sams Town	27.5	18th Sept
		Bus cross-country to Fort Never	11	19th Sept
		Train to Big Easy	35.5	20th Sept
		Bus to Cape Coral	23.75	22nd Sept
		Train to Cape Coral airport	0.25	23rd Sept
		Flight to Meat Island	2.5	23rd Sept
		Flight to Turtle Bay	0.75	23rd Sept
		Wild camping	8 nights	23rd Sept–1st Oct
THE GREATEST ARCHIPELAGO ON EARTH CLEARWATER SWIM SERIES	11th–11th Nov	Cargo ship to the mainland	120	1st–6th Oct
		Bus cross-continent to Lojo	60	7th–9th Oct
		Flight to the Greatest Archipelago	2	10th Oct
		Look for possible job on a boat or camp	32 nights	11th Oct–11th Nov

MALOKODAIDAI ISLAND 10K	19th Nov	Flight to Lojo	2	12th Nov
		Flight to Cape Coral	4	12th Nov
		Flight to El Lay	5	12th Nov
		Sleep at airport	1 night	12th Nov
		Flight to Maloko mainland	12	13th Nov
		Sleep at airport	1 night	13th Nov
		Ferry to Malokodaidai	5	14th Nov
		Wild camping	9 nights	14th–23rd Nov
THE BIG SWIM SERIES IN THE LAND OF KOALAS	24th & 31st Dec/7th, 14th, 21st, 28th Jan	Ferry to port	5	23rd Nov
		Bus to airport	1	23rd Nov
		Flight to the Land of Koalas* *NB Will have buses between swims to pay for when there	5.5	23rd Nov
		Camping – again!	66 nights	24th Nov–29th Jan
THE LAZY RIVER	4th Feb	Bus to airport	0.5	29th Jan
		Internal flight to Bearbrass	1.5	29th Jan
		Sleep at airport	1 night	29th Jan
		Flight to Land of the Rising Sun	9.5	30th Jan
		Sleep at airport	1 night	30th Jan
		Train to the Lazy River	0.5	31st Jan
		Youth hostel	5 nights	31st Jan–5th Feb
THE COLD DROP	14th Feb	Train to Land of the Rising Sun airport	0.5	5th Feb
		Sleep at airport	1 night	5th Feb
		Flight to Fragrant Harbour	5	6th Feb
		Sleep at airport	1 night	6th Feb
		Train to Fragrant Harbour City	0.5	7th Feb
		Youth hostel	8 nights	7th–15th Feb
THE WHALE ISLES	1st March	Train to Fragrant Harbour airport	0.5	15th Feb
		Sleep at airport	1 night	15th Feb
		Flight to Paradise mainland	6.5	16th Feb
		Sleep at airport	1 night	16th Feb
		Ferry to the Whale Isles	0.25	17th Feb
		Camping	42 nights	17th Feb–31st March
THE HOT FJORDS	25th April	Ferry to mainland	0.25	31st March
		Flight to Green Mountain	6.25	31st March
		Sleep at airport	1 night	1st April
		Bus to Al Teeb	0.5	2nd April
		Camping	28 nights	2nd–30th April
THE ANCIENTS TRAIL SWIMS	May	Bus to the Ancients Trail	45	30th April–2nd May
		Camping	29 nights	2nd–31st May

ISLAND-HOPPING	June	Bus to Dut airport	0.5	31st May
		Sleep at airport	1 night	31st May
		Flight to Hella	4	1st June
		Sleep at airport	1 night	1st June
		Bus to Port Peros	0.25	2nd June
		Connecting ferry to Agapi	3.5	2nd June
		Ferry to Zali	2.25	2nd June
		Camping on ten different islands!	24 nights	2nd–26th June
THE SUNRISER	28th June	Connecting ferry to Agapi	2.25	26th June
		Ferry to Port Peros	3.5	26th June
		Bus to Hella airport	0.25	26th June
		Flight to Meli	2	26th June
		Bus to Hal Xemx	0.25	26th June
		Camping	3 nights	26th–29th June
THE MERMAID CANAL	1st July	Bus to Meli airport	0.25	29th June
		Flight to Makkun	3.25	29th June
		Train to city centre	0.25	29th June
		Youth hostel	5 nights	29th June–4th July
THE PILGRIMAGE	22nd July	Train x 2 Sentlia & Mahibo	10	4th July
		Overnight train to the Icy Lake	7	5th July
		Bus to the Pilgrimage	0.5	6th July
		Camping	15 nights	6th–21st July
		Cheap 1* hotel included in event	2 nights	21st–23rd July
		Youth hostel until bus runs	2 nights	23rd–25th July
THE SQUIRLY WHIRLY	11th August	Bus to Oradic (2 times a week)	23	25th July
		Youth hostel until bus runs	1 night	26th July
		Bus to Tuliv (4 times a week)	10	27th July
		Bus to Avana	3.5	28th July
		Youth hostel until event	14 nights	28th July–11th Aug
		Taxi to the Squirly Whirly	2.5	11th Aug
THE CROSS-CONTINENTAL	24th August	Train to Tbilatya	6	11th Aug
		Night train to Kursa	24	12th Aug
		Bus to port	0.5	13th Aug
		Ferry to Banakkala	2	13th Aug
		Bus to event	2.75	13th Aug
		Camping – last time ever!	11 nights	13th–24th Aug
		Bus to Banakkala	2.75	25th Aug
		Ferry to port	2	25th Aug
		Port to Glib airport	3	25th Aug
		Flight home	4.5	25th Aug

GOODBYES

E = T + 3

Our flight to the Foggy City is early tomorrow morning, but first I have some people to say goodbye to. Myrtle and Stella are grinning at me with wide eyes.

"We got you this," they say, shoving a neatly wrapped present into my hands.

"You didn't need to do that," I say, though obviously I'm thrilled.

"Just open the bloody thing!" laughs Stella.

"It's the best underwater camera you can buy," says Myrtle proudly. "You can capture all your adventures *and* upload them to Instagram."

"Oh," is all I can manage because I can't stop blubbing.

Myrtle pulls me into a hug and I bend my head down, resting my wet check on her springy white hair. Then Sage shuffles forward and pushes a bottle into my hand.

"Here," she says. "Take one as soon as you're on the plane."

"What are they?"

"Sleeping pills," she replies. "Don't worry, I've got plenty to spare. Trust me. You'll sleep the whole way. Won't even know you're in the air."

"Thanks," I say. Then I give her a hug. I swear she's lost weight. I can feel her ribcage sticking out. Maybe she's eating less cake now that she's not swimming as much.

"You won't say anything to Mubla, will you?" I ask anxiously.

Sage doesn't reply immediately. Then holding three fingers to her temple in a salute, she says, "I solemnly promise that I, Sage Olander, will not breathe a word of Fig Fitzsherbert's secret. Not to a single soul and very specifically not to Mubla. Cross my heart and hope to die, stick a needle in my eye. If I speak a word of this, may my life be full of … wee!"

Stella and Myrtle howl with laughter until I make them give the same vow.

"Now you have to promise me something," says Sage.

"What?"

"Well, I know you can do this. You obviously always achieve excellence when you set your mind to things. And I know that you'll be careful and sensible because you are. But –" Sage pauses – "you *have* to tell them."

As I start to protest, she holds up a hand to silence me.

"At some point – leave it until you're miles away if you must – you have to do it. It would destroy them if they didn't know you were OK. And listen, if you're ever in any trouble, no matter where you are, ring me. I don't care what time of day or night it is or how far away you are. *Ring me.*"

I nod, slowly raising my three fingers too. "I solemnly promise that I, Fig Fitzsherbert, will ring you, Sage Olander, if I'm ever in trouble, no matter what. Cross my heart and hope to die, stick a needle in my eye. If I fail to call on you, may my life be filled with poo…"

"Good," whispers Sage in a muffled voice. "I'll be rooting for you all the way, my love."

I turn to Stella. "One last word for the road?"

She smiles sadly and says, "Tormented."

"Moonstruck," I respond with a wry laugh, before collapsing into her arms. "I'm going to miss you so much, Stella."

"Me too," she sobs. "Now go and swim the crap out of the world!"

~~~

The last person I say goodbye to is Dab Dabs. He's the hardest one.

"Figaroo," he says, hugging me tight, before dissolving into tears to match mine. "See you in two weeks."

If only he knew…

Our taxi draws away with him still sobbing into his handkerchief. I place my hand on the car window, reaching out to him, then we dip down the hill and are on our way.

CRAZY, STUPID

E = T + 2

"Lemony. Lemony. For heaven's sake. Lemony!"

"What is it?" I ask, looking at a furious Mubla through bleary eyes.

"We're here!"

I look round the now empty plane. When Sage said the sleeping pill would help, she really did mean it. The last thing I remember is having my seat belt checked by a flight attendant.

"Lemony," hisses Mubla. "Come on. I've sent Jago and Aurora on ahead."

"Oh, right," I mumble. "Sorry, Mother."

We take a yellow taxi to our hotel. Mubla must have been in a generous mood when she booked it because we have a whole suite of rooms and I have space to myself. Under the pretence of jet lag ("How can you possibly be tired, Lemony?") I shut the bedroom door and unpack my suitcase. I've managed to squeeze my entire rucksack, tent, sleeping bag and wetsuit into it. ("What on earth have you got in here, Lemony?")

My next challenge is to get it to a storage locker at the train station without anyone seeing me. This turns out to be much easier than I'd imagined, since Mubla, Jago and Aurora all pass out at five o'clock from jet lag, while I'm wide awake on account of having slept eleven solid hours on the plane.

Outside the hotel it's warm and sunny as I sit waiting for a tram to take me to the station. The hills stretch out before me. High-rise buildings line the wide streets. Then I spot the Jailhouse Rock and it takes my breath away. Am I really going to be swimming from out there? Seems a long way…

~~~

"Fig, look!" Jago's eyes are alight as he clambers on the tram seat to look out of the window. "Can we go? Please?"

He's pointing at a poster for *The Human Body Exhibition*. I wonder if it's the same one that Dab Dabs went to years ago. "Really?" I ask, grimacing.

Jago nods eagerly.

Why not? This is my last day with him and I'm going to make the most of it.

~~~

When we arrive, the sight of dead bodies everywhere takes a while to get used to, even for me. All with placards detailing the name and age of each person and what they died of. It's pretty morbid.

"Fig!" calls Jago. "Come see!"

There's a figure with a basketball, arms outstretched, standing on one leg.

"Catch!" he giggles, throwing his jumper at me and making me start.

"Jago," I say in a warning voice. "You can't do that in here." Then I spot a swimmer's body stretched out mid-crawl. It's a cross-section so that you can see inside – all the muscles and tendons frozen in motion. It makes me shudder.

"Are you scared?" asks Jago.

I shake my head. I'm not. It's the thought of tomorrow's swim and saying goodbye to him. "You?"

"No!" he shrieks. "I love it. I can't wait to tell Dab Dabs we've been here. Come on, let's go in there."

We enter a dark and hushed room, where things get a whole lot creepier. Posed bodies playing chess and basketball are one thing, but this room goes further.

"Fig," says Jago, gripping hold of my hand and reverting to baby talk. "Look at dat body."

A torso, sliced vertically into three parts up to the waist, looks more like a dinner jacket than a body. It's equally fascinating and hideous. Next to it is a head, eyes shut like it's sleeping, which has been completely sliced in two to reveal the brain. We continue, pushed forward by the crowd and because we can't *not* look. The body that has been sliced from head to toe and hung in a long row with light shining through each layer, like giant transparency slides for a microscope, is the last straw however.

"I don't like dis," murmurs Jago, hiding behind me.

"It's OK," I say. "Let's get out of here."

But Jago stands stock-still, eyes scrunched up, arms held over his head like he's preparing for a crash. Oh God, he's going to scream. I forget he's such a young kid sometimes.

As the shriek begins to erupt, I shove my hand over his mouth and pick him up like a shop mannequin and stumble out of the dark room, past the rows of dead bodies, until we're back in the lobby area, where I set Jago down and allow him to completely lose it.

The only way to stop him crying is to get him back on a tram. He's so interested in how it works, he completely forgets about the exhibition, and, by the end of the day, we've ridden pretty much every tramline that exists in the Foggy City and have come up with a new mystery for Agents Moonstone and Brown.

Jago's excitement makes me want to cry and I'm full of doubt as to whether I should really do this trip. Maybe I should forget about the swim. These are shark-infested waters after all. I can't possibly swim from the Jailhouse Rock to shore. It's too far! This was a crazy, stupid idea. What was I thinking? I'll go and collect my rucksack from the station in the morning. I won't be swimming the world.

RESOLUTE

E = T

I wake early the following morning when it's still dark outside, my mind on fire with what I hope is excitement. You see I can safely say that I am in fact still leaving today. I cannot bear to be in Mubla's company for a minute more. These are just a few things she moaned about last night:

1. Taking Jago to *The Human Body Exhibition*
2. Letting Jago ride the trams for the rest of the day and therefore not getting enough exercise so that he won't go to bed (see 1)
3. Allowing Jago to eat porridge for breakfast, lunch and dinner
4. Not brushing my hair
5. Wearing the same clothes as the day before
6. Looking at my phone
7. Jago going on and on about the dead bodies (see 1)
8. Being me

But as I watch the sun rise over the Foggy City, seeing the white cloud descend over it like a shroud, I begin to wonder if the swim will even be on.

25 Aug

Stella 06:44
You up, Fig?

Me 06:45
Was just thinking about you. Nebulous. As in the view…

Stella 06:46
Hmm… Lachrymose… Is the swim on?

Me 06:48
Don't know. Can't see a thing at the moment. M doing my head in. I'm leaving regardless. Soz I'm making you sad

Stella 06:50
I'll get over it. Somehow. Good luck today! 📸

Me 06:51
Thanks 😊

"What are you doing on your phone at this hour?" asks Mubla, her sudden presence making me jump.

"What did I do now?" I mutter.

"Jago's been awake all night," she snaps, pacing round my room. "Thanks to you. I've only just got him to sleep."

"And he'll wake up again if you keep on yelling," I moan. "What are you even doing up, Mother?"

"I've got an early breakfast meeting. And don't call me that. Honestly. Your stroppy attitude, Lemony, is the last thing I need. You're responsible for his nightmares, not me. Something about bodies being sliced up?"

"That was the exhibition," I mutter. "He wanted to go."

"You don't say yes to every little thing he asks for, Lemony."

"You do," I counter.

"I do not. I can't understand how you could be so irresponsible. He's six years old, Lemony. I haven't had a wink of sleep…"

"You could try now," I whisper under my breath.

"What was that?"

"Nothing. Did you want something?" I ask.

"I need to run through today's events before I leave for the conference. Aurora's taking Jago out for pancakes later. He needs some fresh fruit after yesterday. What are you going to do with yourself?"

I shrug. "Haven't thought."

"Well, get thinking," snaps Mubla. "I'll be back by eight. I expect to hear a full rundown of today. There's a list on the table of the museums I'd like you to take Jago to. Do you think you can manage that? Or do I need to get

Aurora to take charge?"

I don't bother to argue with her. The fog's beginning to lift and in precisely three hours I'll be on a boat preparing to dive in.

LETTERS

Dearest Mother,

I'm leaving to swim the world. I know you'll think this is a poor reflection on you, but really it isn't and here's why.

1. I've spent the last nine months meticulously planning this trip
2. I've taught myself to swim
3. This is MY resolution. And, when I achieve it, I hope you will be proud of me
4. I know this is an exam year, but I've already got maths and English. And I've checked — I can sit my exams in November. Next year. I know the importance of qualifications. You've taught me that. And I love studying. You should know that by now

So please, don't try to find me. I'll be fine. I've got it all worked out. I'll be back in a year.

Your loving daughter,
Fig

TOP SECRET
For Agent Moonstone's eyes only

Sir, I have gone on a mission of great importance.
I'll be away for some time.
Tell no one what you know. I trust you.
Destroy this message once committed to memory.

Yours, Agent Rose Brown

THE GREAT ESCAPE

SWIM 2 – THE JAILHOUSE ROCK
CONTINENTS: 2 | COUNTRIES: 2

DAY 1

"Swimmers at the ready."

I'm on a boat with maybe one hundred people, all clad in wetsuits, the event's official red swim hats and goggles. I'm so ridiculously nervous I've visited the toilet five times. Not an easy feat on a rocking boat and wearing a wetsuit.

"On your marks!"

I step towards the swimming platform on the back of the boat, toes curling over the edge, staring down into the deep, dark and uninviting water.

"Get set…"

The fog is still lifting and I can just about see the shoreline of where I'm supposed to swim to. The city's enormous black bridge stands stark against the landscape of thick white cloud, the grey ocean meeting it in a line.

"Go!"

I press my goggles on and go to jump. But wait – was that a shark? Too late. Someone shoves me from behind and I plunge into the cold black water. It takes me a moment to realize what's going on, my usual bewilderment at suddenly finding myself in cold water rendering me blind to what I have to do. Then I hear someone yelling, "Swim! You need to swim."

I twist round, trying to get my bearings, as the boat moves away. Where's the shore? I can't see the shore! How did my goggles get so smeared with gunk?

I can hardly see where I'm going, let alone the actual route. God, I hope I'm not swimming the wrong way into the mouth of a waiting shark. What is it you're supposed to do? Punch it on the nose? The panic rises sharply to my throat and I swallow down a mouthful of spit, breakfast having come out a long time ago.

Bubble, bubble, breathe.

Colliding with another swimmer, who angrily tells me I'm swimming the wrong way, turns out to be my saving grace. Finally, I manage to focus on the large yellow buoys marking the route to the finish line. At least I think that's what they are. They look like giant smudges of yellow oil paint. I have to force myself to start swimming front crawl, feeling terrified that, if I put my face in the water, I'll lose sight of my goal again.

Bubble, bubble, breathe.

It's slow going. The water is choppy and I snort a lot of

salt water. I try to tell myself that this was what it was like for the Dinosaur Island swim. But there's no Digbert to help me now.

Bubble, bubble, breathe.

The swim feels like it takes forever. I miss the pool. At least there I'd know how many laps I've done. Even when the final buoy comes into sight, a red one beneath a banner saying *Jailhouse Rocks!*, it feels like ages before I actually reach it. When at last my feet hit the gritty floor and I catch a whiff of the pungent, rotten smell of seaweed, I'm exhausted and close to tears.

"Well done, you did it!" says an official helper in a red polo shirt and beige shorts. "How did you find it?"

I stare, dumbfounded. I hated it. It was terrifying. I thought I was going to die.

"You OK, honey?" says the helper. "Here, take your T-shirt." Then she yells over at an old guy, "Hey, Hal! This one's a bit shell-shocked. Get her a drink, would you?"

I'm shuffled over towards a wide man with a big mop of grey curly hair, who flings a towel round my neck and places a cup of steaming, milky coffee in my shivering hands.

~~~

"Honey?" It's the official from earlier. "The event's over now. Time to go home."

I nod slowly at her. I'm still wearing my swimming hat, smeared goggles and wetsuit, but they're completely dry.

"You OK?" she asks.

"Yes," I say, beginning to smile. "Yes, I am."

I find the changing room and quickly extract myself from my wetsuit. I need to get a move on! My flight's in four hours and I've got to collect my things, get a train to the airport and change my appearance.

Taking a pair of scissors out of my tow bag, I grab hold of my hair and cut off my ponytail. Just like that. All gone. And the perfect bob I had dreamed of now looks like an uneven mess. As I pull on the event T-shirt, the enormity of what I've done suddenly dawns on me and the tears come spilling out. I've just survived the most dangerous swim of my life, with sharks swimming God knows how close to me... And I'm on my own. No one to hug me. No one to congratulate me.

But ... I did it. Despite all my fears.

A grin slowly forms. I completed the swim and I did it *on my own*. I'm poised on the brink of the biggest adventure of my life and I suddenly know that I can do this. I might continue to have my doubts and fears, but I've done it... I have made my escape.

Fig's Swims Round the World

1. ~~Dinosaur Island~~
2. ~~The Jailhouse Rock~~
3. Mount Storm Rough Water
4. The Red Canyon swim series
5. La Isla Bonita
6. Turtle Bay
7. The Greatest Archipelago on Earth
   Clearwater swim series
8. Malokodaidai Island 10k
9. The Big Swim series in the Land of Koalas
10. The Lazy River
11. The Cold Drop
12. The Whale Isles
13. The Hot Fjords
14. The Ancients Trail swims
15. Island-hopping
16. The Sunriser
17. The Mermaid Canal
18. The Pilgrimage
19. The Squirly Whirly
20. The Cross-continental

MISSING

I can't stop looking at myself. Having found shower facilities at the airport terminal, I have dyed my hair as best I can and even managed to tidy up the cut. I actually look like my fake passport photo. Good job. I'll need it for my next swim.

Mount Storm is a rough-water swim, whatever that means, and will be the furthest I've ever swum. It's not for another week. There's just an anxiety-inducing full day of travelling ahead, by train, plane, bus and boat, to get through first.

I don't switch on my phone until I'm safely through border control at the airport, thankful that Jago managed to remove the location tracking. I'm terrified already and Mubla doesn't even know I'm missing yet. She won't do until I'm out of this country.

My phone beeps with two Instagram notifications. One is a picture of a crochet hook from Stella and the other a comment on my photo of the Foggy City bridge rising out of the mist from a @WiseOldOwl who has started following me.

WordBird #word4theday ON TENTERHOOKS, adj.
WiseOldOwl Well done on swim #rooting4u

I post a picture of my event T-shirt to let Stella know that I'm fine.

Ickle_Mermaid Jailhouse Rocks! Swim complete #dodgedthesharks #relieved #swimtheworld

It gets four likes straight away and I gain another follower, though Stella *doesn't* reply. We've agreed that she won't message me for the first few weeks, just in case Mubla checks her phone. We have a code word, *tocsin*, that I'll use if I'm in trouble, so that she can alert the police, but, other than that, I'm on my own.

Gulp.

By the time I'm on the plane, my resolve from earlier has faded and I am about to properly freak out, when a girl points to the window seat and says, "Think I'm here."

I stand to let her past, noticing the similarities between us. Tall with long slender limbs and big shoulders like me, only her braided hair is as dark as mine *was* pale.

"Oh, I did that swim last year," she says, nodding at

my T-shirt emblazoned with the slogan *I broke out of the jailhouse!* "What was your time?"

I frown. "Uh. I don't know." I pull out my fitness tracker, a last-minute purchase with money I received for getting an acceptable English result (I got an A). "One hour and fifteen minutes," I read. "Is that any good?"

"It's not bad. How long you been swimming for?"

"Eight months."

"Eight months?" she gasps. "Well, that's amazing. You'll get faster the more swims you do. Nice watch by the way."

"Thanks," I reply. "How fast did you do it in?"

"Thirty minutes," says the girl proudly. "What's your name? I'm Blue Michaels." And she thrusts a business card into my hand, smiling easily.

Blue Michaels
Professional Open-water Swimmer
Blue@POWS.com
@goldengirl_01

"I'm Fig," I say, then pause, cursing myself. I wasn't supposed to use that name. "Er, that's a nickname. Fay Olander. So what does being a pro mean then?"

"I'm paid to travel round the world swimming!" laughs Blue. "The money's not *that* great, but I get to swim in the most amazing places and they pay for my travel. I mean, being a black sportswoman in professional swimming, that's…"

"Impressive," I jump in.

"Yeah, it is." Blue smiles. "It's taken a lot of work to get where I am."

"So where are you headed next?" I ask.

"The Mount Storm Rough Water swim."

"Oh, me too," I gasp.

I tell Blue about my plans to swim the world. She, in turn, gives me lots of useful information on how to swim better, like not panicking, for one, and how to avoid getting gunk in your goggles. I'm grateful for the company because it takes my mind off everything, including the three-hour flight, and, by the time we land, I feel like I'm saying goodbye to a good friend.

But it's in the port, without Blue nattering in my ear, that the reality of what my life is going to be for the next year hits me hard. No amount of list-writing has prepared me for how it will actually *feel* to be alone.

Day-to-day Logistics

1. Travel to location
2. Find campsite as per location list (budget £10)
3. Put up tent
4. Organize belongings
5. Buy food (budget £10)
6. Swim
7. Sleep

8. Read — dependent on finding books
9. Limit phone time according to when I can charge it (60 mins per day*)

*Based on 8 hours' internet usage per day and assuming I can charge it once a week

I'm not sure I can really do this. And, as the panic rises, I begin to formulate a new list.

Things To Do While Not Swimming

1. Keep a diary
2. Solve some Countdown number problems
3. Keep a log of distance swum, miles covered, etc

I'm saved from worrying about my new list's brevity by an Instagram notification from Blue. It's a selfie she took of the two of us.

goldengirl_01 Meet @Ickle_Mermaid. She's on a mission #swimtheworld #followfriday

All of a sudden I've got a hundred followers, which makes me smile. I've never been so popular. I'm only on Instagram so that I can talk to Stella. But these people are asking me all sorts of questions about my swimtheworld hashtag. I'm not used to having anyone being interested in what I've got to say. I'm temporarily lulled into a state of happiness, which helps me sail through border control without a moment's thought that my passport might not work.

Everything good, however, must come to an end, and as I stand at the bow of the boat, watching Mount Storm grow ever closer, my mind is yet again flooded with the enormity of what I've done. This soon becomes swamped by the realization that Mount Storm is, in fact, a dormant volcano and a new worry is born. What if it suddenly erupts?

DENIAL

To: **Lemony Fitzsherbert**   25 August 23:04

From: **WendyFitzsherbertQC**

WHERE ARE YOU?

Lemony,

What on earth do you mean, you're swimming the world? That's ridiculous! Do you know how many miles that actually is? Perhaps, if you'd spent less time planning this trip and more time studying, you might have got that A* in English, which, by the way, clearly did not preclude you from making spelling mistakes, or is that just your horrendous handwriting?

This won't do, Lemony. I will not take this sitting down. I've alerted the authorities and I've been advised to get a social-media campaign under way – whatever that means.

You're fifteen years old, young lady. Do I need to remind you that you fear everything? You're incapable of doing anything for yourself and you've never even been out of this country before. Do you really expect to manage on your own? I don't think so.

You'll be back tomorrow. Mark my words. You'll soon see that you can't do this.

Your loving mother,
Mubla

PS Damn right you'll be coming home. To sit your exams in June.

THE ERUPTION

What was that noise?

Oh my God, oh my God, oh my God.

I peer out of the tent, half expecting to come face to face with my murderer. Nothing. Must be the wind.

What was that?

Crap!

I sit bolt upright, feeling terrified. There's definitely something out there. I can't do this.

I don't want to die. I don't want to die. I don't want to die.

There it is again. What is it?

"Hello?" I call out.

Crap, crap, crap!

I type 'tocsin' in a text to Stella, my finger hovering over the send button.

I can't do this. I'm going to pack up the tent and go to that late-night café I saw in port.

Then, with my bag on my back, I turn to breathe in the

172

sea view one last time and am immediately struck by its beauty. The moon shining on the sea, as it laps against the shore. The stars in all their vastness, twinkling away. I feel calm again. I can breathe.

Maybe I should give it one more try?

After the sixth time of repeating this cycle, I give up on sleep and stick my head out of the tent. I'm treated to the most beautiful sunrise, which lulls me into a temporary state of calm, making me forget my worries of the night, though last night's list sits in plain view in my notebook.

Top Five Worries

1. Would I be able to outswim the lava if Mount Storm erupted?
2. Can you actually survive a volcanic eruption?
3. When is Mubla going to erupt?
4. What if someone murders me in my sleep?
5. What am I doing?

When I turn on my phone, it buzzes like mad. So many notifications I can't take them all in. The first are notifications of random posts from Stella. One coded, telling me Mubla's state of mind, and the other – a school photo of me from two years ago – because she must act the dutiful friend.

WordBird #word4theday BUFFALOED, adj.

WordBird Please RT – #FindFig

Searching under the hashtags, I'm shocked to discover all sorts of posts. I'm not sure which is stranger – the people I don't know, claiming to have sighted me, or the people I do know, including Cassandra, Maisy and Daisy, who have recorded a video, tearily appealing for me to come home. Like they care…

With a jolt, I realize that I should make my Instagram account private. I can't run the risk of Mubla finding it. I also remember, somewhat guiltily, my promise to Sage and, with quivering hands, I text Dab Dabs, feeling awful that I'd forgotten to do it until now. He was supposed to hear it from me first.

26 Aug

Me 07:00
I'm sorry, Dab Dabs. I've run away. I'm fine. I love you

Dab Dabs 07:01
WTAF, Fig?!

Me 07:03
I'm swimming the world

I don't reply. He'd be like putty in Mubla's hands and I can't risk her finding out. A sentiment I feel even more strongly when I read the email she's sent me. The fact I hate the most is that she's right. I have nearly given up. And then I cry for what must be the gazillionth time. But they're tears of relief because I know that I can't give up now.

MOUNT STORM

SWIM 3 – MOUNT STORM ROUGH WATER
CONTINENTS: 2 | COUNTRIES: 3

Mode of Transport	Number of journeys complete	Distance covered (km)	Time spent (hrs)
Rail	3	275	5
Road	3	445	10
Air	2	9,489	14
Sea	1	320	3

DAY 3

I've decided to update my Fear List. To succeed in this adventure, I've got to overcome some of them.

Fear List

1. Swimming
2. Performing onstage
3. Being on my own
4. Being murdered
5. Jellyfish, crocodiles, water moccasins and pretty much any water creature

6. Spiders
7. Mubla
8. Life

I realize I may be premature in crossing out number three but I've spent two nights in this tent so far and last night I only packed up the tent twice. I'm making progress.

After breakfast, I'm sitting outside my tent, having updated my travelling stats, and happily starting on a new number problem, when I look up to see Blue walking towards me.

"Hello!" she calls. "Your idea of camping under the stars rather appealed to me. And, since I've got some training to do, I thought I'd join you for the week. You don't mind, do you?"

Mind? Is she kidding? It's going to take me quite some time to get used to being on my own. And, besides, two of us could scare away an axe murderer, couldn't we…?

As Blue is an amazing swimmer, I readily join in with her training schedule, which I jot down for future use.

Training

6 a.m.	Yoga
7 a.m.	Gentle 2km swim
8 a.m.	Breakfast
9 a.m.	Note-writing and reading

11 a.m.	Technique practice
12 p.m.	Lunch followed by nap
3 p.m.	4km endurance swim
5 p.m.	Dinner
7 p.m.	Stretching
8 p.m.	Bed

"You know if you swim fast enough," says Blue, one afternoon when we're relaxing in the sun, "it's actually possible to breathe underwater?"

"No," I laugh. "How?"

"Something to do with your head acting like a torpedo and creating a bubble of oxygen in front of you," she says. "When you swim fast enough, you can breathe in that bubble. Try using my fins."

I shudder. Fins are the one piece of kit that I've never liked. What with the painful blisters, and after Maud had me swim with bands round my ankles, I went right off the idea of having anything on my feet. But I'm curious to see whether Blue is telling the truth.

"You're not swimming anywhere near fast enough," she says when I come up, spluttering, with a lungful of water. "Keep those fins if you like. I'll get my sponsor to send me another pair."

"Really?" I ask. "Thanks."

"Oh, sure. Us hard-up swimmers need to stick together, right?"

I nod, feeling like a bit of a fraud. Back home I would have ordered them without batting an eyelid, using Dab Dabs's Amazon account.

~~~

The next morning Blue is teaching me how to sight properly, so that I'll be able to actually look where I'm swimming without doing an enormous zigzagging detour.

"In choppy water you need to sight less," she says. "You've got to lift your head higher which is going to drop your hips. So you'll need to kick more when you're sighting. Oh, and you need to make sure you do it at the top of a wave."

"Is that all?" I laugh. "I'm not sure I've got the crocodile eyes in calm water, let alone rough."

"Don't worry," says Blue, smiling. "You'll get the hang of it. It's as much about the mental challenge as the physical. All you need is self-belief..."

~~~

I'm more than ready for the swim by the time it comes around, though I still feel nervous. There aren't as many swimmers as the last one, but they all look like Blue. Professional. So I slip to the back of the pack and let them battle it out.

The green water is warm and murky with bits of seaweed and wooden debris floating around, churned up by the choppy waves. It is a rough-water swim I suppose...

But I'm used to the large swells now. My daily swimming routine has seen to that and my increased stamina makes completing it seem much easier. I soon settle into the pace that Blue has set me, feeling confident that I won't run out of energy. I plough on, stroke after stroke, sighting every six breaths, just like Blue said, to avoid being smashed in the face by a wave. I do it in two and a half hours. Blue nails it in one.

On our last night together we're lying with our heads sticking out of the tent, staring up at the stars, enjoying that exhausted feeling of having accomplished something.

"So how did you get into swimming the world then?" asks Blue suddenly.

"Fancied the challenge," I reply, trying to be as vague as possible. "Got fed up with the bullies at school and decided my life would be better on the road. You?"

Blue stretches her arms above her head, wriggling her toes. "I'm a miracle," she giggles. "My mum couldn't afford to send me to swimming lessons. Thank God for the free ones at school."

Wow. I feel bad for having given Miss Sally such a hard time now.

"I got spotted by some scout," continues Blue. "I thought I was useless at swimming but they saw something in me that no one else did. They paid for my swim coach and the rest is history. Nicky's great. You'd love her. Comes from some random seaside town too."

"Well, I don't know about miracle," I say, "but you've certainly worked some kind of magic on me. I can't believe I've just completed my first ever six k. And I enjoyed it!"

When Blue doesn't respond, I turn to see that she's fallen asleep already. She looks so peaceful, this beautiful girl who has been my closest friend for the last week.

The next day we say goodbye, with promises to stay in touch.

Fig's Swims Round the World

1. ~~Dinosaur Island~~
2. ~~The Jailhouse Rock~~
3. ~~Mount Storm Rough Water~~
4. The Red Canyon swim series
5. La Isla Bonita
6. Turtle Bay
7. The Greatest Archipelago on Earth Clearwater swim series
8. Malokodaidai Island 10k
9. The Big Swim series in the Land of Koalas
10. The Lazy River
11. The Cold Drop
12. The Whale Isles
13. The Hot Fjords
14. The Ancients Trail swims
15. Island-hopping
16. The Sunriser
17. The Mermaid Canal
18. The Pilgrimage
19. The Squirly Whirly
20. The Cross-continental

POSTCARDS TO JAGO

Agent Hugh Moonstone

c/o Jago Fitzsherbert

The Fitzsherbert Family Funeral Home

Old Mare

England

TOP SECRET

If I go back and I am 18 & U R 6 and 9 respectively then...

14, 12, 12, 13, 8, 7, 12, 13, 22

18/26, 14/12, 16

7, 22, 15, 15/23, 26, 25/ 23, 26, 25, 8

15, 12, 5, 22/ 21, 18, 20

DISASTER DOWNSTREAM

SWIM 4 – THE RED CANYON SWIM SERIES
CONTINENTS: 2 | COUNTRIES: 3

DAY 13

After a horrendously bumpy flight and a restless night at the airport, the bus journey to the camp, my home for the next five nights and location for four different swims down the Red Canyon, is long, but a welcome chance for me to catch up on sleep.

I've been on the run for nearly two weeks and I'm at last beginning to enjoy my own company, or, at the very least, put up with it. Dab Dabs has texted me every day to ask where I am, so I have sent Jago a coded message with reassurances for him.

As I climb down on to the red dirt track signposted as leading to the campsite, the heat encompassing me, I can think of only one thing. Swimming.

"*Howgh.*"

I turn towards the voice. It is deep, rich and gravelly,

the storytelling kind that makes you want to hear more. The man talking to me has long, straight, dark grey hair, streaked with white, and has the craggiest face I've ever seen. Heavy wrinkles map across it to deep-set eyes and a strong nose. He's wearing a dark blue shirt with a beaded necklace and a cowboy hat hanging down his back from a thick red cord around his neck. He's what Mubla would call a hippie.

"Hi," I reply. "I mean, how."

"The last guest. You must be Fay Olander?" asks the man, looking at his clipboard.

I nod. "But you can call me Fig."

"Like the fruit?"

I nod again.

"Welcome, Fig *like-the-fruit*." The man grins a wide smile, revealing a mouth full of gaps. "I'm Bill. Let me show you to your tent."

There's a family of three standing outside the tent next to mine – a boy and his parents. All tall like me, with blond hair and very tanned skin. The boy is going to be very handsome when he's older but for now he's just lanky and ill-fitting in his body. He looks over at me and we make brief eye contact, before both looking away, embarrassed.

"Settle yourself in," says Bill. "We'll do our first swim in an hour. Briefing is where the water runs shallow…"

~~~

In the middle of the group gathered by the water's edge there's a small athletic woman with a swimming hat and goggles on. Her warm-up is like a performance. She knows everyone's watching her and the more she gets their attention, the larger and more showy her exercises become.

"Welcome," says Bill. "Today's swim is a gentle current-assisted seven-kilometre which I expect to take around two hours." He pauses to look at us. "This is not a race. It's a swim to be savoured. The landscape you'll swim past will take your breath away. So please do remember to enjoy yourselves." His face erupts into laughter lines and a deep booming chortle comes out of him. "Well, come on. What are you waiting for?"

The crystal-clear water is incredibly inviting and I need to escape from this stifling heat. As the swimmers begin to dart off, being swept by the current, I'm suddenly gripped by the fear that I don't know what creatures are to be found in this canyon.

"After you," says the lanky boy, grinning at me. He's got the most ridiculously large flashy goggles on.

I nod my thanks, overcome with shyness again. I can't back out of the swim now, can I? The unknown is not on my Fear List and I'm not going to add it now. So I choose my first sighting point, an enormous green cactus, and, with a deep, decisive breath, set off.

It's near the end of the swim that *the thing* happens. For no obvious reason – there are no waves, the current is gentle and the water is peaceful – I suddenly find it much harder to swim. It's as if I'm being pulled back. It's an odd sensation and not one I like. I feel like there's something behind me waiting to pounce and, when my feet are slapped a few times, I go into full panic mode, thinking it's teeth snapping at me. What if it's a crocodile? Do they even have them here?

My fear slowly turns my body to stone and I momentarily forget how to swim, sinking under as if my feet are made of concrete. My breath is stuck and I can't seem to get a full lung of air. I'm not sure this is quite what Bill meant by breathtaking. I'm going to die. Whether it's by drowning or by crocodile remains to be seen. No amount of chanting *bubble, bubble, breathe* is going to help me now.

Just as I've convinced myself I'm about to be gobbled up, the feeling that I'm being snapped at disappears entirely and I can swim normally again. The lanky boy from earlier swims past me, giving me a thumbs up and what looks like a triumphant grin. Was he doing that on purpose? Why? This isn't a competition. Maybe he's like the awful swimmer who swam over the top of me in the Freshwater Quarry.

I tread water and with the relief of remaining alive come the tears. I'm surrounded by astonishing scenery: a sky so blue it's almost purple; deep red rocks reaching high up around me so that the sunlight reflecting from them casts a flaming hue over everything, the skyline defined only by the jagged shapes of the canyon walls. Yet all I can think about is how much I hate that boy and how much I'd like to go home.

"Fig, you're OK?" asks Bill, swimming towards me, his hair plastered to his face. He has the kindest eyes and I immediately feel safe again.

"Lie on your back," he says. "Stay there until you're ready again. I'll hold you."

Bill stays by my side as the current sweeps us along until we finally reach the landing point. I'm so relieved to get out of the water. I'm not sure I can do this any more. Maybe I'm not cut out to be a swimmer after all.

WEAK RECEPTION

"He drafted you."

"What?" I say, turning towards the voice. I almost fall over with my surprise. It's the woman from earlier but only now that she's without her goggles and swim hat do I recognize her for who she actually is. What's the Boss doing here?

"He drafted you," she repeats. "Surfed on the slipstream? No?"

I stare back blankly, which only increases her irritation.

"Call yourself a swimmer," she mutters under her breath. Is she mean like this to everyone or is it just me? "It's where you take advantage of the lead swimmer's speed and you don't need to sight as much. It's an energy-saving measure. Everyone does it. It's part of the fun of swimming... What did you think was happening?"

I shrug. I don't want to admit that I thought it was a crocodile. But she sneers at me anyway.

As I pull off my goggles, I swear there's a flicker of recognition in her eyes. Will she remember me? I doubt it. The Boss isn't interested in anyone but herself. Still, as she stalks away, I breathe a shaky sigh of relief and collapse on to a nearby rock. I need to be more careful.

"Hi!"

The lanky boy is smiling at me, all innocence and light as if nothing's happened. I feel the anger begin to expand in my chest. How dare he? He completely spoiled that swim for me and now I've lost all my confidence. I scowl back.

"OK?" he asks with a slight frown. He has a hard, clipped accent.

I shrug faintly.

"I'm Raif," he continues, offering his hand, which I leave hanging.

"Rife?" I ask, trying to imitate his accent, but it comes out all wrong.

He laughs. "Raif," he repeats, putting a funny growl on the 'R'. "Languages aren't your thing then?"

I stare at him, feeling flabbergasted. Talk about condescending! "Well, Raif," I scowl, virtually gurgling on his name but it still doesn't sound right. "Don't ever draft me again like that. D'you hear?" My voice has become squeaky with emotion and the bottom corners of my lips are wobbling.

He looks at me as if I'm mad. "You don't like swimming?" he asks cautiously.

This makes me even more furious. I thought I was doing

fine and now I feel scared to get back in the water. "Yes, I like swimming," I snap. "Do me a favour and stay out of my way."

I storm off, feeling a strong need to be around people who understand me, so I log on to Instagram. The reception here in the desert is awful, though, and I have to wander round the camp, trying to get a signal. The sun is fading now and the landscape is cast in red and orange, the sky a light blue. Just as I'm taking a photograph of this perfect moment, the Boss appears from behind a cactus, her shadow stepping into view. She snorts grumpily at me, then stomps away, glaring at her phone. Mine vibrates with a dozen notifications of comments under the photo I posted on the bus yesterday.

goldengirl_01 where you at @Ickle_Mermaid?
WiseOldOwl How's the world treating you @Ickle_Mermaid? #rooting4u

Then my nerves mix with laughter when I see the posts and messages from Stella. I don't know where she's finding these awful old photos of me but at least they look nothing like me now!

WordBird #word4theday TEMPESTUOUS, adj
WordBird Please help – my friend is still missing #FindFig

WordBird How's it going? Got through being interrogated by Mubla. Crap. She was scary.

WordBird You still alive??

Ickle_Mermaid Yes, I'm alive. Dodgy reception. Sorry I'm putting you through all this. You know Mubla.

Then I post the photograph of the Red Canyon, the one with the Boss's shadow:

Ickle_Mermaid The Intruder – amazing view, shame about the company #swimtheworld #redcanyon

Blue reposts it immediately, telling everyone to follow me.

goldengirl_01 #repost @Ickle_Mermaid with @repostapp
Sizzling pic! The company?
Ickle_Mermaid Annoying boy.

I'm suddenly inundated with requests for followers, and well-wishers telling me how good the image is. Including the Boss, who shares the photo with *her* followers, with the caption:

TheBoss #repost @Ickle_Mermaid with @repostapp
Not bad. Btw, that's called a crush @Ickle_Mermaid

Ew. No! There's no way I fancy Raif, though I resist the urge to say this to the Boss.

It's a beautiful night, so I leave the tent flaps open and lie in my sleeping bag with my head outside. The campfire is dying down and everyone's returning to their tents.

The silhouettes of people getting ready for bed remind me of the kind of shadow-puppet shows Dab Dabs used to put on when Jago and I were younger. He made this whole theatre from a sheet and an old film studio light, and crafted puppets out of tights. He even persuaded Mubla to be the voice of the villain, which she was always good at, putting the right amount of menace in, which would make me squeal with combined fright and delight... A shiver of guilt runs down my spine. I hope Jago has managed to decode that postcard.

One by one, as the campers switch off their torches, calling goodnight to each other, the galaxy of stars dotted in the cloudless black canvas is allowed to shine through the darkness, revealing their full glory. I'm comfortably mesmerized.

Maybe I won't skip tomorrow's swim after all.

GIRL-WHO-SWIMS-THE-WORLD

In the morning I'm jolted awake by a noise outside my tent. Panic floods my mind, rendering me a quivering mess, and it takes me a moment to remember that I'm in a large group of travellers and an axe murderer would likely be noticed. All the same, I peer cautiously outside. Bill is lighting the fire for breakfast.

"Good morning, Fig," he says in his formal way.

"Morning," I mumble, stifling a yawn.

"Ready for today's swim?"

I shake my head, suddenly feeling the urge to cry.

Bill frowns. "Why the tears? Don't you like the Red Canyon?"

"I'm frightened," I manage before my sobs take over. It only takes someone being nice to me to do it. Bill rests his hand on my shoulder and we sit in silence until my tears are done.

"When I was a boy," he says quietly, "I was afraid of the

water. I thought of it as a monster that needed my breath to survive. I was afraid that if I stepped in the water it would pull me under and eat me up."

"But you're an amazing swimmer," I say.

Bill nods slowly. "Now, yes. But then –" he shakes his head sadly – "I used to watch my friends jumping and splashing in the water on hot days and I'd think, *Fools, you are dancing with danger.*"

I stare at Bill in astonishment. How could this calm and confident person, who had yesterday seen us across some strong currents and made sure each and every one of us had completed the swim, be scared of the water? "What made you change your mind?"

Bill brushes his big hands against his trousers, leaving a smudge of white ash on the fabric. "It was a hot day," he begins. "The hottest of the hottest, when the earth is cracked and the sky is purple. I was sitting in my usual shaded position on the riverside, calling out to my friend. Then suddenly he went under the water and didn't resurface. At first I thought he was joking. I thought he'd jump out, laughing at my fear. My friends were always teasing me. I began pacing around on the shore. The bubbles had stopped floating and the surface of the water was still, as if no one had ever been there."

I gulp, feeling terrified. It's a familiar sensation. "Did your friend die?" I whisper.

Bill stares at me with his piercing eyes. Then he smiles,

shaking his head. "No. No, he didn't. Of course, I thought the monster had come to take his breath. But I also knew I had to try to stop it and save my friend, so I jumped in the water."

"Did you manage to find him?" I ask with a gasp.

"Yes. He'd fainted from heatstroke," explains Bill. "I found him unconscious under the water. So I pulled him to the shore and gave him my air, to replace the breath the monster had taken."

"You saved him," I say. "Did you start swimming after that?"

"No," replies Bill. "I was even more scared after that! It felt like I now had proof of the monster. I learned to swim because of a girl."

I giggle. "A girl?"

"Yes," chuckles Bill, the crinkles round his eyes deepening with laughter. "I wanted to impress the girl who would become my wife. It's amazing how much someone you love can be an inspiration. Now tell me: why are you afraid to swim?"

So I tell Bill my 'learning to swim' story and how I've decided to conquer my fear by swimming the world.

"But yesterday I felt scared again," I say. "All because of Raif." I spit his name out with disgust and realize I've actually said it correctly. "He drafted me and I thought I was going to sink. It felt like I'd forgotten how to swim."

Bill tilts his head at me and then nods. "You were

swimming for the two of you. You must be a strong swimmer, *Girl-who-swims-the-world*. Today you will be fine. Never give up – you have conquered much by being here."

As I watch him walk away, I feel a renewed sense of confidence. He thinks I'm a strong swimmer. No one has ever called me that before. Even Sage, and she was always good at extolling my virtues. I've got to stop letting every little thing get in my way.

ECO UNFRIENDLY

I'm lying by my tent, enjoying the buzz that I get after a long swim. It has made me pleasantly tired and I could happily snooze off with the warmth of the late afternoon sun on my face.

"Well, well, well. If it isn't the Ickle Mermaid. The girl with *all* the questions."

The Boss is blocking my sunlight. Standing with her hands on her hips, her feet apart, she looks a bit like a superhero. I don't tell her that of course. She'd lap it up. So she *does* recognize me then.

"I was only interested," I say.

"I was only interested," she repeats, mimicking me in a most annoying way. "What on earth are you doing here?"

"I'm swimming the world," I reply.

"Yes, I saw the hashtag. Are you the one responsible for it?" Is that a small flicker of approval in her eyes? "Nice move getting Blue Michaels to follow you.

Are you on Twitter too?"

"Twitter's for old people," I retort.

The Boss stares back, unblinking. "My fifty thousand followers would beg to differ. Well, you won't get far keeping your Instagram private. There's no room for modesty on social media, Mermaid. Give me your phone," she says, holding out an expectant hand. "Huh. A thousand followers. Let's see if we can triple that. There." She clicks a few buttons and then returns it to me. I'll change it back later, when she's not looking.

"When you say you're swimming the world, what do you mean exactly?" demands the Boss.

I shrug. "Doing different swims in different countries across most of the continents of the world."

"Oh, is that all?" she says and flops down beside me, looking relieved. "I was ready to be impressed. Nice haircut by the way. Suits you. Blond really wasn't your colour, was it?"

I *think* that's a compliment…

"I almost wouldn't recognize you. Are you on the run or something?" She wags her finger at me. "Is all this a disguise?"

"No," I say, beginning to feel fidgety. I'm sure my face is burning. God, I'm such a bad liar.

"I'm right!" shrieks the Boss. "Who are you running away from?"

I shake my head. "No one. Don't be ridiculous."

"Oh." She almost sounds disappointed. "Well, you're still not as good as me. I'm the Boss. People pay to hear me talk. Even you." She snorts. "All your stupid questions. My God, you didn't half go on!"

"I was *interested* in what you had to say."

"Of course you were." She pauses. "So. Where are you swimming then?"

I list off the next few locations and she nods approvingly.

"I'm doing the Clearwater too. On board the uh, erm, the *Sweet Dreams*, *Sweet Destiny* … sweet something. Bunch of rich rahs paying me for swimming lessons, then easing their consciences by listening to my conservation talks in the evenings… Come on, Mermaid," she says suddenly, motioning for me to follow her. "I need a drink."

Her tent is full to bursting with empty cans and bags of crisps scattered everywhere. Hardly the efforts of someone keen to help the environment.

"I thought you said you were an eco-warrior," I say, nodding at the mess. "Drink much, do you?"

"Oh, who made you the gin police?" retorts the Boss. "You're not better than me, you know. You and your big long legs and youth on your side."

"Yes, you are very short," I say. "And old. How old *are* you?"

"Old enough to have met your sort before," she snaps.

"*That* old," I retort. "Wow."

"Oh, sod off back to your own tent…"

I walk away, feeling bewildered. I've only ever done a handful of open-water swims and I've only just learned what drafting is. So why would the Boss be worried about *me* being better than *her*?

FRESH START

"Is this seat free?"

I instantly scowl when I see it's Raif, all smiles and confidence. I don't reply and look out of the bus window, pretending to be interested in something outside. He sits down beside me anyway.

"Where are you travelling to?" he asks. "NO! Don't tell me." He begins rubbing at his temple like a mind-reader. It's obviously supposed to be funny, but I don't laugh. "It's … La Isla Bonita, isn't it?"

I would love to be able to say no. Wipe that annoying grin from his face. But he's right. I arch an eyebrow, giving a slight nod, and hope he'll take the hint and leave me alone. He doesn't.

"I'm right!" he laughs. "But why are you travelling alone? Where are your parents?"

"Not here," I hiss.

"You're too young, surely."

"First of all," I say, trying to maintain a calm composure, "I'm nineteen…"

"No way," interrupts Raif.

"And, second of all, what's so unusual about me being here?" I snap.

When I see how much his face has fallen, I almost feel sorry for being so aggressive and it dawns on me that I'm being just like Mubla.

"You swam too close to my feet," I mutter. "I thought a crocodile was chasing me."

"A crocodile," repeats Raif, looking puzzled.

"Yes. Back on that first swim, I completely lost my nerve in the water."

"Oh," he says, his face paling.

"I thought I was going to drown," I hiss. "And, while you merrily swam on, I nearly sank to the bottom of that river because I forgot how to swim."

I let out a shaky breath. It feels good to have got that off my chest. But I'm not used to speaking my mind and my bottom lip immediately starts quivering.

Raif rests a hand on my shoulder while I cry. "I'm sorry," he says after a long pause. "You're a strong swimmer. I-I was just—"

"Drafting. I know that now," I interrupt. "I didn't then."

Raif wrinkles his brow, then says, "Hi! I'm Raif. Nice to meet you." He offers his hand in a greeting.

I take it sheepishly. This feels silly but I go along with it.

His puppy-like enthusiasm reminds me of Jago. "Hi, Raif, I'm Fig." And this time I nail saying his name right.

The bus journey south is a long one. Miles and miles of red desert dotted with clusters of colourful and fantastically shaped plants turn into red mountains and lone cacti. The grey road remains consistently straight, reaching towards infinity, making it feel like we'll never get to our destination.

Raif and I spend the time playing silly games like Counting Cars and I Spy, and eventually fall back on answering a favourite maths problem of mine, Completing the Square, which I know well and teach Raif.

"Let's see your passport photo?" he asks when we've stopped at the border, standing at the back of a long queue full of hot, weary passengers.

I show it to him. The one with all the make-up and the wig.

Raif frowns. "It doesn't look like you. Your hair's different. You look less ... intimidating in real life."

This is not what I want to hear at the border. What if they think the same thing? What if they know it's a fake passport? I could get arrested. Thrown in jail. My heart begins to beat faster. Oh my God! I don't want to go to prison.

"It says Fay," says Raif. "I thought you said your name was Fig?"

"It's a nickname," I reply, snatching back my passport anxiously. "Stop asking me questions."

"Sorry," says Raif. "Walk through with us if you want? I'll pretend you're my tutor."

"Tutor?" I laugh.

"*Ja*. I've had plenty of them travel with me before."

"Why?"

"My parents are world-schooling me," he replies.

"Really?" I exclaim.

"*Ja*," replies Raif. "The world is my education. Much better than a stuffy classroom."

"Wow," I say. "I hate school. I wish I didn't have to go."

"Aha! I knew you weren't nineteen."

Crap.

It's Raif's turn to show his passport at the counter. I'm sweating buckets. What have I done? I shouldn't have let my guard down like that. Now Raif knows that I've run away, or at least he'll guess in a minute. What if he tells his parents? They'll tell the police and...

I don't want to go to prison. *Bubble, bubble, breathe*. I don't want to go to prison! *Bubble, bubble, breathe*. I hope to God I'm not saying those words out loud.

I walk up to the counter, my breath hovering around my throat, making it feel constricted. I've got to keep eye contact. I need to act this part. I am Fay Olander, nineteen-year-old swimmer, travelling the world. I smile at the little man with his big brush moustache, ignoring the "try not to look so toothy, Lemony" Mubla comment inside my head, and hand him my passport. He doesn't smile back.

Barely even glances at me or my passport. Then, with a flick of his hand, he waves me through.

Raif is waiting for me in the sunshine. He beams when he sees me. "It worked then?"

"Of course," I say. "Why wouldn't it?"

Raif shrugs and points to a street-food stall selling big tortillas stuffed with chicken and vegetables. "Shall we eat? I'm starving."

The food is delicious. Hot and so spicy that it makes my eyes water and I'm grateful for my ice-cold can of lemonade. Raif wolfs his food down. I've never seen anyone eat that fast. Mubla would certainly have words to say to him about indigestion.

"So," he says, letting out a big burp, "tell me the truth. Why are you using a fake passport?"

I remain silent. Part of me would like to have someone else know what I'm doing, share in my big lie. But I've only just started liking this boy. Twelve hours ago, I hated him.

Fig's Swims Round the World

1. ~~Dinosaur Island~~
2. ~~The Jailhouse Rock~~
3. ~~Mount Storm Rough Water~~
4. ~~The Red Canyon swim series~~
5. La Isla Bonita
6. Turtle Bay
7. The Greatest Archipelago on Earth
   Clearwater swim series
8. Malokodaidai Island 10k
9. The Big Swim series in the Land of Koalas
10. The Lazy River
11. The Cold Drop
12. The Whale Isles
13. The Hot Fjords
14. The Ancients Trail swims
15. Island-hopping
16. The Sunriser
17. The Mermaid Canal
18. The Pilgrimage
19. The Squirly Whirly
20. The Cross-continental

SURFING ON THE SLIPSTREAM

SWIM 5 – LA ISLA BONITA
CONTINENTS: 2 | COUNTRIES: 4

Mode of Transport	Number of journeys complete	Distance covered (km)	Time spent (hrs)
Rail	3	275	5
Road	7	2,347	42.3
Air	3	10,889	14
Sea	3	845	9

DAY 22

"What you have to do is aim for a spot between my hips and ankles," says Raif. "The point of it is to reduce the drag on your swim."

We're treading water in the warm, clear blue ocean of this far-off part of the world, on the country's southernmost tip, and it feels like paradise. Four days ago, I told Raif everything and oh my God it feels so good to have an accomplice! I can't believe how well we get on. We talk about everything. He's as keen a learner as I am and we share a love of maths and music. Raif wants me to play the piano for him, if we ever find one. We've compared swims and he and his parents are doing the same as me until the end of November, when we go our separate ways.

With the La Isla Bonita race in two days, I'm learning how to draft from Raif. The science makes sense. The lead swimmer creates a bow wave creating forward and sideways movement so that anyone swimming close enough to them can take advantage of it, enabling them to swim faster and more efficiently. In practice it's not so easy. I try to do what he tells me but, instead of gliding along effortlessly, I get kicked in the face.

"This is hopeless," I say, gripping my bloodied nose in pain.

Raif tilts my chin up to examine the wound, then grins. "You'll be fine. You didn't need your nose, did you?"

I swipe at him, laughing. "You have more than enough to spare. Can't you give me some of yours?"

He laughs then dives under the water, coming back up to say, "You coming? Practice makes perfect."

I shake my head.

"Why not? Do you still not get it?" he laughs.

"No," I answer in a small voice, feeling worried that he'll be annoyed. I'm used to Mubla. She's not a patient teacher.

"Hold on," says Raif. "Papa! Mama! Can you help us?"

"That was unbelievable," I gasp. "It's like, it's like I didn't have to kick. Like I was … on a wave…"

Raif's father nods. "It's good, *ja*?"

"*Sehr gut*," I reply with a grin, stealing a sidelong glance at Raif, hoping to impress him with my new language skills.

We've been swimming in a pyramid formation, Raif's father at the apex, Raif and his mother set further back to each side, with me swimming in the middle.

"It's what a dolphin is doing when it swims in the wake of a ship," explains Raif's mother. She hesitates for a moment, studying my face. "Would you like to have dinner with us, *mein Liebling*? Spending so much time in that tent isn't good for you and, besides, I would like to get to know the girl my son is spending so much time with."

Anxiety floods over me. Has she guessed that I'm a runaway too? Maybe I'm being paranoid but I'm fairly certain she knows that I'm not nineteen years old. Raif and I are too similar in that regard. Will she tell the authorities? How would she even find out?

~~~

Later on, still in a mad panic, I google 'Find Fig' which makes me go into a tailspin. My face is splashed all over the internet, with headings like *Lemony Fitzsherbert: Missing Schoolgirl*, and I begin to pace round the outside of my tent. Should I leave now? Surely if Raif's mother suspects something the police would be here by now.

By the time Raif arrives from his hotel, I am a bundle of nerves.

"Does your mother know?" I gasp.

Raif grimaces. "She knows you're not nineteen."

"*Scheiße*," I mutter.

Raif doubles over with laughter. "Are you swearing in my language now?"

I dismiss him with a shake of my head. This is no laughing matter. I might only have a matter of hours before the authorities come for me.

"She knows you're fifteen," says Raif. "But she thinks you're an emancipated minor. I said that you didn't get on with your parents and that you wanted to experience the world by swimming round it."

I stare at him in wonder. "And she believed that? Raif, I could kiss you. You're a genius."

"Yes, I know this," says Raif. "Come on. Mama and Papa are waiting for us."

"Hold on," I call. "I need to research my backstory, just in case they ask."

~~~

Dinner is a far more relaxed affair than I anticipated. Raif's mother doesn't ask for information and I don't offer any. The only thing she does say, at the end of dinner while Raif has gone to the loo, is, "If you ever need to talk, *mein Liebling*, I'm always here."

Fig's Swims Round the World

1. ~~Dinosaur Island~~
2. ~~The Jailhouse Rock~~
3. ~~Mount Storm Rough Water~~
4. ~~The Red Canyon swim series~~
5. ~~La Isla Bonita~~
6. Turtle Bay
7. The Greatest Archipelago on Earth
   Clearwater swim series
8. Malokodaidai Island 10k
9. The Big Swim series in the Land of Koalas
10. The Lazy River
11. The Cold Drop
12. The Whale Isles
13. The Hot Fjords
14. The Ancients Trail swims
15. Island-hopping
16. The Sunriser
17. The Mermaid Canal
18. The Pilgrimage
19. The Squirly Whirly
20. The Cross-continental

ANGER

To: **Lemony Fitzsherbert**   18 September 21:45

From: **WendyFitzsherbertQC**

COME HOME NOW!

Lemony,

I will not tolerate your absence any longer.

Do you know what you've done to this family? You have torn it apart. Why? To swim the world? Ha! Not for much longer.

How dare you not respond to my email? I know you've read it. This silent treatment is not going to work. When you come home, you are going to feel the full force of my fury.

No one does this to me.

Come home. Now.

Your loving mother,

Mubla

PS Jago says Moonstone. Something to do with a spy game he's playing.

PPS I have my sources. I know where to find you.

CHANGES

Mubla's latest email arrives at the start of an epic journey to my next destination, Turtle Bay. Five bum-numbing days of buses, trains and planes that will be my most challenging yet. Raif's travelling down on a cruise ship, so I'm on my own again, leaving me with plenty of time for a new list of concerns to form in my mind.

Current Concerns

1. How does Mubla know how to find me?
2. What if she gets in touch with the Fixer?
3. What if the Fixer tells her about my passport?
4. What if she is then able to track me down?
5. Would she let me go to prison?

What's odd about these worries is that they're a list of factors that might prevent my adventure continuing.

The multiple connections, flights and border crossings ahead of me aren't as scary now as they once might have been. Because, having done it a few times now, I know what's coming. My fear of flying is getting better and I know how to get myself through passport control without panicking, how to turn up three hours early for the bus, how to change currency even. Although, while I'm on the subject, they charge you to do it! I lost a whole day's budget converting some money. Thank goodness for Raif's parents buying me dinner...

Something's changed in me. Normally, I'd be panicking by this stage, caught somewhere between yawning for air and vomiting, and having to chant my breathing mantra over and over. But I haven't used it in ages. In fact, I feel so happy and alive at the moment. And it's strange: my mind has been swamped with anxiety for so long now, triggered by the slightest thing, that I don't know what normal is, though being with Raif and his family has given me an insight into it.

I instantly feel guilty for thinking I'd prefer to spend time with them than my own flesh and blood. Then I realize with sadness that it's Jago's seventh birthday today and the postcard I'm sending him from the airport won't get there in time. Dare I get Stella to give him a message?

Birthdays in our family are sacrosanct and Mubla usually finds the exact present that you didn't know you wanted. It's also the one day when you can break all the rules – have breakfast in bed, skip school, eat cake at every meal. I'm going to miss that feeling this year: the one time Mubla actually manages to be like Raif's mum. Nice. If only there were more moments like that.

I'm so thankful to have met Raif. After our shaky start, it feels like we've become good friends. He's been looking out for me, charging my phone, buying me food, that sort of thing. Without his company on this leg of the journey, I fall back on Instagram to keep me entertained. In particular @WiseOldOwl who comments on all my photos. Today she responds to my picture of the back of the bus seat, which I caption, *Twenty-seven hours with this view!*

WiseOldOwl Where in the world are you @Ickle_Mermaid? #rooting4u

Ickle_Mermaid Headed 2 Turtle Bay #thelongwayround #yawn #aching #swimtheworld

WiseOldOwl You're young! You don't know the meaning of aching.

As usual, Stella's coded posts are hilarious, all the more so because they describe Mubla so very accurately and her last photo, of a pug dog, makes me howl with laughter.

WordBird #word4theday WARPATH (ON THE), adj
WordBird #word4theday INCENSED, adj
WordBird #word4theday BELLICOSE, adj

I get the idea. Mubla is furious and itching for a fight. I wonder if she realizes that she's making me even more determined to finish this? I'm only sorry that Dab Dabs and Jago are the ones who have to endure it. If only I could get in touch with Dab Dabs in some way that Mubla wouldn't ever think to look for…

I almost drop my phone when a Google search for Tom Fitzsherbert reveals a new Instagram profile, @BalmyEmbalmer, complete with a selfie of Dab Dabs and a series of his death portraits under the hashtag #DeathBecomesThem. Dare I message him? But, as the Boss replies to @WiseOldOwl on my photo, I'm reminded that my account setting is still *public*.

TheBoss I love Turtle Bay! Say hello to the turtles for me.

A new worry begins to creep into my head, sending out feelers to every part of my body. What if Mubla can see all this? I wouldn't put it past her to be trawling the internet, looking for clues, and here I am laying a trail for all to see! I'm not being careful enough. This realization comes just in time and I delete the draft message to Dab Dabs, making my account private once again. I mustn't forget what Mubla is like.

POSTCARDS TO JAGO

Agent Hugh Moonstone
c/o Jago Fitzsherbert
The Fitzsherbert Family Funeral Home
Old Mare
England

If you were six on your last birthday and eight
on your next, how is this possible?

CLOSE CALL

DAY 30

"Where are you going?"

The border-control officer has been taking his time looking at my passport, flicking from page to page, scrutinizing my photo. I don't like the way he's peering at me and I'm beginning to wonder if he suspects something. Of course that makes my cheeks flush red.

I desperately try to remember some of the things Mubla looks for when attempting to spot a liar. A lot of them involve the eyes: rapid blinking, eyes darting around, closing them for too long, that sort of thing. But, as Sage once said, "If you stick to as much truth as possible, any lie will have some plausibility to it."

So I look directly at the border-control officer and answer, "Turtle Bay," clasping my hands tightly together so that I'm not tempted to scratch my face (another sign apparently).

"What are you doing in Turtle Bay?" he asks, returning my stare unwaveringly.

"Swimming," I reply, trying to hide the fact that I'm not breathing.

As if rubbing it in, the man exhales noisily, frowning down at my passport. "You've been in and out of this country a lot recently. Why?"

"I'm a professional open-water swimmer," I lie. "It just depends where the race locations are."

He grunts at me, then, standing up to look over the counter at my feet, his eyes travel slowly up my body, as if he's sizing me up.

"You're very tall," he says eventually.

"Well, yes."

"How tall are you?"

"Five foot ten." I can feel beads of sweat forming on my scalp. I hope to God they don't start to drip down (another sign).

"No," he says firmly, with a shake of his head.

"No?" I ask, confused. Is he saying no to my height or to my passport?

"No," he repeats and for a long painful moment, in which time seems to stop, there's silence.

I watch helplessly as the officer jumps down from his stool and comes to stand alongside me, continuing to look me up and down.

"See?" he says. His breath stinks of onions. Makes me

want to retch. "I'm five ten. You're at least an inch taller. Like I said, you're very tall."

I begin to wonder if this is some kind of delaying tactic. Has this weird man pressed a secret button that alerts the police when a runaway is found? I don't get it. My passport has worked before. There's no reason it should fail now, is there?

"Well, go on then," he says, nodding towards the exit. "What are you waiting for?"

"Sorry," I murmur and turn to walk away. I almost make it too.

"Wait!"

My blood runs cold and a shiver shoots down my spine. He knows. Why else would he be stopping me again?

Oh my God, oh my God, oh my God. I don't want to go to…

"Your passport?" he calls, offering it to me with a dismissive roll of his eyes.

Quite how I manage to keep my cool when I'm in fact screaming inside my head, *I'm a runaway, it's a fake passport, arrest me!*, I don't know. Nor how I manage to walk out of there, given the wobbliness of my legs.

TROUBLE IN PARADISE

SWIM 6 – TURTLE BAY
CONTINENTS: 2 | COUNTRIES: 5

Mode of Transport	Number of journeys complete	Distance covered (km)	Time spent (hrs)
Rail	5	2,689	40.75
Road	10	6,239	104.85
Air	5	12,703	17.25
Sea	3	845	9

DAY 31

Turtle Bay is beautiful. Palm trees everywhere. Blue skies, white sand, crystal-clear water. Your basic paradise. Except I'm too weary after my gargantuan journey and, with my belongings spilling everywhere, I'm half tempted to curl up and sleep under the stars, leaving my tent until the morning.

I'm still sitting there when Raif arrives, and the joy of seeing him and having a conversation with someone familiar floods over me.

"Raif!"

He grins sheepishly at me, then colours as he extracts

himself from my overeager hug. "I brought you this," he says and hands me a thick book. *Moby Dick.*

"Thanks," I mumble, stifling a yawn.

"Well, don't be too enthusiastic," he laughs. "I thought you said you liked reading."

"I do," I reply. "I'm just really tired."

"Oh. Well, have you seen any turtles yet?" he asks.

I shake my head.

"Let's go find some then!" Raif bounces to his feet, grabbing hold of my hand to pull me up. I don't understand why he's being so fidgety. It's like he can't sit still.

"I can't swim now," I moan, snatching my hand out of his grasp to wave helplessly at the mess surrounding me. "I've got to tidy up and this tent's not going to put itself up, you know."

"What's wrong with you?"

I could say the same thing but instead mutter, "Journey from hell."

"Oh. Sorry." He bites nervously on his top lip. What's got into him today?

"How was your cruise?" I ask.

He shrugs dismissively. "Boring. Full of old people," he moans. "Give me adventure any day. I wish I could've travelled with you."

"No, you don't," I frown. This spoilt act of his is really beginning to bug me.

"What's wrong?" Raif asks again.

My bottom lip begins to wobble as I say, "I told you. Bad journey. And now I'm tired and aching and I don't have any energy."

As my tears start to flow, Raif finally reacts the way I want him to and takes the tent from my hands. I'm so grateful to have someone to help me. This is possibly one of the hardest things about my round-the-world adventure. Having to do absolutely everything for myself. It's exhausting.

"Sit," orders Raif when we've finished. He perches behind me and begins to massage my shoulders, working on a particularly hard knot in the right side of my neck. "You need to practise breathing on your weak side," he says. "It needs loosening up."

"I know," I murmur. His hands are warm and I feel secure in them. "How are your parents?"

Raif shifts uncomfortably behind me, taking too long to clear his throat.

"What is it?" I ask.

"Erm…"

"Raif," I say. I was just beginning to relax as well. What isn't he telling me?

"Erm…"

"Raif. What is it? What's wrong?"

"Mama knows."

MUBLA'S DAUGHTER

"Mama knows," is still hanging in the air between us.

I want to ask, "Knows what?" but Raif's face says it all. All memory of relaxed muscles goes straight out of the window and I lose it. "Your mother knows!" I shriek. "Why didn't you say something sooner? All you've done is moan. Poor little Raif. Being world-schooled in the lap of luxury. You're such a spoilt brat!"

Raif looks shocked by my anger but I don't care.

"This is all your fault. If you hadn't pushed me to tell you, then she wouldn't know, would she? You could have saved me the bother of putting up the tent. I can't stay here. What's she going to do? Tell the authorities? I might as well get off this island now. I can't believe it. Why didn't you say something?"

"Because I knew you'd react this way," says Raif calmly. "It will be OK."

"How exactly?" I shout. "I'm all over the internet thanks to Mubla."

"Mama says she won't do anything until she's talked with you."

"Oh, that's just great. So I get to have a rubbish night of sleep, dreading having a chat with your mother? I wish I'd never met you."

"But—"

I shove Raif away. "Leave me alone! I'm tired."

I'm so furious I can hardly think. Is this my last night of freedom? Should I expect to be sent home tomorrow or, worse, arrested? I ignore the fact that Raif's sad face makes me feel awful. He can go back to a nice comfortable hotel and sleep in a bed. All I get is this bloody sleeping bag. Stella was right. Camping sucks.

I don't know how I manage to get any sleep, but I do. My worries flood my mind but, for the first time ever, they don't keep me awake. I'm too tired. That's progress for you, even if it is bittersweet.

In the fresh light of day I can see things more clearly and my anger with Raif has subsided. It's not his fault. No doubt his mother would have guessed anyway. I don't know what to do. Should I stay for the race or should I make my escape now? I don't want to go home. As much as it's hard work fending for myself, I'm mostly enjoying it. Even the camping. Especially when I wake up on mornings like this to a view of turtles crawling round the beach. I decide to go for a swim to meditate. I may as well make the most of this paradise before I lose it.

I don't know which hotel Raif is staying in but I take an educated guess and pick the most expensive one on the island. The hotel receptionist is cagey with me and won't allow me to go up to the room. Small wonder, I realize when I catch a glimpse of my appearance in one of the many shiny surfaces. My hair's a mess. It needs a cut and I really must sort out the colour, which has faded badly. My clothes are scruffy and I look exhausted. This won't do. I am Mubla's daughter through and through, and this is not the right way to do things.

Three hours later, I'm back in the lobby, with brushed-back hair and clean clothes. And I have prepared my case.

Raif's mother is not a scary lady in the slightest and she greets me with a smile and a hug. "Fig. I'm glad you're here. You've lost weight. Can I get you some food?"

I shake my head, though I'd love to be able to say yes – I can't afford to eat here – but I don't want to show any sign of weakness.

"My treat," insists Raif's mother.

So we order milkshakes and lobster rolls that arrive piled high with tropical fruit, and which I devour in seconds, and then she sits back to listen to what I have to say. I tell her the whole story. From my life under Mubla's control, to learning to swim and planning this trip. I make sure to emphasize that Sage knows where I am, and would happily

227

rescue me, and that I've also been in touch with Dab Dabs.

Raif's mother, in turn, listens and considers everything I say. Then it's her turn to question me. "How did you get here from La Isla Bonita?"

"Three buses, two trains and two plane rides."

"Did you ever feel scared?"

I shake my head. It's only a small lie and I push the image of the border-control officer out of my mind.

"How are you getting back?"

"By ferry," I say. Actually, it's five days by cargo transport because it's cheaper, but I keep that quiet.

Raif's mother stares at me intently, then asks, "If I were to tell the authorities, what would you do?"

"Run away," I answer immediately. "I'd be gone before the night is over. My tent's already packed." Another unavoidable lie, which I feel bad about. "I'd swim to the next island if I had to."

Raif's mother laughs, her face softening. "I don't doubt you would." She hesitates, taking me in with her pale blue eyes. She's very pretty. I can see where Raif gets his looks from.

"OK," she says. "It's clear that you're determined to continue. I still don't agree with it. If it were my son, I would never stop hunting him down and I would hope that other parents would help me find him too. So … that puts me in a difficult position, doesn't it?" She rubs the back of my hand gently and sighs. "You must do two things for me."

"Anything," I murmur, wondering whether she's about to tell me I have to go home after all.

"I want to talk to this Aunt Sage. I'd like to hear what she thinks about all this."

I don't bother to correct her assumption and say, "OK. What's the other thing?"

"You must write another letter to your parents. Reassure them that you're alive and well," says Raif's mother. "They must be beside themselves." She smiles at me. "And if you're ever in trouble, *mein Liebling*, you must talk to me. Is that understood?"

"Yes." I feel so relieved, I could cry. "And yes, I'll do both those things. I promise."

"Good. Now go and put my son out of his misery. He hasn't left his room since your argument last night, and he's driving me and his father insane."

"OK," I laugh. "I'll take him swimming. There are some turtles on the beach I wanted to photograph anyway…"

Fig's Swims Round the World

1. ~~Dinosaur Island~~
2. ~~The Jailhouse Rock~~
3. ~~Mount Storm Rough Water~~
4. ~~The Red Canyon swim series~~
5. ~~La Isla Bonita~~
6. ~~Turtle Bay~~
7. The Greatest Archipelago on
   Earth Clearwater Swim series
8. Malokodaidai Island 10k
9. The Big Swim series in the Land of Koalas
10. The Lazy River
11. The Cold Drop
12. The Whale Isles
13. The Hot Fjords
14. The Ancients Trail swims
15. Island-hopping
16. The Sunriser
17. The Mermaid Canal
18. The Pilgrimage
19. The Squirly Whirly
20. The Cross-continental

BARGAINING

To: **Lemony Fitzsherbert**   11 October 06:32

From: **WendyFitzsherbertQC**

Please come home

Lemony,

Thank you for your letter, though it was a little short and lacking in much detail. My main concern is that you have no intention of coming home yet. Please, Lemony. You must. Your family needs you. All will be forgiven. Come home now. We'll just be glad to have you back. I promise.

Your loving mother,
Mubla

PS I know you're behind the postcards to Jago – the turtles are a bit of a giveaway, don't you think? Why are you sending them in code?

PPS It's obvious where you are.

LIFE ON BOARD

SWIM 7 - CLEARWATER SWIM SERIES
CONTINENTS: 3 | COUNTRIES: 9

DAY 55

The Greatest Archipelago on Earth is a vast set of volcanic islands lying on either side of the equator, home to an abundance of plants and animals, and where the Clearwater swim series, a set of iconic weekly swims round the volcanic craters, takes place.

I've been on board the *Sweet Destiny* for a week, as a guest of Raif's parents. I think they felt sorry for me and/or wanted to keep an eye on me, even though I did send the letter to Mubla as promised. Whatever the reason, I'm savouring every moment while it lasts. Though, by some unhappy coincidence, it's also the boat the Boss is staying on too.

It's peaceful on deck tonight and I'm updating my budget. Something I haven't done in a long time, not since La Isla Bonita, partly because I'm a bit scared that I haven't stuck to it very well. I blame the continued cost of currency conversion and the fact that I've had to buy more hair dye.

Budget last checked 18 days in = £7,124

Allowance for days 19—27 doing swim 5 La Isla Bonita = £187.47

Actual:

Accommodation   9 x 200 = 1,800MEX$ x 0.04 = £72

Food   245 + 230 + 250 + 120 + 320 + 250
                + 400 + 100 + 500 = 2,315MEX$ x
                0.04 = £92.60

Currency Costs 625MEX$ x 0.04 = £25

Extras   750MEX$ x 0.04 = £30

Total   £219.60

That's an overspend of more than £30 and I've still got twenty-nine days to account for.

"Well, if it isn't the Ickle Mermaid. What *are* you working on?"

I look up to see the Boss standing over me, her face scrunched up in its usual scowl. I suppose I was bound to run into her at some point. I hold up my notebook.

"Maths!" she laughs, clumsily leaning over my shoulder and spilling her drink on me. "Oops. What are you doing that for?"

"Some of us have a budget to stick to," I retort.

The Boss squints at my sums. "Well, you're not doing very well, are you?"

I wrinkle my nose at her. "Should you be drinking that much with the swim tomorrow?"

"Oh, here we go," she cackles. "I forgot you were the gin police. Nothing wrong with losing control every now and then, Mermaid. You should try it."

"I can't," I mutter. "I'm too scared."

The Boss snorts. "Of what?"

"Everything," I reply. Then I reel out my list to her.

"Sea creatures!" she laughs. "Have you seen what you've been swimming with this past week? You can't be scared of jellyfish. So what if they sting you? Just swim on – unless it's a giant jellyfish in which case you're dead. Just don't go anywhere near them."

Her logic is full of holes but I admire the way she's so blasé about things.

"You're getting to be a very good swimmer, Mermaid," the Boss mutters. "Nowhere near my level of course. Getting quite a following on Instagram too. Though why I don't know…"

"Why don't you like me?" I ask.

The Boss frowns. "Like? What's like got to do with

anything? Do you see many friends around me now?" She shakes her head. "I have followers. My swimming life is a lonely one, but it's part of my make-up." She hesitates. "I'm the greatest swimmer on earth, d'you know that? The only person to swim the Six Seas in under a year. I've got so much influence in the swimming community. It's amazing where a bit of money will get you—"

"Is that how you survived that thunderstorm then?" I interrupt. "Did you pay for it to disappear?" The image of her holding up a wad of notes to a black sky crackling with lightning makes me splutter with laughter which is not appreciated by the Boss whose face clouds over as she stomps off.

RELATIVITY

DAY 72

"A top swimmer had a brother who died. What relation was the top swimmer to the brother who died? The answer isn't brother…"

Raif and I are taking our usual afternoon swim, in which we ask each other maths questions. I don't want my brain to shrivel and I find the best way to challenge myself is with brainteasers, of which Raif knows many.

"Too easy," I reply. "Sister."

"OK," says Raif. "How can you add eight 8s to get the answer 1,000, only using addition?"

"888 + 88 + 8 + 8 + 8," I answer quickly. "Still too easy!"

Raif laughs. "You're too good. I need to think of some more… Are you coming to hear the Boss talk tonight?"

"You mean drone on more like," I laugh. It took her a whole week to talk to me again after our last conversation.

"She's such a fraud," I say. "Considering how much she's goes on about saving the planet, she doesn't exactly practise what she preaches. Hold on a sec…"

I dive down beneath the water, camera at the ready, as a sea lion shoots past. It's almost impossible not to get a good shot here, what with the perfect light conditions and the most insane wildlife imaginable. It's like swimming in a giant aquarium.

"Get it?" asks Raif as I resurface. I nod.

"You're getting pretty good at that, you know?" he says, pulling me aside to let a turtle drift past, munching happily on some green algae. At Turtle Bay, we couldn't stop gawping at them, and all I could think about was swimming alongside them and capturing it on camera. Here, however, they're nothing special among the multitude of other sea creatures. Mentally I write a list.

Wildlife I have seen in the Greatest Archipelago
on Earth

Marine iguanas
Sea lions
Turtles
Manta rays
Dolphins
Whales
Flightless cormorants

"Fig," says Raif urgently, interrupting my thoughts. "Did you hear me? I said it's our last swim together next week. Then we'll be on opposite sides of the world."

"I know," I say sadly. "Aren't there any others we're both doing? What about the Pilgrimage? Or the Squirly Whirly?"

Raif shrugs miserably.

I take a huge breath then pull my way down towards the seabed. It's beautiful. Where the sunlight passes through the water, the shadows cast a complex pattern of organic shapes on the sand, and the seaweed and coral reef explode in a riot of colour. Oranges, purples, yellows and reds. The amount of fish down here is mind-blowing. Sometimes I really wish it was actually possible to breathe underwater.

Raif swims down and motions for me to go back up, a big smile spread across his face. "I've got it," he says when we get our breath back. "We *are* going to the Pilgrimage. Papa's always wanted to see the church in the middle of the Icy Lake. If you're doing that, why not meet me for the Time Travel swim first?"

"The Time Travel swim?"

"Yes. Trust me, you'll want to do this. It's in the Land of the Midnight Sun in July. Starts at midnight and, if you do it fast enough, you finish the swim the day before you start it."

I agree in a heartbeat, feeling completely intrigued by this notion, and wishing I'd paid more attention to those relativity classes last year…

Fig's Swims Round the World

1. ~~Dinosaur Island~~
2. ~~The Jailhouse Rock~~
3. ~~Mount Storm Rough Water~~
4. ~~The Red Canyon swim series~~
5. ~~La Isla Bonita~~
6. ~~Turtle Bay~~
7. ~~The Greatest Archipelago on Earth~~
   ~~Clearwater swim series~~
8. Malokodaidai Island 10k
9. The Big Swim series in the Land of Koalas
10. The Lazy River
11. The Cold Drop
12. The Whale Isles
13. The Hot Fjords
14. The Ancients Trail swims
15. Island-hopping
16. The Sunriser
17. The Mermaid Canal

Bonus swim - The Time Traveller

18. The Pilgrimage
19. The Squirly Whirly
20. The Cross-continental

SEASICKNESS

SWIM 8 – MALOKODAIDAI
CONTINENTS: 4 | COUNTRIES: 10

Mode of Transport	Number of journeys complete	Distance covered (km)	Time spent (hrs)
Rail	5	2,689	40.75
Road	11	8,826	158.85
Air	6	14,015	21.75
Sea	4	1,762	132

DAY 87

"Swimmers at the ready!"

I glance nervously around me. This is a big swim. A marathon 10k swim. The furthest I have ever swum in one go and I don't know what to expect. Should I have been training over longer distances? Should I swim differently? Should I even do this? I don't know. At least I'll have Raif by my side, though no doubt he'll storm ahead.

I arrived on Malokodaidai five days ago, in stormy weather, which didn't encourage me to get in the water, especially after a particularly rough crossing by ferry where all the passengers, me included, vomited our guts up over the side of the boat. I swear I was green and empty by the time I stood on dry land. I must have really stunk of sick too, because Raif pulled away pretty quickly from our hug. I was even ill when I went for a short swim the next day. The waves were big and choppy, and I found myself gagging. I didn't know you could get seasick swimming. It was not a happy discovery.

"Take your marks."

My swimming training has subsequently hit a wall and I'm not the enthusiastic swimmer I once was. The water here is cooler and murkier and full of debris. Getting in for a swim feels like a chore and I'm tired of doing it. It's not surprising really. I was bound to hit a low at some point. If only Dab Dabs was here to give me a hug and a word of encouragement.

After the first few rotten days here, I've spent my time exclusively with Raif, swimming and answering more and more complicated riddles. And, when Raif hasn't been around, I've been taking photographs, which I'm becoming equally obsessed with. It's all about light and texture for me, and in an idyllic place like this, where palm trees line the fine white sandy beaches and the dramatic clifftops stare out at the dark blue ocean, there's plenty to capture. The sunlight is warm and intense, and, as it changes position in the sky, the landscape is continually transforming into not-to-be-missed photo opportunities.

"Go, go, go!"

I run into the water, bounding over the waves alongside

a thousand other like-minded, orange-capped swimmers. I've never seen this many people in the water before. It's overwhelming and I naturally pull back until there's more room. I've taken a seasickness tablet just in case. It's tough going and I'm soon hit in the face by a giant wave just as I'm breathing in and I get a mouthful of seawater. My stomach churns painfully and I hurl it back up in one violent motion. There goes my medicine. This is not going to be easy.

Getting to the halfway point feels like it takes forever. Marked by two large wooden poles sticking out of the water, a row of multicoloured flags festooned between them, there are boats where volunteers are handing out water and encouraging words, but I daren't go near. The water will make me sick and the words will make me cry.

"Fig!"

I have to wait for the wave to fall before I see Raif waving at me. In a few short strokes he's by my side.

"Are you OK? You don't look OK," he says. He seems worried.

"Seasick," I manage to say. Then I throw up again, bright yellow bile coming from deep within my stomach, burning my throat and making me retch even more.

"You should get out," says Raif.

I shake my head. I'm over halfway. I can't stop now. I've always said that I don't mind failing but I know, deep down, that I just cannot fail at any of these swims. "No. Just give me a minute."

Raif stays by my side, treading water. He won't go on, even though he knows his time won't be good if he waits.

"Come on," he says. "Your body won't like you if you don't start swimming soon."

I agree to follow him but make him promise to swim on at his own speed, which he does unwillingly. I fall into a slow crawl, gagging to the side occasionally, as my waves of nausea coincide with the swell of the sea. I hope there isn't anyone swimming in my wake...

The last five kilometres feel like they stretch on to infinity. When I finally see the finishing posts, perhaps five hundred metres out, I'm so relieved, I could cry. But it takes such a long time and I have to dig deep to find the energy to keep going. *Bubble, bubble, breathe* comes to mind. At the final hundred metres I see Raif and his parents standing on the beach. They're jumping up and down, chanting my name. It gives me that last push I need and I kick my feet until I feel like my chest will explode with the effort.

At last the water temperature changes back to warm and I sink my feet into the sandy seabed. My legs are like jelly. I'm the most exhausted I've ever been and end up crawling on hands and knees over the finish line, where a swim official is waiting to hang a flower garland round my neck.

"Fig, you did it!" yells Raif. "Are you all right?"

"Yes," I murmur. Then, "No." And I spew the remaining seawater left in my stomach all over his feet.

WHAT A DIFFERENCE A YEAR MAKES...

"I'm impressed," says Raif that evening. "I didn't think you'd keep going today."

"Why would you think that?"

"When I first met you, you nearly gave up when you thought I was a crocodile."

I laugh. Seems such a long time ago now. "I was a different person then."

"A much grumpier person," says Raif.

"I was not!"

"OK. You're still grumpy," he laughs. "But I'm glad I met you."

"Me too. I was full of fears then. The world doesn't seem quite as scary now."

Raif grins. "So what's your biggest fear about swimming now?"

I consider this for a while. "Probably a Portuguese man-of-war jellyfish or a crocodile. You?"

"Sharks," says Raif.

"Sharks? Pah!" I tease. "I've swum in shark-infested waters already."

"You have not!" laughs Raif.

"Well, kind of," I admit. "I did the Jailhouse Rock swim. The island is surrounded by leopard sharks."

"And did you meet any?"

I giggle nervously. "No, they're scared of humans. But I was ready to punch one if I did."

"You *Trottel*!" Raif doubles up with laughter and I shove him over, making him howl even more.

The next morning I lie in my sleeping bag, thinking about what I've achieved since my last birthday. I meant what I said the night before. The world isn't as scary any more. I used to quake with fear at so many things. Now look at me! I'm nearly halfway through my swims and I can honestly say I've conquered my fear of water. This gets me to thinking about Sage and all she did for me.

I dial the number with shaking hands. It's a funny ringtone. Far off and distant. After a few clicks, Sage picks up.

"Hello?" she says.

For a moment, I can't say anything. I can't breathe.

"Hello?" she repeats.

"Sage," I whisper.

"Fig! Is that you? Are you OK? Is everything all right?"

"Yes," I say quickly. "I'm fine. I was just thinking about you."

"Thank goodness for that... It's so wonderful to hear your voice. You know, I had the strangest of phone calls. Some woman with an accent asking questions. She seemed to know *everything* about you. Seemed to think I was your aunt..." I give another sniff. "Fig? Are you OK?"

Oh, how I wish I was at home right now, even though it's probably raining and cold. I'd be sitting in my bed, eating lemon drizzle cake and enjoying the fact that Mubla has already rung school to say I'm not coming in.

"Yes, I'm fine," I eventually manage. "Hearing your voice has made me homesick. And it's my birthday."

Sage gasps. "Of course it is! Happy birthday!"

"Thanks," I reply. "Oh, Sage! This is the best thing I've ever done in my whole life! I've met so many lovely people. Someone called Blue, who's been teaching me everything about open-water swimming. And there's this boy called Raif. We've been swimming together loads. He's that woman's son. She found out and the only way I could convince her not to tell Mubla was if I gave her your number. You did tell her you know who I am?"

"Yes, don't worry," says Sage. "I guessed something like that had happened, after your father came round."

I gasp. "Dab Dabs! But—"

"Mubla found out about the Mermaids."

My fingers whiten as my grip tightens on the phone.

"She's building quite a case against you, you know. Even tried to question me," says Sage, cackling. "Don't worry. I know how to handle people like Mubla."

I breathe out slowly, my nausea beginning to pass. I'd love to have been a fly on the wall of *that* interrogation. Mubla meeting her match in a former secret-service agent.

"How was Dab Dabs?" I ask. "And was Jago with him?"

God, I wish I could see them right now.

"Both fine," replies Sage. "You don't need to worry about either of them." Her laughter is distant and crackly. Or is that her coughing? I can't tell. "Just keep going, Fig. What you're doing is fantastic."

"Oh, Sage," I gush. "Thank you so much for helping me. I feel like I've finally done something that I can call mine. I'm so happy."

"Good for you, my love. Good for you."

Fig's Swims Round the World

1. ~~Dinosaur Island~~
2. ~~The Jailhouse Rock~~
3. ~~Mount Storm Rough Water~~
4. ~~The Red Canyon swim series~~
5. ~~La Isla Bonita~~
6. ~~Turtle Bay~~
7. ~~The Greatest Archipelago on Earth~~
   ~~Clearwater swim series~~
8. ~~Malokodaidai Island 10k~~
9. The Big Swim series in the Land of Koalas
10. The Lazy River
11. The Cold Drop
12. The Whale Isles
13. The Hot Fjords
14. The Ancients Trail swims
15. Island-hopping
16. The Sunriser
17. The Mermaid Canal

Bonus swim - The Time Traveller

18. The Pilgrimage
19. The Squirly Whirly
20. The Cross-continental

POSTCARDS TO JAGO

Agent Hugh Moonstone

c/o Jago Fitzsherbert

The Fitzsherbert Family Funeral Home

Old Mare

England

Countdown to coming home!

Using any of the numbers below, can you work it out?

75

1 2 3 4 5

THE PERFORMANCE

DAY 91

The airport is small and deserted. Outside the rain is lashing down so hard, I half hope there'll be no flights tonight. This is where Raif and I say goodbye for the next seven months. He's travelling home. I'm heading to the other side of the world to the Land of the Koalas.

"Fig," he says, nudging me. "Look."

There's a lime-green upright piano plonked in the middle of the airport, its keys open to the world, enticing me to touch them. It wants to be played... No. There are too many people about. I can't.

"Are you going to play it then?" asks Raif.

I shake my head.

"Why not? You always promised you'd play for me, if we ever found a piano."

I shake my head again. "What if someone hears me?"

"They're supposed to," he laughs. "Go on. Please?"

So I sit at the piano and cautiously run my fingers over the keys. It sounds wonky and out of tune but, as I continue to play, it seems to warm to me. Dab Dabs's favourite piece of music springs to mind, but the piano is loud and jarring. I turn to look around but no one's paying attention, and I have no audience, except Raif.

"Keep going," he whispers.

'Scenes from an Italian Restaurant' starts off gently, with a catchy melody, then builds to a rock-and-roll style that is so energetic my forearms throb with the unfamiliar movement and I can feel the sweat forming on my forehead. Then, as the catchy melody finally returns, I take the music to its grand climax, finishing it so abruptly that the silence engulfs me. It's broken by a sudden gust of applause and I turn to see an audience of passengers have gathered, staring at me in awe. Raif looks stunned.

"More!" someone cries. Then it becomes a chant. "More, more, more!"

Raif nudges me. "Go on. They're not going to stop until you do."

I nod willingly – I'm actually enjoying myself – and, turning back to the piano, I begin another piece. Once again I get lost in the music. It feels wonderful to play, and the achiness in my fingers and wrists soon slips away. It's like riding a bike and the memory of all the music I've ever played comes flooding back. When I turn round, the audience has grown even larger. Countless people are filming me on their phones. They erupt into cheers.

"Take a bow," whispers Raif. "You've earned it."

So I do. It seems Mubla's dream of my becoming a concert pianist has finally come true.

"Did you see those people, Mama?" gushes Raif. "They were all there for Fig. Can you believe it?"

Raif's mother nods, smiling at me. "You are a girl of hidden talents, *mein Liebling*!"

"I just like to do things well," I reply, grinning back. I feel so proud of myself. Why haven't I done that before?

"Look! Someone's uploaded it already." Raif shows me his phone.

In the video you can clearly make out my face. My eyes are closed and the music is seemingly pouring out of me. The title makes my heart freeze, though.

STRIKING A CHORD – FIG OLANDER
WOWS THE WAITING CROWD

"Final call for passenger Fay Olander. Please make your way to gate three."

"How did they get my name?" I ask, ignoring the announcement, half wondering if it's even safe to fly in a storm like this.

The blood drains from Raif's face. "Someone asked me. *Scheiße*. Fig, I'm sorry. I forgot."

I turn to him, the panic rising in my stomach. I need to puke.

"This is the final call for passenger Fay Olander. Please make your way to gate three."

Raif takes me by the shoulders. "You need to go – you can't miss your flight. You'll be fine. Message me when you get there."

I nod.

"And you won't forget the Time Travel swim?" he asks. "Promise me."

I nod again. "I promise." I don't want to say goodbye. I reach out to hold his hand and he grips mine back.

"Till we meet again?" he says.

"Till we meet again." I finally manage to pull my hand away. I'm full of anxiety. For the flight. For the video. For the storm.

Raif looks panicked too, and calls, "She won't know to look there, will she?"

The breath is stuck in my throat and I have to resist the urge to throw up. My last words as the flight attendant shuffles me through the gate are, "You don't know Mubla…"

DEPRESSION

To: **Lemony Fitzsherbert**   24 December 12:04

From: **WendyFitzsherbertQC**

You're never coming back

Lemony! I've just got back from Malokodaidai. Twenty-four hours on a plane. Twice! You were supposed to be there.

You're never coming back, are you? What did I ever do to deserve this? Why don't you want to be found? It's our Resolution Dinner next week and you're not here. It won't be the same without you.

Oh, Lemony, why are you doing this?

Your loving mother,

Mubla

PS Jago says 276. I've given up trying to work it out.

PPS I'm offering a £10,000 reward for information that ensures your safe return. I'm not giving up on that.

MESSAGES

SWIM 9 – THE BIG SWIM SERIES
CONTINENTS: 4 | COUNTRIES: 11

DAY 123

Ickle_Mermaid Wishing you a Saturnalian Xmas! I miss you so much, Stella. Without you here to keep me sane, I feel lonely and depressed. Every day something happens that I want to tell you about, which just makes me realize you're not here.

WordBird Ha! Love it. And a convivial Christmas to you too! Miss you more. Like crazy. How's it going on the other side of the world?

Ickle_Mermaid Hot! Give me cold, frosty weather any day. The Christmas trees here look ridiculous on the beach. And a full traditional Christmas-day turkey is not the best thing to eat in the heat. Especially before a swim.

WordBird Not more vomiting, Fig!! Walked past your house the other day. Even more decorations than usual!

Ickle_Mermaid You know Dab Dabs. Bet it looks magical, though. Have you seen Jago? I hated not getting to see him open his Santa stocking.

WordBird You sound homesick, Fig. Keep going. You're amazing!

Ickle_Mermaid 🖤🖤🖤
Btw, you are deleting these messages?

DAY 130

To: **Raif**   1 January 16:31
From: **Fig Fitzsherbert**
Frohes neues Jahr

Hi Raif,

Happy New Year!

You'll never guess who turned up the other day. Blue! It was apparently some last-minute gig and she needed the money. She's even camping with me so it's been like old times. Living together, swimming together. I've had such a good time. We've taken to comparing crazy swimming stories to while away the hours, so I've been telling her about the Boss.

Did you celebrate New Year's Eve? Blue got us invited to a party. My first one ever. Turns out Mubla was wrong. It *is* fun counting in a new year, especially with friends! Also guess what? The world doesn't end if you don't make a New Year's resolution...

I got an onslaught of DMs from the Boss, bragging that she's still number one (like I care). I thought about her when I did the annual New Year's Day swim this morning. Think there were quite a few hangovers.

I also got an email from Mubla, which made me feel awful. She loves New Year's Day. She's offering a £10,000 reward. Don't you dare cash me in!

Till we meet again,

Fig xox

PS Don't worry. I know you'd never do that to me. I'm so glad I've got people like you and Blue and Stella in my life!

DAY 136

> **Ickle_Mermaid** Narcoleptic! I swam the *Long One* today. Quite similar to the Malokodaidai 10K but much warmer and I didn't throw up over anyone!

Ickle_Mermaid Stopped for a chat with the ladies handing out water at the halfway point. Good job they were there because my goggles broke – again. Think I ate too many jelly babies. Blue said we all looked like seals at feeding time, which made one of the ladies laugh so much she almost fell in the water! Blue's really funny like that.

WordBird Green-eyed! Blue's still swimming with you then?

Ickle_Mermaid Nothing to be jealous of, Stella. You're still my BFIATW. Guess what? The Boss followed me on Instagram. OMG! MISSING YOU LIKE CRAZY!

DAY 143

To: **Raif**   15 January 18:07
From: **Fig Fitzsherbert**
I survived!

Hi Raif,

I swam the *Medium One* today and *nearly* encountered a Portuguese man-of-war jellyfish. Obviously I survived. There were tons of people yelling at us from the fishing boats, telling us to move in the other direction. No one got stung, though, which seems a miracle considering the amount of detached tentacles floating around. Blue got me through it. Thank God she's here.

I researched Portuguese man-of-wars and it turns out it isn't in fact a jellyfish. It is a colony of individual organisms called polyps! Maybe I should knock jellyfish off my Fear List? Actually no. Just googled them again. There's apparently an immortal jellyfish that can *live forever*. Sting symptoms range from mild headache to death...

Till we meet again,

Fig xox

DAY 150

Ickle_Mermaid Languishing... Today's swim was the *Short One*. It was fun but over too quickly. I've spent too much time online and now I'm almost out of phone data.

No phone data + No you = Boredom.

WordBird 😁 and yes, I'm deleting them. Even as I type... 😆

DAY 157

Hi Raif,

I'm writing you this email from an internet café which I stumbled on after my last swim (the *Big One*).

I was told it would be hard and to expect difficult conditions, but it was dead calm for days. Then, this morning, it was like someone had played that tablecloth trick and replaced it with a completely different ocean, with strong winds and swells coming in all directions. Thankful that you told me to practise breathing on my weakest side, as that's the only side I could breathe on. Found out the hard way and swallowed a lot of water. You'd have been proud of me. I wasn't sick. I also managed to ignore my feelings of doubt in the first 500 metres of the swim, like you said. And my skin tingled today when I heard the waves breaking and the crowd cheering at the end. Still felt relieved when it was over. Will that ever change?

Blue reckons she can get me a job as a photographer on the Whale Isles so I can earn a bit of extra cash. Says my pictures are more than good enough. Had a dig at me for not sharing my photos publicly. But I couldn't exactly explain the real reason, could I? She laughed when I said I was shy. Made me promise to change my Instagram status back to public. Not sure how much of a good idea it is, since Mubla seems to be getting closer. But a promise is a promise.

Oh and I checked my swimming stats. If I count only the event swims, that's 115 kilometres of the world, which is only a meagre 0.2875 per cent.

I miss you.

Till we meet again,
Fig xox

Fig's Swims Round the World

1. ~~Dinosaur Island~~
2. ~~The Jailhouse Rock~~
3. ~~Mount Storm Rough Water~~
4. ~~The Red Canyon swim series~~
5. ~~La Isla Bonita~~
6. ~~Turtle Bay~~
7. ~~The Greatest Archipelago on Earth~~
   ~~Clearwater swim series~~
8. ~~Malokodaidai Island 10k~~
9. ~~The Big Swim series in the Land of Koalas~~
10. The Lazy River
11. The Cold Drop
12. The Whale Isles
13. The Hot Fjords
14. The Ancients Trail swims
15. Island-hopping
16. The Sunriser
17. The Mermaid Canal

Bonus swim - The Time Traveller

18. The Pilgrimage
19. The Squirly Whirly
20. The Cross-continental

DISTANCE OF DOUBT

SWIM 10 – THE LAZY RIVER
CONTINENTS: 5 | COUNTRIES: 12

DAY 164

Lap one. Oh God, why am I doing this? It's cold. I want to get out. I can't do this. I've still got nineteen laps to go.

Lap two. OK, it's not so bad after all. I've at least warmed up. Only eighteen laps to go. Yawn. This is such a dull swim.

Lap three. Maybe I should work out my budget – I've got plenty of time.

So, I've got 201 days to go and with my daily budget allowance that's roughly...

20 x 201 = £4,020

Eek! So why have I only got £3,802 left?!

Laps four to seven. How could I let this happen?

*Bubble, bubble, breath*e.

Lap eight. How can I call myself a mathematician? I'm useless.

Bubble, bubble, breathe.

Lap ten. Halfway there. This is boring. Twenty laps of a 500-metre course. Why did I choose this swim? It was a pain to get here and I hate the idea of them stopping the current of a river. I bet the Boss would have something to say about that.

Lap eleven. How can my budget have gone so wrong?

Obviously, there's the extra cost of the hostel and all the lovely sushi. Mmm. But I thought I'd accounted for that, what with Raif's parents paying for me for that month on the boat.

Lap sixteen. Oh, I know. I must have mucked up the conversion rate. Of course!

Lap seventeen. No, I know what it was. It was my stupid handwriting. Mubla was right. I thought I was spending £100 on these five days, which I wrote down as 43,764 yen when it's actually 13,764 yen. That's a difference of:

43764 / 137.64 compared with 13764 / 137.64…

Which is £217.96. Rounding that up to £218 and taking it away from the budget I thought I had equals … £3,802.

Lap twenty. Oh. It's over. Phew.

Fig's Swims Round the World

1. ~~Dinosaur Island~~
2. ~~The Jailhouse Rock~~
3. ~~Mount Storm Rough Water~~
4. ~~The Red Canyon swim series~~
5. ~~La Isla Bonita~~
6. ~~Turtle Bay~~
7. ~~The Greatest Archipelago on Earth~~
   ~~Clearwater swim series~~
8. ~~Malokodaidai Island 10k~~
9. ~~The Big Swim series in the Land of Koalas~~
10. ~~The Lazy River~~
11. The Cold Drop
12. The Whale Isles
13. The Hot Fjords
14. The Ancients Trail swims
15. Island-hopping
16. The Sunriser
17. The Mermaid Canal
Bonus swim – The Time Traveller
18. The Pilgrimage
19. The Squirly Whirly
20. The Cross-continental

NIGHT SWIMMING

SWIM 11 – THE COLD DROP
CONTINENTS: 5 | COUNTRIES: 13

Mode of Transport	Number of journeys complete	Distance covered (km)	Time spent (hrs)
Rail	8	2,775	42.45
Road	16	9,870	168.35
Air	13	46,140	66.25
Sea	6	1,952	134

DAY 174

The sky is clear tonight and the stars burn brightly out here in the Eastern Sea, away from the light pollution of the city. The full moon has been given the stage to shine in all its splendour, casting a sparkly path over the expanse of water before me. I'm ready. Complete with glow sticks tied securely (and believe me I've triple-checked) to my goggles. I even have glow paint on my face. I look like a strange, luminous pink bug with a bright red body.

I pause to have my photograph taken by the event photographer, then take my place with the other fifty or so swimmers. I'm feeling incredibly nervous. This is the biggest leap of faith I've ever taken. I've never swum in the water at night and I don't know where I'm going. The organizers haven't told us. We're just supposed to follow the sound of the music as it leads us back to shore. I'm terrified.

Piano notes suddenly echo into the night sky, accentuated by the strike of chords. It silences everyone. Then the singing begins – a low and mournful voice and a song about a quiet night.

HONK!

As the siren sounds, I join everyone, like a lemming, and jump into the pitch-black sea. It's freezing and we all howl up at the moon as we try to acclimatize to the temperature. Red fireworks shoot into the sky, one after the other, forming the shape of a heart. It is Valentine's Day after all. Everyone cheers. It's a strangely exhilarating feeling, like I'm part of something.

Then we're off. Slowly at first, to get used to the feeling of swimming blind. All I can see is the faint light of the glow sticks by my face and I can just about make out my gloved hands in the water. Every now and then I become aware of someone's feet in front of me so at least I know I'm going the right way. As long as they keep the music loud, I'll be all right. Flashlights shine over the water, shouts from the safety kayaks, yelling, "Keep right!"

I'm ridiculously calm, considering I'm me. The water isn't cold any more and I'm not quite as stranded as I feared I would be. The song is still blaring out, the mournful voice still warbling. How nice to swim to music! I've never thought to do that before. I roll on to my back to look behind me and am rewarded with a heavenly sight. A trail of multicoloured lights slowly floating across the water. They are the other swimmers but they look like fairies dancing. It feels magical.

I'm forced to continue, as I'm getting rather cold and I can feel my wrists growing stiff. It doesn't take long to reach the shore. I call out the number written on my hand, so the organizers can mark me as finished. Then I sit on the beach among the other finishers and stare out to sea to watch the rest come in. What a feeling! I'm so glad I did this swim. Then, as the moment of elation passes, it's replaced with a moment of fear. Isn't it always? I hate how I can be so happy one minute and paralysed with anxiety the next.

There's a swim official standing by the soup stand. She's wearing the usual garb of beige shorts, which appears to be the uniform of every official going, with a white sports shirt saying *The Cold Drop* in a large red heart. She looks exactly like Mubla. I feel like the wind has been thumped out of me. *Is* it Mubla? No. Surely not. How could she be here? I'm on the other side of the world. This place is, literally, a drop in the ocean.

I stare for a long time at the woman. The darkness doesn't help and I still feel a little bit woozy from the cold water. The likeness is uncanny: red hair piled on top of her head, a full face of make-up. The only difference is her clothes. There's no way Mubla would ever be seen dead in anything like that. Dab Dabs would ensure that...

As I nibble on a corner of flapjack, a towel wrapped round me, I turn to my phone to settle my nerves. I've really come to rely on it. It's no wonder I keep using up all my data. My notifications have gone wild. Then I see the cause. Thanks to the Boss reposting it, the airport concert video has gone viral.

> **TheBoss** #repost @Ickle_Mermaid with @repostapp
> Blimey @Ickle_Mermaid. You kept that quiet
> #HiddenDepths
> **Ickle_Mermaid** Thanks for the tag.
> Thought I'd go one better than the ukulele
> #pianosarebetterthantinyguitars

My post sparks a most enjoyable back and forth with the Boss and I can feel my nerves calming down. Then she sends me a direct message with a web link:

> **TheBoss** 'World's most badass swimmer swims the most dangerous shark-infested swim on earth.' Sorry @Ickle_Mermaid, looks like the title is already taken.

> **Ickle_Mermaid** No danger of me swimming with great whites. That is unless I count you @TheBoss

> **TheBoss** Haha. I can unfollow too.

Somehow the Boss brings out a sarcastic side of me that I never knew I had. I kind of like sparring with her. I take a photo of the Cold Drop logo on my swimming hat and caption it:

> **Ickle_Mermaid** Happy Valentine's Day @TheBoss Whose day are you spoiling?
>
> **TheBoss** Yours. Spending it with lover boy?
>
> **Ickle_Mermaid** If you mean Raif, he's on the other side of the world.
>
> **TheBoss** Aw, never mind. Find yourself another. Or can't lightning strike in the same place twice?

I'm suddenly reminded of the Q&A session the Boss held when I first met her and how cagey she got about her last swim, apparently swimming through lightning. I message her the link to a science article online about lightning conducting in water and post a picture of someone with their hair standing on end.

> **Ickle_Mermaid** Well, you would know @TheBoss

She doesn't reply. It's like a virtual tumbleweed floating around in the ether. Then my follower count goes down by one and I know what she's done.

Fig's Swims Round the World

1. ~~Dinosaur Island~~
2. ~~The Jailhouse Rock~~
3. ~~Mount Storm Rough Water~~
4. ~~The Red Canyon swim series~~
5. ~~La Isla Bonita~~
6. ~~Turtle Bay~~
7. ~~The Greatest Archipelago on Earth~~
   ~~Clearwater swim series~~
8. ~~Malokodaidai Island 10k~~
9. ~~The Big Swim series in the Land of Koalas~~
10. ~~The Lazy River~~
11. ~~The Cold Drop~~
12. The Whale Isles
13. The Hot Fjords
14. The Ancients Trail swims
15. Island-hopping
16. The Sunriser
17. The Mermaid Canal
Bonus swim - The Time Traveller
18. The Pilgrimage
19. The Squirly Whirly
20. The Cross-continental

SMALL WORLD

SWIM 12 – THE WHALE ISLES
CONTINENTS: 5 | COUNTRIES: 14

DAY 203

"So where are you girls from?" asks the skipper of our boat, the *Whale Whisperer*. We've been sailing this patch of water for over an hour now, watching, waiting for and willing the whales to come.

"Small seaside town," I say. "You won't have heard of it. Although it is famous for producing some brilliant swimmers. Of which I am one!"

"Brilliant, eh?!" laughs Blue, digging me in the ribs. "You've improved loads since I first met you. I'll give you that much. You weren't far behind me on that last swim either. Well, by an hour. But, by most people's standards, that's amazing."

I grin back. I've had the most incredible few weeks. The Whale Isles race is done. I swam it well and I even enjoyed it. And, as promised, Blue got me a job on board this whale swimming tour boat as the photographer, thanks to them having seen my Instagram account.

I have swum with whales, even heard them sing. I could quite happily turn into a mermaid and live here, swimming and taking photographs every day. Every picture I take looks amazing. And, what with taking underwater pictures for these tourists every day, I think I'm becoming good at it too. Myrtle would be proud of me. As soon as I get back to civilization, I'll upload them to my account for her. And I'll send Sage all of my swimming cap trophies. They're weighing me down and I think she'd appreciate them.

"I'm from the Big Smoke," says Blue. "My coach is from a town famous for its swimmers too. Hey, Fig. Wouldn't it be hilarious if it was the same one?"

I nod slowly, trying to work out the likelihood in my head. Surely not. I mean, I know the world is a small place and all that, but that would be *some* coincidence. And rather dangerous.

"Where *are* you from?" asks Blue. "You've never said."

"Whale!" yells Skipper and our conversation is thankfully put on hold.

"If you could sit down until we've stopped, please," I call, ushering the tourists back to their seats. "Skipper's got to speed up if we want to be the first to get to the whale."

It's amazing how much authority I now have in my voice. People are actually listening to me and doing as they're told. We're too late, though, and another boat has the whale.

Etiquette says it's theirs and we must move on to find our own. It could mean another hour of sailing around without a sighting, though chances are we'll soon find our own.

I settle back in my seat, preparing for another long wait. "Did you hear about the woman who swam thirty kilometres in a cage so that she wouldn't be eaten by creatures along the way?" I ask, hoping to move the subject away from home.

But Blue isn't taking the bait. "So," she says, "what's with the secrecy?"

"I don't know what you're talking about," I laugh nervously, leaning back in my seat, trying to look as casual as possible, while inside my head I'm screaming, *She knows you're a fake!*

Blue pouts. "I thought we were friends."

"We are," I say. "You just wouldn't have heard of it, that's all."

"Try me," laughs Blue, though there's an edge to her voice. "How many seaside towns are famous for producing good swimmers?"

I shrug. "A few?"

Blue looks confused. She knows I'm being evasive.

"Well, if you won't tell me," she says, "I'll guess. Is it Old Mare?"

My stomach plummets when she says that and I have to concentrate hard on the horizon to stop myself from puking. I hastily cover this up by making a show of looking for our own whale, scanning the water for the telltale signs.

"Well, am I right?" asks Blue.

I don't answer her but instead yell, "Whale!" because I've spotted one.

And we're off. This time it's ours and it's a pod of three. I climb into the water, camera at the ready, waiting to capture any moments with these beautiful creatures.

The larger whale swims round us, curious about the strange humans in wetsuits. The others are smaller and cute. They stick their snouts out of the water, blowing and slapping their tails so that we get splashed. They're playing. Teasing us and enjoying our squeals of laughter. The larger one breaches out of the water and dives back down, swooping right under us. It's a breathtaking moment and one that I think I've caught on camera.

All too quickly, though, there are three *eek* sounds, as if they're saying, "Enough playing now. It's time to go home." They slowly rise out of the water and, with a graceful flick of their tails, they're gone.

The tourists are happy. They've seen the whales and we can take the boat back to base. Blue is looking at me in a funny way, though. Like she's trying to figure out a conundrum.

HOME TRUTHS

"This is you, isn't it?"

I haven't seen her in a few days. Not since the funny looks on the boat. Blue thrusts her phone under my nose. It's an old school photo of me, with the caption, *Growing concerns over missing sixteen-year-old schoolgirl Lemony Fitzsherbert, known to her friends and family as Fig.*

"Is this why you wouldn't tell me where you're from?" snaps Blue. And, with one look at my guilty face, she snorts, sitting down heavily opposite me. "So you thought you'd lie to me?"

"I couldn't tell you," I say. "You don't know my mother."

"No, but my swim coach Nicky does," she replies. "Everyone knows *Mubla* in Old Mare apparently. I can't believe you lied to me. I thought we were friends. Friends don't keep big secrets from each other."

"I'm sorry," I say. "You have to understand. It's not all it's cracked up to be living with Mubla."

"Oh, sure," snaps Blue. "Living in an enormous house. Must be hard having someone pay for everything you've ever wanted. Poor little rich girl. I bet your parents paid for this trip, didn't they?"

"I'm using savings," I say feebly. "And I'm going to pay it all back. Honest. I've been working where I can and spending as little money as possible. It's been hard."

"You wouldn't know hardship if it came up and bit you on the butt," snarls Blue. "I thought you were the same as me. All your constant worries about money. I should have known when I saw your posh fitness tracker. I thought you'd stolen it or something!" She shakes her head angrily. "I was wrong about you. Turns out you're just another ungrateful, privileged white girl…"

The harsh realization of what I've taken for granted my whole life hits me full on. She's right. I am spoilt. The feeling doesn't sit well with me.

"I'm sorry," I say. "I've never thought of it that way. I didn't realize… I … I guess I've never thought that other people might not get the same opportunities… But…" I pause. "You don't know Mubla… She's never been there for me…"

Blue stares back, her eyes steely and unfriendly. I don't recognize her.

"She's been there enough for you to do everything you've ever wanted to do," she sneers. "She's given you *everything* you have *ever* needed."

"Except love," I want to say, but I don't think she'd hear me.

"I'd take that over having to send home half of what I make each month," continues Blue. "I scrape by so that my mum and siblings don't have to. What have you ever done for your family? Like I said. Spoilt brat."

"You're right," I say. "I *am* ungrateful and I didn't realize it. But Blue. Please believe me. I wanted to tell you so many times. I'm so sorry. I really do value our friendship. You've helped me through some of the toughest swims. You even got me this job. When I started out on this adventure, I never expected to meet someone like you. Never expected to have the fun that we've had. You've really made a difference…"

For a moment, I think Blue's going to forgive me and I allow my shoulders to relax a fraction. "You won't tell the authorities, will you?" I ask with a hopeful smile.

But Blue's expression changes and, with a shrug, she says, "It's too late. I've already reported you."

Fig's Swims Round the World

1. ~~Dinosaur Island~~
2. ~~The Jailhouse Rock~~
3. ~~Mount Storm Rough Water~~
4. ~~The Red Canyon swim series~~
5. ~~La Isla Bonita~~
6. ~~Turtle Bay~~
7. ~~The Greatest Archipelago on Earth~~
   ~~Clearwater swim series~~
8. ~~Malokodaidai Island 10k~~
9. ~~The Big Swim series in the Land of Koalas~~
10. ~~The Lazy River~~
11. ~~The Cold Drop~~
12. ~~The Whale Isles~~
13. The Hot Fjords
14. The Ancients Trail swims
15. Island-hopping
16. The Sunriser
17. The Mermaid Canal
Bonus swim - The Time Traveller
18. The Pilgrimage
19. The Squirly Whirly
20. The Cross-continental

THE BREAK-UP

DAY 221

The moment Blue said she'd reported me, I got out of there quick. I left a note trying to explain myself. I thought it would help and we could go back to the way things were. But then she started direct messaging me relentlessly:

goldengirl_01 How could you lie to me?

Ickle_Mermaid I'm sorry.

goldengirl_01 I thought we were friends.

Ickle_Mermaid We were. We ARE. I'm sorry.

goldengirl_01 Were.

This morning delivers her most fatal blow, a repost of a selfie I took swimming alongside a whale.

goldengirl_01 #repost @Ickle_Mermaid with @ repostapp. I've found her! #FindFig #swimtheworld

I don't reply. The damage is done. Our friendship is clearly over.

Then, a few hours later, Stella sends me a link to an article on our local newspaper's website, along with *that* photo. My cover is well and truly blown.

INSTA SWIMMING STORM

The long-distance swimmer, eighteen-year-old Blue Michaels, who took the open-water swimming world by storm two years ago, has found herself embroiled in the compelling case of missing schoolgirl Lemony Fitzsherbert. (Yes, you read that name correctly in case you think I've got a hankering for a boiled sweet – Ed.) Fitzsherbert, commonly known as Fig, has been missing since August 25th last year when she left her hotel room in the Foggy City. Her mother, barrister Wendy Fitzsherbert QC, has been running her 'Find Fig' campaign ever since.

The police received a tip-off via Instagram from Miss Michaels – @goldengirl_01 – who claimed to have been spending time with her abroad while Fig – @Ickle_Mermaid – completes her #swimtheworld challenge. A note has been handed in, purporting to be from Fig herself, confirming Miss Michaels had no knowledge of her being a runaway. It is unclear whether she has been given the reward money.

DAY 232

I feel awful. Stuck here in the hot desert, waiting for my next swim, with literally no one to talk to. I keep my head down, swimming cap firmly on, and stick to my tent, only going out for training swims and to get food. My nerves are frazzled. Everywhere I look, I keep thinking I see Mubla. It can only be a matter of time. I've never felt more alone. And I've never wanted Dab Dabs to come to the rescue more.

HOT WATER

SWIM 13 – THE HOT FJORDS
CONTINENTS: 5 | COUNTRIES: 15

DAY 243

On the morning before my next swim I get this well-timed direct message:

> **WiseOldOwl** Don't give up @Ickle_Mermaid.
> Remember. When all else fails, BE A MERMAID.

Oh my God! It's Sage. She's on Instagram! She's been with me this whole time and I hadn't realized.

I breathe slowly. Finally feeling calmer. Too calm perhaps because I don't see the inevitable – a torrent of Mubla finally coming for me...

> **BalmyEmbalmer** I'm using your father's account, Lemony @Ickle_Mermaid. What sort of name is that anyway? You need to come home. Where are you?

> **BalmyEmbalmer** Lemony. Where are you?

> **BalmyEmbalmer** Lemony. You need to come home.

> **BalmyEmbalmer** Lemony. Why would you do this to us?

> **BalmyEmbalmer** Lemony. When did you learn to swim?

> **BalmyEmbalmer** Lemony. Why have you done this?

> **BalmyEmbalmer** Lemony. Is it so bad at home? You have a roof over your head, a loving family.

What do I do?

Oh my God, oh my God, oh my God.

Bubble, bubble, breathe.

I've got a swim to do today. How am I going to make it through?

Bubble, bubble, breathe.

No. I've got to get this swim done. I can't let Mubla into my head.

~~~

The water is beautiful and warm. Perhaps a tad too warm for swimming 3k but at least I don't need to wear a wetsuit. It won't take me long, and I'll be away from my phone and those wretched messages.

That's it! That's what I've got to do – switch my phone off.

I'm so focused on getting Mubla out of my head that I don't see it until I'm in it. Mushroom soup. Or at least that's what it looks like to me, though the technical term is actually a bloom, which is far too nice a name for a group of such terrifying, if quite pretty, creatures.

My breath is suddenly well and truly stuck in my throat and I gulp down a mouthful of salty water that burns my throat.

Bubble, bubble, breathe.

I'm surrounded by jellyfish. There's nothing for it but to keep going and hope to goodness that they won't all sting me.

But what if they do? Surely that number of stings would be fatal.

Bubble, bubble, ow.

~~~

I don't know how I complete the swim but, when I get out of the water, I have an awful burning sensation down my back, which turns out to be big red stripes of searing pain that make me look like I've been given ten lashes.

I'm ushered quickly to a makeshift first-aid area, where other swimmers are being treated for similar wounds. Nurses desperately try to keep at bay the crowd of reporters who are clamouring for comment.

"What happened?" calls one, handing me a tissue.

I find myself croaking out my story in between tears. "I'm alive. I can't believe I'm alive. I was terrified. There were so many of them. I thought I was going to be stung to death."

"Thanks," says the reporter. "Oh, and what's your name?"

And, in my woozy, panic-fuelled haze, I do the worst thing possible: I give her my real name.

Fig's Swims Round the World

1. ~~Dinosaur Island~~
2. ~~The Jailhouse Rock~~
3. ~~Mount Storm Rough Water~~
4. ~~The Red Canyon swim series~~
5. ~~La Isla Bonita~~
6. ~~Turtle Bay~~
7. ~~The Greatest Archipelago on Earth~~
   ~~Clearwater swim series~~
8. ~~Malokodaidai Island 10k~~
9. ~~The Big Swim series in the Land of Koalas~~
10. ~~The Lazy River~~
11. ~~The Cold Drop~~
12. ~~The Whale Isles~~
13. ~~The Hot Fjords~~
14. The Ancients Trail swims
15. Island-hopping
16. The Sunriser
17. The Mermaid Canal
Bonus swim - The Time Traveller
18. The Pilgrimage
19. The Squirly Whirly
20. The Cross-continental

POSTCARDS TO JAGO

Agent Hugh Moonstone

c/o Jago Fitzsherbert

The Fitzsherbert Family Funeral Home

Old Mare

England

Going off grid. I'm alive and well. Don't worry.

Yours,

Agent Brown

OFF GRID

DAY 245

Oh my God, oh my God, oh my God.

Oh my God, oh my God, oh my God.

I haven't felt this anxious in a long time. My breath sticks in my throat and I'm once again reduced to yawning in the air, gagging as my throat constricts with panic. Rereading the article from the *Musandan Chronicle* for what must be the hundredth time doesn't help either.

ATTACK OF THE JELLYFISH

Swimmers taking part in the annual Hot Fjords 3k swim will have received quite the surprise today. A giant bloom of jellyfish flooded the water, putting all participants in danger. Swimmer Fay Fitzsherbert was visibly traumatized when she got out of the water, saying, "I was terrified. There were so many of them. I thought I was going to be stung to death." Climate change is thought to be the cause.

Oh my God, oh my God, oh my God.
Oh my God, oh my God, oh my God!
Bubble, bubble, breathe.
At least they got my name wrong.
Bubble, bubble, breathe.
I need to get out of here…

DAY 246

I take the first bus I can find, thankful that I have three days of being on the move.

Oh my God, oh my God, oh my God.

Bubble, bubble, breathe…

DAY 249

Climbing off the bus at the start of the Ancients Trail, a tired-looking beach resort with palm trees standing proud in the dark violet sky and a band of deep blue sea stretching across the horizon, I keep my eyes peeled for Mubla. She's not here. Yet.

Bubble, bubble, breathe.

There are police officers everywhere, sitting around

on camels, but thankfully they look more bored by than interested in me.

Bubble, bubble, breathe.

I need to swim. This heat is something else and I need to think things through.

The water is as cool as the sun is hot and I'm grateful to finally stretch out in it, letting the gentle lapping of the sea lull me back to my senses.

Bubble, bubble, breathe.

I need to get my head straight if I'm going to evade Mubla. If only I could remember which swims I'd told Blue about.

Oh my… No. *Bubble, bubble, breathe.*

I can get a job on another boat as a photographer. I've been doing it for the last month. I've got tons of examples of my work and they're good! I can do this.

DAY 251

I have a job! On a live-aboard with a local called Seth, a Voyage of the Water Treaders coach of all things. I recognized the T-shirt and asked him if he knew Barry. He didn't but it at least got the conversation going.

"I can't give you a salary," he said. "And you'll have to pay for food. But I can offer you board on the boat in return for taking photos of the tourists."

I said I didn't mind, as long as I could take part in

the Ancients Trail swims. We went on to have a lengthy discussion about all the swims we've done.

We leave tomorrow. Just one more night to get through without Mubla finding me.

Bubble, bubble, breathe.

This heat is something else. I can't wait to get on to the water and away from shore.

DAY 255

This place is amazing! I love it here. Swimming is easy in these calm waters. And the sights! Great ancient tombs sticking out of the sand. I've never seen anything like it.

Seth and I have bonded over our love of swimming. He says he's desperate to do the Dinosaur Island swim one day. But that sounds like nothing compared to the kind of swims he's done. He could rival the Boss for stories.

DAY 265

I'm growing tired of this boat. The constant rocking. The enclosed space. How I long for land!

I've heard all of Seth's stories. Numerous times. I've seen the monuments and swum round the shipwrecks. And while the swims are refreshing, with tons of beautiful, colourful marine life, how can anything compare to the Greatest Archipelago on Earth? Those long days I spent swimming alongside Raif, solving his silly riddles. I'd give anything to have one now. Setting my own *Countdown* ones just isn't enough.

DAY 273

I hate sailing! I'm sick of this trip. Three times now I've swum round these lagoons. Photographed swimmers grinning in front of lighthouses and coral reefs; swimmers hugging underwater among the throngs of colourful fish; swimmers raising their glasses around the communal dining table. I don't have their holiday spirit.

I'm lonely. I miss Raif ... Blue ... Stella ... Sage ... even the Boss! And without a phone I'm without them all.

Fig's Swims Round the World

1. ~~Dinosaur Island~~
2. ~~The Jailhouse Rock~~
3. ~~Mount Storm Rough Water~~
4. ~~The Red Canyon swim series~~
5. ~~La Isla Bonita~~
6. ~~Turtle Bay~~
7. ~~The Greatest Archipelago on Earth~~
   ~~Clearwater swim series~~
8. Malokodaidai Island 10k
9. ~~The Big Swim series in the Land of Koalas~~
10. ~~The Lazy River~~
11. ~~The Cold Drop~~
12. ~~The Whale Isles~~
13. ~~The Hot Fjords~~
14. ~~The Ancients Trail swims~~
15. Island-hopping
16. The Sunriser
17. The Mermaid Canal

Bonus swim - The Time Traveller

18. The Pilgrimage
19. The Squirly Whirly
20. The Cross-continental

MAMMA MIA

ISLANDS HOPPED: 2

DAY 285

It's been forty days since I last turned on my phone. My budgeting is now meticulous, and I know exactly where I've been in the world and how far I've swum.

Budget

Remaining money = £1,472

Days left = 80

Budget remaining = £1,472 ÷ 80 = £18.40/day

Original budget = £20.83/day

Giving a variance of −£2.43

Distance swum after 15 swims: 255.5km

Proportion of the world:

100 x (255.5 ÷ 40,000) = 0.64%

Mubla hasn't yet found me. But that hasn't stopped me spending much of my time looking over my shoulder, wondering whether my next swim is my last and if the police, or worse – Mubla herself – are going to turn up to bring me home. Though I have managed to keep my anxious thoughts in check now that I'm hopping between islands, spending little more than two or three nights on each.

ISLANDS HOPPED: 8

DAY 300

The swim to the next island is a glorious one. Clear, cool, turquoise water, where you can see all the way to the bottom. Rocky brown coastline dappled with greenery. Fine sandy beaches waiting for us to collapse on. This could be my favourite one. But, then again, that's what I said about the last seven…

Lunch is to be served in a local taverna and, as usual, we're famished after the morning's 3km swim, visiting sea caves and secluded beaches only accessible from the water. We traipse up the pathway towards the bright white building with its blue shutters thrown open in welcome. Ready-laid tables await us on the covered veranda, and we sink into the wooden chairs, grateful for the shade.

"Fay!" calls Heather. She's from a town not far from

the Foggy City. We of course got on immediately when I said I'd swum the Jailhouse Rock. "Come sit over here. It's cooler."

As I take a step towards her, a flash of red hair from a table *inside* the restaurant catches my eye and my heart stops.

Mubla?

I shrink back against the wall.

"You all right, Fay?" asks Matt, Heather's boyfriend.

I don't reply. I'm too busy trying not to hyperventilate.

"Sit down," suggests Heather. "Probably got a bit of heatstroke while swimming."

I nod slowly, sinking into the nearest chair.

"Here, have some water," says Matt, which I take willingly.

I peer at the door, half expecting Mubla to walk out.

Bubble, bubble, breathe.

"You look like you've seen a ghost," laughs Heather.

I smile weakly.

They chatter about the cave where we met a particularly friendly dolphin. I don't really listen. My attention is firmly on the door. What if it is Mubla?

A shriek of laughter from inside sends a shiver running down my spine. It sounds *just like her*.

Bubble, bubble, breathe.

I need to get away from here…

"Can I borrow this?" I ask Heather, holding up her large

floppy straw hat. "Think I need to walk this nausea off."

Heather smiles. "'Course. Want me to order for you?"

My appetite has completely vanished but I nod anyway, asking for the cheapest thing on the menu. "Just a salad. Thanks, Heather." And, donning my disguise, I edge away from the building, trying to keep clear of the door.

I stroll through the shade of the olive trees, attempting to breathe, trying to comfort myself that, if this *is* it, I've had a good stab at swimming the world. But the idea doesn't sit well with me. I need to know if it's her. I can't go on worrying like this.

Slowly, I wander back, smiling at my friends and nodding that I'm going to the loo. I take a tentative step towards the doorway, where a beaded curtain gently sways in the breeze.

Bubble, bubble, breathe.

There's that laugh again.

Bubble, bubble, breathe.

My eyes struggle to adjust as the bright sunlight switches to the cool darkness of the restaurant. I can hardly see with these sunglasses on! The woman with the red hair has her back to me. She's tall – like Mubla. Pale – like Mubla.

Bubble, bubble, breathe.

It *must* be Mubla.

Oh my God, oh my … ow.

The chaos as I bang into a table, sending cutlery clattering to the floor, gives me what I don't want – the attention of the entire restaurant.

"Sorry," I gasp, looking around wildly and coming face to face with the red-haired woman.

Oh.

Bubble, bubble, breathe.

It's not her.

Fig's Swims Round the World

1. ~~Dinosaur Island~~
2. ~~The Jailhouse Rock~~
3. ~~Mount Storm Rough Water~~
4. ~~The Red Canyon swim series~~
5. ~~La Isla Bonita~~
6. ~~Turtle Bay~~
7. ~~The Greatest Archipelago on Earth~~
   ~~Clearwater swim series~~
8. ~~Malokodaidai Island 10k~~
9. ~~The Big Swim series in the Land of Koalas~~
10. ~~The Lazy River~~
11. ~~The Cold Drop~~
12. ~~The Whale Isles~~
13. ~~The Hot Fjords~~
14. ~~The Ancients Trail swims~~
15. ~~Island-hopping~~
16. The Sunriser
17. The Mermaid Canal

Bonus swim - The Time Traveller

18. The Pilgrimage
19. The Squirly Whirly
20. The Cross-continental

PLAYING CATCH-UP

CONTINENTS: 6 | COUNTRIES: 18
DAYS WITHOUT PHONE: 63

Mode of Transport	Number of journeys complete	Distance covered (km)	Time spent (hrs)
Rail	9	2,777	42.95
Road	22	13,598	215.1
Air	17	56,318	85
Sea	12	2,440	146

DAY 308

It's no use. I can't do it any more. I'm sick of writing lists. I miss my friends. I'm turning my phone back on.

There are 1,099 Instagram notifications from Mubla, who has now created her own account. I ignore them and message Stella.

Ickle_Mermaid Hey.

WordBird WTF, Fig! Where have you been? It's been months!

Ickle_Mermaid Off grid. Couldn't handle Mubla.

As I hit the block button, I suddenly realize that I'm over three quarters of the way through my adventure and it won't be long until I have to go home. I've never considered this. How am I going to face Mubla? Then I see the article about her online.

TOP QC FIXES THINGS FOR THE FIXER

Top barrister Wendy Fitzsherbert QC has secured the release of Alfredo Morani, aka the Fixer, in a court case that lasted two months and took the jury just four hours to deliberate on what was a unanimous 'not guilty' verdict.

The thirty-five-year-old Morani, living a seemingly quiet life in the sleepy seaside town of Old Mare, was arrested two months ago after a six-month undercover operation by the Serious Organized Crime Agency (SOCA). Morani was accused of organizing fake documents, including visas, passports and currency, for the firm known as the Mobley Mob, which SOCA have been trying to infiltrate for years.

Wendy Fitzsherbert QC was unavailable for comment.

It doesn't surprise me that she's been representing the Fixer, though it certainly alarms me. What if he's told her about me? Is it actually possible to track someone down via a fake passport?

That's when I start making a mental list of all the times I haven't been as careful as I should have been.

1. The viral video from the airport concert
2. All the selfies of me posing in idyllic locations
3. The statement I gave to the newspaper reporter after the Hot Fjords swim when I freaked out and used my real name
4. My Instagram feed

I once again change my Instagram account to private and message Stella, hoping she'll calm me down, but all I get back is that she doesn't think there's much chance Mubla will have seen a small article on page 12 in some random desert newspaper. My answer, as always, is, "You don't know Mubla..."

The message and web link from Sage is the final nail in the coffin and I know my days really are numbered.

WiseOldOwl You're an award-winning photographer now! And well deserved too. Myrtle submitted it.

Runner-up in the Young Landscape Photographer of the Year

(THE INTRUDER by sixteen-year-old Fay Olander)

There's been too much online coverage of Fay Olander, making it ridiculously easy to trace me around the world, if you know that's my alias. And when I see Stella's latest post – a meme of a hairy puppet going crazy on the drums – I know for certain.

WordBird #word4theday CORYBANTIC, adj.

Mubla must have good reason to feel excited and it's only a matter of time. All my sightings of her have been mere premonitions. Mubla is coming for me.

Fig's Swims Round the World

1. ~~Dinosaur Island~~
2. ~~The Jailhouse Rock~~
3. ~~Mount Storm Rough Water~~
4. ~~The Red Canyon swim series~~
5. ~~La Isla Bonita~~
6. ~~Turtle Bay~~
7. ~~The Greatest Archipelago on Earth Clearwater swim series~~
8. ~~Malokodaidai Island 10k~~
9. ~~The Big Swim series in the Land of Koalas~~
10. ~~The Lazy River~~
11. ~~The Cold Drop~~
12. ~~The Whale Isles~~
13. ~~The Hot Fjords~~
14. ~~The Ancients Trail swims~~
15. ~~Island-hopping~~
16. ~~The Sunriser~~
17. The Mermaid Canal

Bonus swim – The Time Traveller

18. The Pilgrimage
19. The Squirly Whirly
20. The Cross-continental

ACCEPTANCE

To: **Lemony Fitzsherbert**   30 June 18:42

From: **WendyFitzsherbertQC**

You win.

It's been nearly a year now, Lemony. If you're reading this, you win. I give up. Stay away if you want to. I know exactly where you are.

THE LITTLE MERMAID

SWIM 17 – THE MERMAID CANAL
CONTINENTS: 6 | COUNTRIES: 19

DAY 311

Mubla's email is the last thing I should read the night before
a swim but I do and, of course, instantly regret it. I'm not
sure I believe that she's really accepted that I'm not coming
home, and, when I see the three photos that Stella posts in
quick succession, I feel certain that she hasn't.

WordBird #word4theday SPLENDOROUS, adj.
WordBird #word4theday PORTENDING, adj.
WordBird #word4theday CATACLYSM, noun.

I suppose it's not really surprising. She was bound to find
me sooner or later. I had just hoped that I'd make it to the
end of my list. I'm not ready to go home yet and I'm not
ready to see Mubla.

I idly thumb through my notebook, looking at the

various lists and notes that I've written over the last ten months. Each swim carefully noted down with location, distance and particular details that I wanted to remember. I've tackled strong currents, swum big distances, sometimes with jellyfish stinging my body, and have endured long periods of time on my own. I have, on the whole, enjoyed it. And, as the page falls opens on my Fear List, I'm suddenly seized by the realization that I can cross more things off it.

It's an odd feeling knowing that you're no longer scared of something. For example, I can't for the life of me understand why I was scared of being on my own. I love my own company now. And I've managed to survive without being murdered, mauled or kidnapped as previously feared.

I only have two fears left (not counting water moccasins – they're never coming off). Spiders and Mubla. More similar than you'd think. Both are more than capable of spinning elaborate traps to capture their prey. And they both like silk... Thinking about her makes my neck tense, so I focus instead on tomorrow's swim.

≈≈≈

The following morning, as I stand in the waiting pen for the race to begin, my head is throbbing and I feel like a trapped animal. After all this time and all these races, those feelings don't change. Anxious, nervous, excited, jittery all rolled into one. A short swimmer in a neon orange suit is jostling everyone, pushing through to the front. It's unnerving.

When they let us out on to the jetty, I can see everyone cheering us. Big banners spell out good luck or something similar. Everyone is speaking in another language. It's confusing and my fuzzy brain hurts.

I'm in group six, with the blue caps, made up of a variety of swimmers, young and old, even a group of wheelchair users who have floats attached between their legs. I'm full of admiration for them. The memory of Maud tying my legs together, and feeling like I was sinking, still haunts me. My eye catches the professional mermaids in the group behind. A group of lively, bikini-clad women clutching their tail-shaped fins. They remind me of home.

The water is cold and I'm feeling achy and shivery even though I'm wearing my wetsuit, which I haven't worn since the Whale Isles. My breakfast is still fresh in my stomach, sitting there like a lead weight. It's making me feel sick and I'm worried that it will repeat on me when I start swimming.

As the whistle blows, it's the usual mad dash to get out in front and away from the other swimmers, which always results in swimming on top of each other and getting kicked in the face. But I don't mind it any more. Even when I clash arms with the swimmer in the neon suit. I slow down and let her go. I'm in no rush. I want to savour this swim.

The course is made up of four seawater canals running round a square section of the city. It's surprisingly clear and clean, and pleasant to swim in, though the first tunnel

I swim through is a shock. It's so low and dark, and I can't help thinking about the people standing on the bridge above my head, wondering what would happen if it was to collapse. Still, I'm through it in only a few strokes and my fear subsides.

About halfway round the course there's another one. Two hundred metres long. It's the part I've been dreading. The part that kept me up last night visiting the loo. It's pitch-black. I might as well be swimming with my eyes closed. What if I get trapped in the tunnel, forget which direction to swim in? But the odd thing is it doesn't bother me when I actually swim through it. My pulse doesn't race. My breath doesn't get stuck in my throat. I pound on regardless.

Then, in the light at the exit, I see a figure smartly dressed in grey. It's only a quick glance as I breathe to the right, but it looks exactly like Mubla. My blood runs cold. Am I never to be free of these apparitions? I slow down to a gentle breaststroke to get a better look. Even through my foggy goggles, I know and, despite my many sightings of redheads, this time it feels different.

I become hyper aware of my red wetsuit. It's like wearing a giant bullseye on my back, yelling, "Here I am, Mubla!" But, as my worry begins to engulf me, I'm suddenly surrounded by the mermaids of group seven, as they come shooting past. Their blue, sparkling tails flip through the water as they dive down deep into the water and up again, gliding at a crazy fast pace, like dolphins in their graceful ease. I try to keep up but it's no good – they're too fast and my kick is no match for their fins, so I dive under the water to hide from Mubla's searching eyes.

At the bottom of the canal I spot some childlike figures. They look so lifelike I have to do a double take to check they're not actually drowning, but the seaweed gives them away. I wonder briefly if the fever has gone to my brain. Maybe it's not Mubla after all and I'm just seeing things as usual. Fear always clouds my judgement.

I resurface like a crocodile, body submerged with eyes peering out so that I can observe unnoticed. It's her. No doubt about it. My breath halts in my throat. I try to swallow but the lump stubbornly stays put and I resist the urge to gag. The moment her head turns towards me, the air splutters noisily out of me, like a demon being expelled. I'm certain we make eye contact, a flicker of recognition registering on Mubla's face. I allow myself to sink again to the canal bed.

The underwater sculptures are covered in brown furry moss, posed crying, laughing and sleeping. It reminds me of the quarry I swam in last year, though I didn't get to see the sculptures there. It's peaceful down here and I have a sudden longing to stay with these water babies. They're arranged in a circle round a lone central figure resting her tail on a rock, her head in her hands as she cries. I want to comfort her, this little mermaid. Tell her it's going to be OK.

A glimpse of yellow fins moving amid the seaweed snaps me out of my reverie and I slowly focus on a diver with a bulbous underwater camera pointed directly at me. Somehow I manage to smile. It's only taken me sixteen years and I'm not wearing a tutu, but nevertheless I'm not in tears. With a strong kick of my feet and my lungs about to explode, I resurface. I've got to get to the finish line before Mubla does.

THE CONFRONTATION PART I

When, at last, I'm through all the tunnels, there's a huge banner across one of the bridges saying '2,800 metres'. That means I've only got 200 metres to go until this race ends. That's my signal to start kicking hard. The swimmer in the neon suit from earlier is just up ahead. I set my target on them and, as we swim round the corner of the canal, the last strait in sight, I turbo-kick past. It's a strong finish and as I climb out of the water, the crowd going wild, there's a camera on us and my face appears on the big screen.

"*Godt klaret!*" says a young official, placing a medal round my neck.

I nod my thanks, then dash quickly to the changing room, ripping off the red wetsuit. I need to be away from here before Mubla finds me. I can't let her stop me completing this round-the-world challenge. I'm not ready to go back to her telling me what to do and how to do it. Not yet. Not when I've spent the best year of my life doing something I truly love.

"How dare you! No one beats me."

I turn to see the swimmer in the neon orange suit.

"Oh," I gasp. "It's you…"

As the swimmer removes her swim cap and goggles, I can't help but grin.

"It's no laughing matter," snaps the Boss.

I ignore her and continue to get dressed. I haven't got time for this.

"I'm talking to you. Why aren't you responding? Oi, you!" The Boss begins angrily poking at me. She's half naked now and I can see the tendons in her neck and shoulders sticking out, her breasts jiggling with every prod. "You're just a silly little girl who has no business being here."

"You can't tell me what to do!" I yell suddenly. After my Mubla sighting, I'm not in the mood to be picked on. "You're not my mother! You don't control me."

"Of course I'm not your mother," snaps the Boss. "I'm too young for one thing. And anyway what are you doing letting your mother run your life?"

I have nothing to say to that. She has a point.

"How old are you?" asks the Boss. "Really."

"Sixteen. Fifteen when I left home."

"Fifteen?" she snarls. "I left home at fourteen."

Of course she did. The Boss and her tall stories. I can't help an eye roll, which only makes her madder.

"Grow up, Fig. Or should I call you Lemony?"

I gasp. I'm not really surprised but I wonder how long she's known.

"You need to stand up for yourself," snarls the Boss.

"I can't," I mutter. "You don't know Mubla."

"Yes, you can."

"No, I can't! I can't do it. I don't know how."

"Yes. You. Do." The Boss emphasizes each of her words with a jab of her finger into my chest. "What are you doing right now? I've been a complete bitch ever since I met you. I've pushed you around, ridiculed you, called you names and you've taken all of it. As if you deserve it or something. But you don't. And now you're finally, FINALLY, doing something about it." She pokes me again. "Go on. Do something."

The prodding continues. My tears are streaming, heart pounding in my ears, fists clenched tight, and I realize how angry I am. With the Boss. With Mubla. With Dab Dabs even.

"Stop it!" I yell. "Stop it. What did I ever do to you?" Then I shove her so hard, she stumbles backwards over the changing bench, and lands between it and the wall, her wetsuit-clad legs sticking up in the air. She starts to laugh. Hysterical laughter that makes her cry. She looks like a beetle trapped on its back. It makes me giggle too. I offer her a hand and pull her up, so that we're face to face in fits.

"Ow. You've given me a stitch," says the Boss, digging her fingers into her waist. She grins. "I knew you could do it."

"What?" I say. "Is that why you've been so mean to me?"

The Boss shrugs. "And I feel threatened by you."

My mouth drops open in shock. "*I threaten you.*"

"Yes, Ickle Mermaid. You can put your tongue away now! It's hardly surprising. You're half my age, immensely tall and turning into a not-half-bad swimmer. You've got a keen eye for photography too."

I can't speak. I can't get past the fact that she's complimented me. "You like my photos?"

The Boss rolls her eyes. "Well, duh! Of course I do. And you've got one hell of a story to tell too. Learning to swim. Finding a passion for adventure in the face of a controlling mother and a hippie father. People will lap it up."

"Have you known all along?" I ask, wondering why she hasn't handed me over to the authorities the way Blue did.

The Boss nods. "Course. The question now is what are you going to do?"

I twist my lips. I don't know. The thought of actually seeing Mubla again is a daunting one. "Do you really think I can stand up to her?"

But I don't hear the Boss's reply because my eyes are frozen on the changing-room entrance, where Mubla is now standing.

THE CONFRONTATION PART II

"Lemony?"

I stare, open-mouthed, not wanting to believe it's really her. She doesn't look any different, maybe a little older, a few more wrinkles to add to the collection. Then, like a forgotten nightmare, my old feelings wash over me. My palms are clammy and my breath gets stuck in my chest. I want to be sick.

I manage a strangled, "Mother?"

"Lemony," she repeats, her smile swiftly being replaced with a frown as she places the back of her hand on my forehead. "You're not well?"

"I'm fine," I mutter, batting her hand away.

Mubla raises herself up to her full height, although I'm the taller one now. "You're not fine. You've got a temperature." She goes to hug me, only it's awkward and uncomfortable. I don't want this. I don't want her to be here.

"You all right, Fig?"

My eyes fall back on the Boss, who's still half naked.

"Yeah. Yeah, I'm fine," I say.

"And who might you be?" says Mubla, towering over her. "Have you been helping my runaway daughter? Because there are plenty of charges I can bring against you, you know. I can do a lot to hurt a person—"

"Yes, I'm well aware of how much harm you can do, Mrs Fitzsherbert," retorts the Boss.

Mubla glares at me. "And what's that supposed to mean? Lemony, what have you been saying?"

"Doesn't she prefer to be called Fig?" says the Boss.

Mubla ignores her and grabs my arm. "Come along, Lemony. We have a plane to catch."

"What?" I say, tearing myself from her grip. "But I don't want to go."

"What you want and what you need," says Mubla firmly, "are two very different things. Now come along."

"No," I say, feeling the adrenaline begin to pulse through me.

"No?" repeats Mubla.

"No."

I'm surprised at how calm I sound. Inside my head is a whole other matter.

Mubla tilts her head and stares at me, her eyes narrowing in thought while she figures out her next move. "You must be hungry after that swim," she says. "Come and have lunch with me. You at least owe me that..."

"How could you do this to me, Lemony?"

We're sitting in a café overlooking the canal, watching the remaining swimming heats go by. Mubla slowly shakes her head, the familiar disappointment plastered across her face. "Honestly. I thought you were dead."

"I'm sorry," I mutter. "How are Dab Dabs and Jago?"

Mubla frowns at me and for the first time I see the deep lines etched in her forehead, which weren't there a year ago. "Distraught. Worried. Missing you. I can't believe you did this."

I take a deep breath, bracing myself for the onslaught of her lecture. Mubla has her court persona on.

"After all the opportunities I've given you," she mutters.

"I know," I say. "But I would have given them up in a heartbeat if it would have meant more time with you."

I can see I've made her uncomfortable. Mubla's never been someone to confide in. She shifts in her chair, clearing her throat. "Why on earth did you pick swimming? Why not something else? You could have asked me," she says, fixing me with her steely gaze. "I could have helped you."

"But I didn't want your help…"

I can't tell whether she hears me or ignores me, as she drones on. "I can't understand it. Swimming?"

I sit there dumbly, letting her comments wash over me. I'm not sure I've got the strength to fight her. My head is throbbing and all I really want to do is sleep.

"Thank goodness you left such an enormous trail of evidence. Posing for all those photos in that red wetsuit, Lemony. I spotted you immediately. And your friend Blue? She was most helpful. Told me all the swims that you'd talked about doing. Gave me access to all of your social-media activity too. Selfies, Lemony. Really? From that, I was more than capable of working out where you were heading. Perhaps she wasn't the best person to confide in after all? If *I* had done it, *I* would have disappeared without a trace."

Oh, how I wish she would! But I don't say it and my throat throbs with the pain of swallowing that down.

"You're going to have to pay it back," says Mubla suddenly. "The credit-card bill? And where *exactly* did you get the rest of the money from?"

"My savings account."

"I see." Mubla sighs deeply, her jaw pulsating as she grinds her teeth together. "Well, come along then," she mutters, leaving some money on the table. "Our flight's in three hours. We need to go."

This time I don't argue with her. I haven't the strength. I obediently follow her out of the café, crushed. I've failed in my swim-the-world challenge. And, though I've failed at many things before, this time it hurts so badly because I know I would have succeeded.

PART 3
THE FINAL FEAR

"Courage is knowing what not to fear."
Plato

MY PEOPLE

"I brought your *real* passport," says Mubla quietly, when we're in the taxi to the airport. The flicker in her eyes confirms what I already suspected. She knows I got my fake passport from the Fixer.

I start to mutter an apology but the brisk shake of her head silences me. So I go back to staring at the swimming list on my phone. I can't believe how far I've come. I've nearly finished it.

Fig's Swims Round the World

1. ~~Dinosaur Island~~
2. ~~The Jailhouse Rock~~
3. ~~Mount Storm Rough Water~~
4. ~~The Red Canyon swim series~~
5. ~~La Isla Bonita~~
6. ~~Turtle Bay~~

Why don't I stand up to her? I *want* to finish it! This challenge is so much more than a list of swims. It represents all the fears I've overcome. It's shown me what I am capable of when I'm motivated. I've seen the world and I like what I see. I've shown it who I truly am. Completing this list means everything to me. And now I feel like a complete failure. Why don't I stand up to her?

"Are you going to look at that thing the whole way?" asks Mubla.

I shrug. "I won't be long."

Me 14:09

I'm sorry, Raif. Mubla found me. I'm not coming

I take a quick selfie, looking glum and ignoring Mubla's disapproving noises. I post it with the caption:

Ickle_Mermaid #swimtheworld is over. #FindFig #Found

I turn off my phone and look out at the scenery speeding by. I've never felt so low. I don't want to go home. I want to keep on swimming. Why is Mubla forcing me to do this? I thought we weren't supposed to fail at things. The Boss's words ring in my ears. "You need to stand up for yourself…" But can I really do it?

"Mubla," I whisper, feeling the nerves begin to course through my veins. "Why can't I stay?"

She stares at me. "What? You need to speak up."

"I want to finish the swims," I say.

Mubla remains silent, her lips pursed as she concentrates on her laptop screen.

"There's only two months left," I say. "I promise I'll come home straight after."

"Absolutely not, Lemony," says Mubla firmly. "You've got far too much studying to catch up on."

"But…"

She sighs heavily, closing her laptop with a snap. "There are no buts. A no is a no."

~~~

There's some kind of delay with the flight and the check-in queue is reaching out of the door. It hasn't moved for the last hour, so we haven't even gone through security yet. Mubla has stormed off to ask someone what's going on and left me in charge of the bags, so I switch my phone back on to help with the boredom. It instantly goes wild with notifications. I read Raif's first.

Raif 14:30
What d'you mean you're not coming? I wanted to time travel with you!

Raif 14:31
How did Mubla find you?

Raif 14:32
You can't give up now. You're so close!

Stella posts a random photo of a guitar saying:

WordBird #word4theday DIRE STRAITS, noun.

And then the comments on my selfie come flooding in.

WiseOldOwl Don't give up! #swimtheworld
#rooting4u

TheBoss You're kidding me. What happened to
standing up to her?

TheBoss Now you've made me really mad @Ickle_
Mermaid.

TheBoss DM me. NOW.

WordBird @WiseOldOwl is right, Fig. Don't give up
now!

TheBoss OK, if you won't DM me, let's have it out
here.

TheBoss You stood up to me, didn't you? Didn't you?

TheBoss And don't give me your usual 'you don't
know Mubla'.

TheBoss I've met enough Mublas in my time. You do
realize not many people dare stand up to me?

I feel overwhelmed by the support from everyone, like I've finally found my people. But it's when I see the text from Dab Dabs that I completely go to pieces.

Dab Dabs 14:45
Figaroo. Don't come home. Finish what you started.

He thinks I should carry on! Oh, if only he was here to

help me get through to Mubla! But hang on. I don't need him to. I can stand up to her. I've done it before, haven't I? By choosing my own resolution and doing all these swims? I can do this…

TheBoss I'm outside the airport in a taxi. Come on, Mermaid.

I take a deep breath. Mubla may well have tracked me here but she doesn't know where I'm going next and everyone else thinks I can do it. Maybe *I* should believe in myself.

On the back of the luggage tag attached to Mubla's suitcase, I write:

I'm sorry.
Please don't try
to find me.

THE TIME TRAVELLERS

It's been a week since my second escape from Mubla. I've spent most of it recovering in a warm bed and being waited on hand and foot. Raif at my feet, reading aloud and talking non-stop. He's changed loads in the seven months since I last saw him. Taller for one thing.

Today's swim, my first since the Mermaid Canal, is from one side of the river running through the Land of the Midnight Sun to the other, crossing a time zone and landing some five kilometres downstream. We'll be swimming in cold water and, even with wetsuits on, it will be a challenge.

There's a small group of us standing by the water's edge, doing warm-ups and windmill arms. It's 11.45 p.m. and it's a most peculiar feeling. This is a night swim with a difference – the sun is still in the sky and it's broad daylight. I've drunk more coffee than I care to remember, in an attempt to stay alert and awake, and it's made me incredibly

*Where F = number of days until final swim and T = today

jumpy. I glance over at Raif and his family. They're having their usual group hug before a swim. Raif waves me over, pulling me into the huddle.

"*Viel Glück, meine liebste,* Fig," says Raif's father, kissing me on the forehead.

"*Viel Glück,*" I reply.

"*Swimmers, please acclimatize,*" calls the official over the tannoy.

"Fig," says Raif, grinning wildly at me. His voice has changed. It's deeper and has lost that squeaky tone that used to embarrass him. "See you on the other side?"

"*Swimmers to the starting buoy…*"

I nod. "If I make it."

"You'll make it," he replies. "I'll be swimming by your side the whole way."

"*Swimmers, on your marks…*"

"But I haven't swum for a week. What if I'm not fast enough?" I gasp. "You won't be a time traveller."

"You'll be fast enough," says Raif firmly. "I'm going to make sure you are. Time travellers together, eh?"

Gold fireworks burst open in the sky, forming the numbers 12:00. It's midnight and I have less than an hour to do this. As the group of swimmers dashes into the water, I don't hang back like I used to. I've been kicked in the face enough times to know that everyone always finds their place in the group eventually. And, with Raif by my side, I feel like I can do anything. At least I think it's him.

It's kind of hard to tell people apart when you're all wearing the same yellow swimming hat.

It's tough going at first – my shoulders are aching and my feet are numb with cold – but, as my body adjusts, I settle into the pace. I'm full of energy and can feel, as my hand catches the water, my pull growing stronger. The course is easy too. There's only one way to go once you get to the middle of the river, where the current picks up and begins to shoot me downstream. I sight less and concentrate on my stroke. *One, two, three, breathe, one, two, three, breathe.* The monotony allows my mind to wander and I marvel at where I'm swimming and the fact that I'm even doing it. A week ago, I was sitting in the airport with Mubla, feeling like my life was over.

"Fig! Help."

Raif is up ahead, waving frantically at me.

"What's wrong?" I ask.

He holds up his flashy goggles. "They're broken. I don't know what to do."

I look around me. There aren't many swimmers nearby and I have no idea whether they're in front or behind. All I know is that we need to keep going.

"We'll share mine," I say. "You take them first and I'll draft off you. Then we'll switch over. Come on." I take his hand. "We can do this. Time travellers together."

Bearing in mind that the only time I've managed to do this correctly was when I was swimming in the dolphin formation with Raif's parents, I'm still not sure I can do it. I thrust my goggles into Raif's hands and begin to swim slowly, waiting for him to go past. It's strange swimming without goggles and I tentatively open my eyes underwater, expecting them to really hurt. They don't but I can't see much. Raif is just up ahead and all I need to do is get by his feet and let him do the rest. It doesn't work at first and I wince with the pain of being kicked in the face. Then suddenly it's easier and it feels like we're flying through the current.

We swim this way for the remainder of the course, switching over with the goggles and the drafting position, until I spot the end of the swim, marked by a large yellow banner saying *Time Travel is Possible...* I clamber out of the water after Raif, who stands and waits for me, so we can cross the finish line together. Someone takes our timing chips off our ankles and hustles us towards a near-empty waiting area.

"Where is everyone?" I ask. "Have they gone home already?" I can feel the disappointment welling up inside me.

Raif bursts out laughing.

"It's not funny," I say.

"They haven't finished yet. Look." He points to the clock. "It's only eleven forty p.m. We travelled back in time."

I stare at him with wide eyes, my excitement quickly overcoming the disappointment. "You mean we did it?

We finished the swim the day before we started? Oh my God! We are time travellers!"

Raif laughs with me, his eyes shining with fondness. That's when I do something I hadn't planned to do. I pull him to me, my arms round his neck, standing slightly on my toes, and I kiss him quickly on the lips.

Fig's Swims Round the World

1. ~~Dinosaur Island~~
2. ~~The Jailhouse Rock~~
3. ~~Mount Storm Rough Water~~
4. ~~The Red Canyon swim series~~
5. ~~La Isla Bonita~~
6. ~~Turtle Bay~~
7. ~~The Greatest Archipelago on Earth~~
   ~~Clearwater swim series~~
8. ~~Malokodaidai Island 10k~~
9. ~~The Big Swim series in the Land of Koalas~~
10. ~~The Lazy River~~
11. ~~The Cold Drop~~
12. ~~The Whale Isles~~
13. ~~The Hot Fjords~~
14. ~~The Ancients Trail swims~~
15. ~~Island-hopping~~
16. ~~The Sunriser~~
17. ~~The Mermaid Canal~~
~~Bonus swim - The Time Traveller~~
18. The Pilgrimage
19. The Squirly Whirly
20. The Cross-continental

GOING TO THE CHAPEL

Ickle_Mermaid Going to the chapel #swimtheworld
#3togo #pilgrimage

The Icy Lake is unlike any other place I've visited, with its sparkling emerald water set against a backdrop of mountains swathed in lush greenery and fluffs of cotton-wool clouds floating serenely across the royal blue sky. Deer scamper round the shore while swans glide majestically across the lake and butterflies dance among the flowers. Perched on a large rock is an old white church with a scarlet rooftop accessed via a set of steep stone steps. Quite how they managed to build it in the middle of the lake is beyond me. A sentiment echoed by my many followers when I post a photo of it.

The Pilgrimage is an annual nine-kilometre swim round the island. A little known race favoured only by locals, thanks mainly to the early morning two-hour hike to get here.

But it's been worth every step. I've been on cloud nine ever since the Time Traveller swim and not just because of that kiss either, though I haven't stopped thinking about it...

"Come on, Fig," says Raif, grabbing hold of my hand and pulling me out of my reverie. I follow him into the warm water to begin the now familiar pre-swim ritual and then stand with the water up to my waist, solemnly contemplating the challenge ahead, enjoying the silence of the swimmers as they do the same.

"OK?" asks the swim leader, a short stocky woman called Branka, who beams as murmurs of assent ripple among us. She goes on to explain, in three different languages, the details of the course. "Lunch will be here onshore," she says. "But nine k is hungry-making in these waters, with no currents to push you along, so there'll be refreshments on the island. Of course, walking up the two hundred steps *is* optional but I promise you the views from the church tower are worth it. And for those – how do you say? – *lovebirds* among us, it's traditionally good luck to carry your loved one up the steps before making a wish in the church. That's if you have the energy of course..."

I catch Raif grinning soppily at me, the new pair of goggles squished against his face making his eyes look ridiculously big.

"Sorry, Raif," I say with a splutter of laughter. "I think you're a little too heavy for me to carry..." And I peck him on his burning cheek and dive under the shimmering, clear water, to cool my own.

> **TheBoss** Chapel? WTAF! Taking it a little too far there, Mermaid. It was only a kiss.
>
> **TheBoss** Ah, the happy couple #dingdong
>
> **WordBird** I hope you're joking @TheBoss
>
> **BalmyEmbalmer** Steady on there, Figaroo. I haven't even met the chap.
>
> **WordBird** It was just a kiss @BalmyEmbalmer
>
> **TheBoss** Yeah, but she kissed him.
>
> **WiseOldOwl** Ickle_Mermaid is in love? 🖤

And so they go on. For, during the nearly four-hour swim, the Boss has cooked up a social-media frenzy about me and Raif. Even Dab Dabs joins in. I don't know what to be more embarrassed about: the fact he knows I kissed a boy or that Raif might actually see some of these comments.

Then Stella posts a photo of two kittens in a cute embrace:

> **WordBird** #word4theday SMITTEN, adj.
>
> **TheBoss** Raif and Fig up a tree, k-i-s-s-i-n-g.
>
> **TheBoss** Rig or Fife – which do we prefer?
>
> **WordBird** Definitely Fife 😹

I have to put a stop to this!

Ickle_Mermaid IT WAS ONLY A KISS!

"Hi," says Raif, flopping down next to me on the blanket and nosily trying to peer at my phone, which I quickly clutch to my chest.

"OK?" he frowns.

I nod, trying to ignore the phone buzzing in my hand but can't because, well, the Boss is having a field day over this.

TheBoss Oh, but what a kiss! #Rig #Fife

I'm half tempted to mute her if only to get her to shut up…

"Mama says I can travel with you," says Raif.

"Where?" I ask, preoccupied with trying to think up a good comeback.

"To the Squirly Whirly. She said that we can meet them there."

Ickle_Mermaid 😭 @TheBoss

"Fig," says Raif, throwing a crisp at me.

"What?"

"Aren't you excited?"

I frown. "About what?"

TheBoss Oh, you found the picture of me when I heard about the 😢

"Fig! Would you stop looking at your phone? I'm trying to tell you something."

I throw my phone on to the blanket and peer guiltily up at him.

Raif grins. "Mama says I can travel with you."

"Why would you want to do that?"

"For the adventure of course," he frowns. "And to spend as much time with you as I can."

"I don't know that sitting on three buses is much of an adventure, Raif. Are you sure about this?"

Raif nods eagerly. "Absolutely. I've been dying to do it."

"Well, OK," I sigh. "The first one is in three days and it's a twenty-three-hour journey."

Raif pales. "And the second?"

"Ten."

He slumps back on to his elbows, frowning. "I daren't ask about the third. How is that even possible? We could get there by plane in a fraction of the time."

I nod. "I know but I didn't much like flying when I booked this trip."

"And now?"

"Well, I don't love it… But I don't hate it either."

"In that case," says Raif decisively, "we're flying. I'll get Papa to buy you a ticket. But on one condition."

"What's that?"

"No more talking about us on Instagram..." he says and leans in to kiss me.

Fig's Swims Round the World

1. ~~Dinosaur Island~~
2. ~~The Jailhouse Rock~~
3. ~~Mount Storm Rough Water~~
4. ~~The Red Canyon swim series~~
5. ~~La Isla Bonita~~
6. ~~Turtle Bay~~
7. ~~The Greatest Archipelago on Earth~~
   ~~Clearwater swim series~~
8. ~~Malokodaidai Island 10k~~
9. ~~The Big Swim series in the Land of Koalas~~
10. ~~The Lazy River~~
11. ~~The Cold Drop~~
12. ~~The Whale Isles~~
13. ~~The Hot Fjords~~
14. ~~The Ancients Trail swims~~
15. ~~Island-hopping~~
16. ~~The Sunriser~~
17. ~~The Mermaid Canal~~
Bonus swim – ~~The Time Traveller~~
18. ~~The Pilgrimage~~
19. The Squirly Whirly
20. The Cross-continental

A SUDDEN UNDERSTANDING

On the evening of my penultimate swim, I look out miserably over the course of the Squirly Whirly, a ten-kilometre race down the Black Gorge. My feelings of disappointment are mingling with frustration and upset. There's a high chance the event will be cancelled.

The weather is atrocious. Heavy rain lashing against frothing water. Gale-force winds whipping the trees into a frenzy as angry black clouds threaten to unleash even more fury. Naturally, I'm drawn to thinking about Mubla and the fact that I'll soon have to face her rage. And, if I don't complete *this* swim, I'll have to admit that I've failed even at my own resolution, a thought that does not sit well with me.

"Is it on?" I anxiously ask Raif who has been to find out more information, though his gloomy face isn't a good sign.

He winces. "Not looking good. The event organizers have said if there's even a hint of thunder..."

And, as he utters those last few words, a distant rumble confirms my greatest fear and I start to cry, the distress of my imminent defeat bubbling out of me.

Raif enfolds me in a hug as my tears spill.

"You haven't failed," he says. "Even if you don't do this swim. You've swum on six continents in places that people only dream of going. In waters where many would never dare to go. And all this when you'd only just learned to swim. That's amazing, Fig. Missing this one doesn't matter. You can't do anything about the weather."

The sky fills with a multitude of lightning flashes as the storm gets going and I sob my heart out, unable to shake the feeling that Mubla is going to relish my failure.

"It doesn't matter what your mother thinks," murmurs Raif.

"I know," I wail. "But I wanted to finish my list. For *me*. Not *her*. It's … it's … allegorical."

Raif bursts out laughing. "Have you and Stella been swapping words again?"

And I laugh because it's better than crying.

"I've never known someone like you, Fig," says Raif. "How am I going to cope without our regular maths conversations? How can I go back to a normal life? Can I come with you?"

"Yours is hardly a normal life," I retort. "And I'm not sure Mubla would like you. Well, the thought of you anyway."

Raif snorts. "Everyone likes me, Fig."

"You don't know Mubla," I reply and rest my head on his shoulder, going back to miserably contemplating the stormy scene, feeling helplessly annoyed with the weather. If it wasn't for the rocks and the fuming water... If it wasn't for the danger of the lightning... If only it was completely safe to swim in a thunderstorm... I'd do the swim in a heartbeat.

I gasp, wide-eyed, slapping my hand dramatically across my mouth. Because I suddenly know exactly how the Boss felt when she was up against her final swim across the Strait of Knar.

"What?" asks Raif.

But I don't get to answer him because his mother is here with news.

"They've made a decision," she says. "They're postponing until Monday. The weather looks better then."

A smile spreads across my tear-stained face. "You mean it's not cancelled?"

She shakes her head.

"I can still do the swim?"

Raif begins to laugh. "Yes, Fig. You can."

My disappointment instantly vanishes to be replaced with gratitude that I can still do the swim. Because, unlike the Boss, it doesn't matter to me that it will be two days late.

Fig's Swims Round the World

1. ~~Dinosaur Island~~
2. ~~The Jailhouse Rock~~
3. ~~Mount Storm Rough Water~~
4. ~~The Red Canyon swim series~~
5. ~~La Isla Bonita~~
6. ~~Turtle Bay~~
7. ~~The Greatest Archipelago on Earth~~
   ~~Clearwater swim series~~
8. ~~Malokodaidai Island 10k~~
9. ~~The Big Swim series in the Land of Koalas~~
10. ~~The Lazy River~~
11. ~~The Cold Drop~~
12. ~~The Whale Isles~~
13. ~~The Hot Fjords~~
14. ~~The Ancients Trail swims~~
15. ~~Island-hopping~~
16. ~~The Sunriser~~
17. ~~The Mermaid Canal~~
~~Bonus swim - The Time Traveller~~
18. ~~The Pilgrimage~~
19. ~~The Squirly Whirly~~
20. The Cross-continental

REUNION

F = T + 1

As Raif and I walk hand in hand through the town square to register for my final swim, I can hardly believe that I've made it to the end and that Mubla hasn't come after me, though I suspect I have Dab Dabs to thank for that.

"Fig!"

His voice is unmistakable and I spin round, getting the shock of my life when I see it really is Jago pelting towards me.

"Jago," I say, smiling as he flings himself into my arms.

Now he's *really changed*. Lost all of his baby chubbiness and he's grown loads. It makes me feel sad, like I've missed out on something.

I stand to attention with a salute and, in my best plummy voice, I say, "Agent Rose Brown at your service, sir! Reporting for duty following a successful mission, sir!"

Jago's face lights up. "Really?" he says. "You're not mad at me?"

"How can I be?" I ask. "I haven't seen you for a year."

"But I told Mubla about your mission. It was supposed to be top secret."

"Oh, that," I laugh. "Most agents would crack under that level of interrogation."

"Yes, but … don't you see?" Jago's serious brown eyes search my face. "I gave information to the enemy. I defected!"

"No, you didn't," I say, pulling him to me again. "It's fine. I completed the mission, didn't I? Or will do, once tomorrow's swim is over."

Jago buries his face in my chest. God, I've missed him.

"How did you know I'd be here?" I ask.

He grins up at me and taps his nose. "Hugh Moonstone will not be revealing his sources any more."

I laugh. "Then who are you here with?" I ask, becoming aware of Raif watching all this with an amused glint in his eye.

"Dab Dabs. He wanted to watch your last swim," says Jago, eyeing him suspiciously. "Who's he?"

"Erm, this is my friend, Raif. Dab Dabs is here?"

"Figaroo?"

Flipping hell! Dab Dabs is standing right in front of me. In a foreign country. Away from home. We both immediately start to sob and he pulls me into a tight hug, the kind that I've been longing for all year.

"Dab Dabs," I sob. "You're here. You got on a plane. That's…"

"Unbelievable?" he says, grinning at me. "Believe me, it took a lot of gin to get me on that flight."

"Oh, Dab Dabs," I laugh. "I've missed you so much."

"And I've missed you too." He kisses the top of my head. "My daughter the swimmer, eh? I can't believe you did it… I'm so proud of you." Then he whispers in my ear. "Don't tell Mubla I said that—"

"You're still alive then, Lemony?"

Speak of the devil.

"Mother," I reply.

Mubla winces. "You know it's Jago's feelings you're hurting by calling me that. Not mine."

"Lovely to see you again too," I say with a smile.

Mubla's mouth sets in a line as she takes in the boy who's holding my hand.

"And is this the young man who helped you run away?"

Uh-oh. Time to face the firing squad.

THE GULF BETWEEN

SWIM 21 – THE CROSS-CONTINENTAL
CONTINENTS: 6 | COUNTRIES: 27
F = T

Mode of Transport	Number of journeys complete	Distance covered (km)	Time spent (hrs)
Rail	12	4,119	58.75
Road	35	14,894	235.6
Air	23	61,943	104.25
Sea	14	2,553	148.5

"*Swimmers at the ready...*"

My final swim. I can't believe it. I'm not sure I want this to be over yet. There's still so much more of the world's oceans to swim out there.

"*On your marks...*"

I pull on my goggles for the final time, pressing them firmly against my face. Check my timing chip is secure around my ankle. Adjust the straps on my well-worn swimming costume. Stare out at the blue expanse, mentally planning my best route. Another gorgeous day. Another iconic swim to conquer.

"*Go!*"

Two thousand swimmers swarm across the starting

mat into the clear, cool water. A prospect that would have terrified me a year ago but I'm a seasoned swimmer now. I pick my route carefully so as not to get kicked in the face by overzealous competitors. Fall into a confident stroke, breathing every five, sighting every ten. Taking my time, trying to enjoy the last few hours of my swimming challenge. And the water matches my mood. Calm and clear. This is going to be a good swim...

~~~

"Well done, Fig!" yells Dab Dabs, patting me on the back as I clamber out of the water.

"Woo-hoo!" shrieks Jago, jumping up and down.

No Mubla. But then that doesn't surprise me after last night's showdown. I can't help feeling disappointed. I've actually completed a resolution and I'd half hoped that she would be there to see it.

"What an accomplishment," continues Dab Dabs. "My daughter swimming between two continents. How far was that swim?"

"Five point five k," I reply. "That brings my final total to three hundred and seventy-three kilometres."

"Wow!" shrieks Jago. "That's nearly one per cent of the world's oceans."

Their enthusiasm makes me want to cry. Having completed so many swims in the last year, the one thing I missed the most was having someone to cheer me out of the water. And now they're here and it feels … wonderful.

"Where is she? The local museum?" I ask, half joking.

Jago nods sheepishly.

Dab Dabs squeezes my hand. "You know what she's like. She'll forgive you eventually."

I'm not so sure, judging by her tirade where she made it clear that we will be discussing "my disappointing behaviour" as soon as we get home. Can't wait for that…

We stand looking out across the vast blue expanse over which I have just swum.

"She didn't use to be like this," murmurs Dab Dabs. "You know, you're the spitting image of her, Fig. And just as intelligent and determined. Perhaps even more so." He clears his throat. "She does love you. I know she doesn't show it very well but she only wants the best for you."

"No, she doesn't," I say, my voice beginning to rise.

"That's not fair," says Dab Dabs. "After everything she's done for you—"

"What, look after me?" I snap. "Isn't that what every mother is supposed to do? She loves controlling me."

A flicker of anger appears on Dab Dabs's face but it's soon replaced with his soppy, lovesick smile. "Complicated woman, your mother…" he murmurs, patting my hand softly and looking out to sea again.

"I can't continue to let her control my life any more," I say.

"Her heart's in the right place," is all Dab Dabs replies.

We stare out at the water in tense, nervous silence,

watching the last swimmers finishing the race in dribs and drabs.

"Talking of which," says Dab Dabs excitedly. "You'll never guess what I worked on last week."

I blink, a chill beginning to creep over me. "What d'you mean?"

"You remember," he replies, "I've always wanted to work on a body with situs inversus… Well, I worked on one."

My heart plummets. The chances of it being someone else in Old Mare are pretty slim, something like one in ten thousand. My bottom lip starts to wobble and then suddenly I'm bawling my eyes out.

"Figaroo," says Dab Dabs gently. "What is it?"

I can't answer for a long time, my throat throbbing with sadness. Why didn't Stella tell me?

"Fig. Why are you crying?"

"Was your client a little old lady with different coloured eyes?" I manage to ask.

Dab Dabs nods. "Yes. How did you know?"

I dissolve into fresh tears much to the dismay of Jago who comes to wrap his arms round me. "It's Sage," I mumble into the top of his head. "She's dead…"

REMEMBERING

"Look at this one," says Stella.

We're lying on her bedroom floor, looking through some old black-and-white photos of Sage that Myrtle has given us. Stella hasn't stopped hugging me. We've slotted straight back into how things were before and it's like I've never been away. Except *I've* changed.

"She was stunning, wasn't she?"

I peer at the photo. Sage must be twenty something and is wearing a swimsuit with her usual flowery swim hat. She was beautiful. The corners of my lips begin to quiver. "I wish I'd been here for her."

"She didn't want you to be," says Stella. "She wanted you to finish your swims."

"Yes, but I wanted to tell her all about my adventures."

"She knew, Fig," says Stella. "Talked about them all the time. Even in the hospital."

This last bit of information sends me into floods of tears

again and Stella throws her arms round me.

"Oh, I can't believe you're here," she gasps. "I've missed you so much. I'm … *intoxicated*."

I laugh. "Nice. Me too. I'm…" I fish around for the appropriate word, "*heartsore*. Good words by the way. I enjoyed looking those up."

"Thanks," grins Stella. "My favourite was corybantic. Can't wait to use that on the teachers at school. Doubt they'll know what it means."

My shoulders sag. School starts on Monday and I'm dreading returning to that hellhole. Not least because I've got to attend all the revision classes for the November resit.

"Not sure I'm ready to see people like Cassandra again," I shudder.

Stella snorts. "Don't worry about her. She's not queen bee any more."

"What? Why?"

"Maisy and Daisy met Kaisy!" she laughs.

"You're kidding…"

"I'm not," says Stella. "It's true. They got fed up of Cassandra ordering them around."

I sigh. "I so don't want to go back there."

"Don't blame you," says Stella, hugging me tight as if she's saying goodbye. "You will stay in touch, won't you?"

"What d'you mean?" I ask. "I've only just got back."

She shakes her head. "Not for long, though."

I frown at her. "I'm here, Stella. I'm back. You don't need to be lonely any more."

Stella sighs. "Yeah, but you shouldn't have come back, Fig. You could take your exams with your eyes closed. No reason for you to be here, is there? Just stay in touch. Promise me? Instagram, email, however you like. Just promise you'll never stop being in my life."

I find myself promising this, even though I don't have a clue what Stella is talking about.

THE FLASH MOB
FUNERAL

Stella looks amazing in her costume. It's gold and sparkly, and suits her perfectly. I, on the other hand, don't really feel comfortable being dressed as a mermaid. Myrtle has made me an extra-long tail, which hangs down to my ankles then swoops up to hook on to a piece of elastic round my wrist. I feel ridiculous in it, though I do like the colour – a sort of aquamarine blue that I imagine you'd get if you combined Sage's blue and green eyes together.

There's an enormous crowd standing by the sea pool, all wearing different coloured mermaid outfits, complete with the kind of flowery swimming hats that Sage used to wear. I think she'd approve. On Myrtle's signal, we wade into the water. Row upon row of us, until we're all submerged, faces turned in the direction of a giant picture of Sage that has been erected for the occasion.

The music comes on and we begin to move in unison. A routine that has apparently been rehearsed over the last few weeks, though I only learned it from Stella the other day. It's a simple water ballet that Myrtle dreamed up. Good old Myrtle. She's been such a rock. "It's what Sage would've wanted," she said on the phone.

At the end everyone congregates at the edge of the water, standing around, hugging, chatting, remembering. I think Sage would be proud of the amount of people that are here. She could always draw anyone in, was completely at ease with the most withdrawn of people and could get you to tell her your deepest secret.

A microphone pops suddenly and we collectively turn to listen to Myrtle, though, for a brief moment, I forget and think it's Sage and my breath freezes.

"Thank you for coming here today," says Myrtle quietly. "And thank you for taking part in the water ballet. Sage would've loved seeing it. She firmly believed that grief doesn't have to be just about sadness. She wanted us to gather here to celebrate her life, doing the things she loved best, *with* the people she loved best. If you'd like to come up and say a few words, the floor is open. Bottoms up!"

"Bottoms up!" repeat the audience. We've been handed small shot glasses of amber brown liquid, which the others raise and down in one go.

"Not you two," hisses Maud, snatching the glasses away from me and Stella. "It's whisky!"

There are picnic blankets spread on the beach, laden with great platters of cake. It's a perfect funeral and I spend my time chatting with the Old Mare Mermaids, wowing them with details about my swimming adventures.

"Myrtle! This is bloody marvellous," cries Stella, jumping up to give her a hug.

I gaze up at her standing in front of me. She looks so sad and lonely. I can't imagine what it must feel like to lose a twin. Probably like losing a limb. Or worse. I stand up to give her a hug. "Myr. It's so good to see you. Sage would've loved this."

"I know," she smiles. "She helped me plan it. She'd be so pleased to know that you made it."

The three of us stand together, holding hands, biting our lips, trying not to cry. But it's no good – the hole is too great.

"I still talk to her, you know," says Myrtle. "Old habits die hard, I suppose. But it was her time to go." She wipes my tears away with one of her usual scrunched-up tissues from her sleeve. "She really suffered these last six months. But, oh my goodness, Fig, your Instagram feed certainly kept her entertained."

"And she kept me going," I reply. "We had such lovely conversations about swimming. I miss those chats."

Myrtle grins. "Your adventure was what kept her going. She had all your swimming caps framed, you know. That was a nice thing you did. She just couldn't quite make it to the last one. She knew *you'd* make it, though. There was never any doubt in her mind."

"I wish I could've said goodbye," I murmur. "I would've come home with Mubla."

"That's why she never told you," says Myrtle. "Now are you going to say a few words? Sage wanted you to."

My breath immediately catches in my throat. "What, speak in front of all these people?"

Myrtle nods.

I take a deep breath. I can do this. *Bubble, bubble, breathe* comes to mind. I don't need to fear them. We're here for the same reason. So I ignore the sudden desire to run off to the nearest loo and make my way to the microphone.

"Ahem," I say, wincing as it squeaks loudly. "I, er, I just wanted to say a few words about Sage. She was the nicest person. Instantly put me at my ease when I started swimming with the Mermaids. At least I think she did. I talked with her and Myrtle for a good hour before I was sure who was who." I pause here as a ripple of laughter sweeps through the audience, boosting my confidence. "Sage took me under her wing. I saw life differently from there and for that I will always be grateful. She gave me courage. Convinced me to do things that I would never normally have done, including eating some of her cooking."

Another murmur of laughter. Then I go on to talk about the time Sage convinced me to swim in the demonstration pool at the Swimmers Show. It has everyone in stitches and I smile, knowing that that's what Sage would've wanted.

Tears of laughter. I look up at the photo of Sage with her flowery swim cap on, grinning away at the camera.

"Here's to you, Sage. I hope there's a pool and a good bar wherever you are…"

FACING BULLIES

I meet Stella by the school gates on the first day of term. I'm feeling as nervous as hell about being back in this place. "*Butterflies*," I tell her, which makes her laugh because that's what she was going to say, too.

"Not glad to be back then?" she says.

I laugh. "What do you think? Back to everyone calling me names. Can't wait."

Stella glances around. "I don't think so, Fig. You've just done something half these people will never achieve…"

"All right, ladies?"

Stella groans as Billy steps towards us.

"Ugh. Went on a date with him over the summer," she whispers under her breath.

"And?" I ask.

She shrugs. "I dumped him. Let's just say we didn't get on."

"Nice haircut," says Billy obliviously.

Stella frowns. "That's such an old line. Or don't you have any other vocabulary?"

"I wasn't talking to you," he sneers. "Little Miss World Swimmer here. Houdini. Grim. Fug. She's finally got something right."

I flinch at the names. So much for no more contempt. Nothing has changed. Billy may have got a bit taller, older, hairier but he's still the same old douchebag.

"I'd ask you to stop using such derogatory names, Billy," I say, "but I don't think you'd understand. Thanks for the compliment, though. Wish I could say the same about your boy beard." Stella snorts with laughter. "Hasn't your dad taught you to shave yet?"

"Yeah, well, I…" Billy stammers into silence and, with face flushed an extreme scarlet, he stomps off angrily, in the wake of our howls of laughter.

"Where did that come from?" asks Stella.

I shrug. "Had enough of being pushed around."

"Well, if it isn't Grim! The wanderer returns, eh?"

"Cassandra," I reply with a curt smile.

"What did *you* come back for?" she asks.

"Nice to see you too," I retort adding, "not," for Stella's benefit.

"Look who's here," calls Cassandra to Maisy and Daisy, who make a show of ignoring her.

"You three not friends any more?" I ask.

Cassandra snorts. "They were hardly friends of mine!"

"Funny, I thought that's exactly what they were," says Stella.

"You were always so *palsy-walsy*," I add, casting a sidelong glance at Stella who is clearly enjoying the new me.

Cassandra scowls at me. "You and your big words, Grim. You think you're so clever. Although…" She takes a long pause and I can actually see the idea slowly forming in her head. "You missed taking your exams, Bug. That means … that means I'm cleverer than you. Ha ha. Ha ha ha!"

She walks away, cackling to herself, leaving me with the words, "You're light years behind me in intelligence, Cassandra," poised on my lips.

Strange that she didn't expect me to come back. Even Stella assumes I won't be staying. When I think of all the places I've been, the things I've learned, it dawns on me that, by staying in Old Mare, I'm just treading water in a millpond sea. What exactly that means I should do now, I don't know.

In the science revision class I find myself sitting among the usual suspects.

"Billy, can you work with Fig, please?" asks Miss Denny.

"What, Boffhead?" he sneers.

"Don't call me that," I say, my cheeks flushing indignantly.

"Shouldn't Fug be in the year below us cos she's missed so much?" chorus Maisy and Daisy.

Billy sniggers. "Yeah… I'm not working with *Fug*. She won't know what we're doing."

I sit quietly, listening to their digs and not-so-wise cracks, and a smile forms slowly as I finally let out what I've been wanting to say for years.

"Do you really think this is what life is?" I ask, sweeping my arm around. "Life is out there. In the real world you don't get to hang out with people just because their name rhymes with yours." Maisy and Daisy's cheeks flush red and I think I get a slight smile from Cassandra. "You don't go around being mean to people and calling them names. You get to know as many people as you can and, if you're lucky and you get on, you can call them friends. I've seen what life is. And it most definitely is not this…"

~~~

As I sit outside the headmaster's office, it feels good to have finally got that off my chest, though I don't think Miss Denny appreciated my diatribe. God knows what Mubla's going to say when she gets home.

THE JOB OFFER

There's a message from the Boss waiting for me. I haven't heard from her in ages.

> **TheBoss** @Ickle_Mermaid I've got a job for you. Here's my number. CALL ME.

It goes through to a long dial tone. She must be abroad somewhere.

"Hello? Hello?" There's a lot of noise in the background, clanking bottles, shouting and loud music. Sounds like she's in a bar. I wouldn't be surprised. "Hang on. I'll go outside... Hello. Mermaid, is that you?"

"Yes," I reply.

"Good. Well, look – I'll cut to the chase. I'm writing a book and I want you to take the photographs."

"What?"

"Yeah, why not?" says the Boss. "I'm paying, if that's what

you're worried about."

"No, it's not that," I say cautiously. Apart from the glaringly obvious point that I'm a sixteen-year-old schoolgirl, there's something bothering me about the Boss that I need to get to the bottom of. Especially if I'm going to consider working for her. "Can I ask you one question?"

"Ask away…"

"What happened during that lightning storm? The one on your Six Seas swim."

She doesn't respond immediately. It's always been a touchy subject with her. "I thought you knew," she says.

I remain silent.

"If I tell you," says the Boss, "you cannot breathe a word to anyone. Not even to lover boy."

"I solemnly promise," I say, raising three fingers in a salute, even though she can't see them, "that I, Fig Fitzsherbert, will not tell anyone. Cross my heart and hope to die, stick a needle in my eye. If I ever breathe a word, may my life be full of turd."

"A simple yes would've been fine… OK. If you must know, I had to postpone the swim to the next day. And yes," she says, "that does mean I completed it in three hundred and sixty-six days, not three hundred and sixty-five. So technically I'm no different to the rest who've done the Six Swims."

"How did you get away with it?" I ask.

"Money," she replies and I imagine her rubbing her

thumb and fingers together. "We paid off the officials and the local press. Got them to run the story as if it were a day earlier."

"Oh," I say. It all makes sense now. "Wait, what year was that?"

"It was 2012. Why?"

"Wasn't that a leap year?" I say, trying to remember whether Stella had thrown one of her epic 'every four years' birthday parties that year.

"So what if it was?" says the Boss.

"Well, if it was, then technically you did complete the challenge within a year."

I realize there's a gaping hole in my logic – no one else is allowed 366 days to complete it – but the Boss doesn't notice. She's whooping away as if I've solved all of her problems. "You're a genius. That's it! This calls for a celebration."

"About that," I venture. "Now that I've stood up to Mubla – thanks in part to you – maybe you could face up to your own demons?"

"Oh, here we go," snorts the Boss. "The gin police are back."

I giggle. "It's up to you if you do it. But … it's affecting your swimming now, isn't it? I mean, even I managed to catch you up in the Mermaid Canal…"

The Boss inhales sharply and I think that's it. I'm in for it. Instead, she says, "All right. Maybe I will… Now about the job. You've got until this evening to decide.

More details to follow."

"Wait," I say. "What's your real name? I can't go on calling you the Boss if I'm going to work with you."

"Sorry, Mermaid. You said one question…" And with that she hangs up, leaving me with an enormous decision to make.

DECISION MADE

"You're suspended?" shrieks Mubla at dinner that evening. "You've been in school for less than one day, Lemony."

"I'm sorry, Mother," I say, though I don't really feel it. It felt great to finally speak my mind. I've been quiet for far too long.

"I can see I'm going to need to take you in hand," says Mubla, curling her top lip. "It really won't do, you going around behaving like this. These are important years, Lemony. Without qualifications, you won't get anywhere in life."

"I've got maths and English already," I mutter. "I could take the other exams tomorrow and pass them."

"That's not the point," says Mubla. "Tom, can I have a little support here, please? Your daughter seems determined to ruin her life."

Dab Dabs looks up. "What was that?"

Mubla ignores him. "I suppose that *woman* put you up

to this? What did you call her? The Boss." She takes a long swig of wine, studying me all the while. "What did she ever do for you?"

Stood up for me, I think. *That's what.*

I glumly look at my plate. It's Aurora's night off, which always makes Mubla more stressed, but she has at least made my favourite dinner: roast beef with all the trimmings.

"There's always world schooling," says Jago suddenly, putting his hand on mine, in an act of solidarity. He's actually eating the same meal as us tonight, which is nothing short of a miracle. I guess I'm not the only one who's changed.

Mubla clears her throat. "Yes, thank you, Jago. I don't need your input." She glares at me. "I called Andy, by the way."

I freeze, fork halfway to my mouth.

"Andy," repeats Mubla. "For your acting lessons. You didn't think I'd forgotten, did you?"

"But I don't want to be onstage." There. I've finally said it.

Mubla carefully places her knife and fork on her plate and stares at me. We've been circling this moment ever since I got back. "I've never had a resolution fail, Lemony," she says in hushed tones. "Never. And you've had far too many. That needs to change."

"She learned to swim, Wendy," interrupts Dab Dabs, looking like a rabbit caught in the headlights.

"Yes, I know that, Tom."

"She swam nearly four hundred kilometres," he continues. "Visited twenty-seven countries. That's thirteen point eight per cent of the world. You've got to admit that's impressive."

Mubla shifts uncomfortably in her seat, her cheeks beginning to flush. "Well. Yes… It is but … Lemony needs to—"

"It's Fig," I say suddenly.

"What?" says Mubla. "Lemony, you're mumbling again. I do wish you'd learn to speak properly."

"It's Fig," I repeat. "I don't answer to Lemony and I don't want to learn to act. My so-called failings are exactly that. Mine. Not yours. It's OK to give up sometimes. I've learned to swim and I've visited six of the world's continents. That's the biggest achievement of my life so far. Look, I'm truly grateful to you for all the opportunities you've given me. I should've said that more often. But I want to choose my own goals now." I breathe nervously, knowing that I've finally made up my mind. "I'm leaving home."

"Lemony," says Mubla quietly, "I forbid you to do that. Tom? Tell her she can't do that." But Dab Dabs remains silent, giving me a hint of a smile and a barely perceptible wink.

The blood has completely drained from Mubla's face and her usual milky white skin looks almost transparent. "You can't leave me again. I won't allow it." She hesitates again, looking distraught, then adds quietly, "Fig. Please…"

"I'm not leaving *you*, Mubla. I've been offered a job. It's just a few years earlier than planned." Then I hug her and leave the room.

OUT OF THE BLUE

My phone is blinking on the bed. I assume it's Raif. He hasn't stopped texting since I got back. But it's a message from the Boss with a phone contact attached, saying ring for job details.

A familiar voice answers but I can't quite place it.

"Oh, hello," I say. "This is, uh, I'm Fig Fitzsherbert."

Silence.

"Hello?" I say.

Nothing. I stare at my phone, wondering if I've lost reception, but the seconds are still ticking away and, just as I'm about to hang up and give it another try, I hear the familiar voice again.

"Fig? What are you doing ringing me?"

And then I realize who it is and I nearly drop the phone.

"Blue? Oh my God. It's so good to speak to you. How are you? Are you still swimming? Where are you? Oh, it's so nice to hear your voice."

I half expect her to hang up on me. But she doesn't.

"You're not mad at me?" she says in a small voice.

"Mad?" I reply. "Why would I be? I'm the one who lied. You were right. I was being an ungrateful spoilt brat. I'm so sorry about all that."

"But I sent Mubla after you… I didn't take the reward you know. It wasn't about that. I was … *mad* at you for lying. Thought you were different. But that doesn't make me much of a—"

I interrupt her. "You were one of the best friends I had out there, Blue."

"And I still want to be," she says quietly. "I'm sorry too."

We chat for ages after that. Blue tells me about the swims she's been doing and I tell her about completing my swimming challenge and how I'm back in school, facing the bullies, as if nothing has changed.

"But everything *has* changed," she says. "From the sound of it, you stood up to them all. And the Boss has offered you a job, hasn't she? That's why you're calling me."

"Yes, I was wondering why she'd given me your number," I laugh. "Building bridges isn't exactly her thing, is it?"

Blue giggles. "No. But I think she stands to gain something by the two of us getting along again because she's offered me a job too. Wants me to be a case study in her self-help book."

"Now that," I snort, "doesn't sound like the Boss. I thought everything was always supposed to be about her."

"It is," agrees Blue. "By the way, do you know what her real name is? She wouldn't tell me."

We collapse into more giggles and, after Blue gives me the details about where and when to meet, I ring off.

A message flashes up telling me that the Boss has tagged me in a story. It's a photo of a mermaid posing underwater, with giant text splayed across it:

WELL @ICKLE_MERMAID?

Then come a load more direct messages. The Boss is an impatient person. And *very* persistent. I can quite see how she gets everything she wants…

TheBoss Come on, Mermaid. What's taking so long?

TheBoss I'm not getting any younger, Mermaid…

TheBoss I guess Mubla's actually won then? Old habits really do die hard.

And, without any more hesitation, I reply to her message:

Ickle_Mermaid Well, you'd know about being old @TheBoss. Btw, I'm in…

ACKNOWLEDGEMENTS

A book about a list-loving girl would not be complete without a list of acknowledgements. Here, therefore, is my list of amazing, beneficial, exquisite people who all played a role in helping get my debut novel out of my head and on to the printed page.

<u>My Thank You List:</u>
- My agent, Gill McLay
- The Publishing team at Stripes, including (but not limited to):
  - Ruth Bennett
  - Katie Jennings
  - Lauren Ace
- Rachel Boden
- Robert Kirby
- Rachel Leyshon
- Lou Morgan
- The Bath Children's Novel Award (for longlisting it)
- My husband Joe
- My swimming buddy Jo-Anne Hale who took the underwater photo
- And last but not least, Grace, Evie and Teddy

ABOUT THE AUTHOR

Lou Abercrombie grew up in Essex, studied at Durham
University, where she gained a first class Maths degree,
and then moved to London, where she worked in
television. Lou now lives in Bath with her husband,
fantasy novelist Joe Abercrombie, and their three children.
As a portrait photographer, alongside projects such as
Shooting the Undead (a series that required Lou to learn
how to do zombie make-up) and Age Becomes Her (a
series celebrating the older woman), Lou's camera has
been deftly focused on a large number of children's,
fantasy and crime authors.

Lou has always been a keen swimmer, but a chance reading of an article a few years ago, about Lord Byron, inspired her to follow in his footsteps and swim the Hellespont, a 5km stretch of water between Europe and Asia. Since then she has swum a 10km marathon swim down the River Dart, learned to free dive like a mermaid, swum round Burgh Island and Brownsea Island, competed in the annual Copenhagen TrygFonden swim and completed a night swim with glow sticks. She is always on the lookout for the next exciting swim.

@LadyGrimdark
louabercrombie.com